The House on West 10th Street

An Absolutely Gripping Horror Story

HELEN PHIFER

Fabrian Books

Cover design by Gina Dickerson @Rosewolf Design

ALSO BY HELEN PHIFER

<u>The Annie Graham Series</u>

The Ghost House
The Secrets of the Shadows
The Forgotten Cottage
The Lake House
The Girls in the Woods
The Face Behind the Mask

The Good Sisters: A stand alone horror story

<u>Detective Inspector Lucy Harwin Series</u>

Dark House
Dying Breath

This book is dedicated to Gail and Paul O'Neill,
the kindest, most supportive friends a writer
could ever hope for.

Xx

Prologue

December 3rd, 2014

Homicide Detective Maria Miller stared at the television screen as the camera panned around the crowds of spectators; thousands of them all crammed into the Rockefeller Plaza underneath the huge Christmas tree. Sam passed two cardboard coffee cups over to her. 'Have a good one Maria.'

'You too Sam, thanks.'

She juggled the scalding cups of coffee along with the heavy door of Sam's Deli on Waverly Place. Frankie Conroy, her partner, watched her with a grin on his face. He knew there was no point in jumping out and opening the door for her. She'd complain that she could manage, so he pretended to be interested in the woman across the street on the second floor of the Brownstone, who was decorating her window with Christmas lights. Maria reached the car and he leant across to open the door for her. As she got in, the aroma of the fresh coffee and a hint of perfume filled the front of the Toyota Prius.

'Do you miss working the streets on days like this?'

He turned to stare at her. 'Let me see, it's cold and there are probably around thirty thousand people currently in midtown. Every single one of them trying to get a glimpse of the tree-lighting ceremony. We would be stood there for a full shift smiling and talking to tourists and you miss standing around for hours.'

'You know what I mean. It's always such a good atmosphere. Sting and Mary J Blige are singing tonight. I like both of them.'

'You'd be lucky if you got to hear them; you never get close to the plaza unless you've been ass kissing all year. No thank you, give me my warm car, hot coffee and a homicide any day of the week.'

'You're so full of crap. I bet you'd be there if Frank Sinatra was playing.'

He shrugged. 'I wouldn't be there even if old Frank had come back for one night only just to croon to the crowds and flick the switch on that tree.'

Maria rolled her eyes, took a sip from the cardboard coffee cup and sighed. 'You can keep your Starbucks, this is the real deal.'

Both of their cell phones rang in unison and Maria shook her head.

'Hell no, tis the season to be jolly. What's wrong with people? Where's their Christmas spirit?'

Maria smiled. 'It's probably in the same place as yours.'

She answered the call. 'Yep, we are. What address?'

Tucking her cell under her chin, she pulled a pen from her top pocket and wrote the address on the back of her hand. 'Right, on our way.'

'Homicide West 10th Street. Officers on scene, suspect at large.'

'Be nice for once if we weren't the ones catching all the calls.'

'Quit complaining, we get paid, don't we? Did you not just wish for a homicide? You need to watch your mouth Frankie, the universe is always listening.'

Frankie parked as close to the circus as he could. The usually quiet tree-lined street was lit up with flashing red and blue lights. Maria looked around. The street was deserted apart from the police cars and an ambulance. She took a large gulp of the coffee knowing that it would probably be cold by the time she got back into the car. Frankie did the same. 'Just as well we haven't eaten yet.'

She nodded, put the cup in the holder and got out of the car. Tugging her ID out of her pocket she flashed it at the officer standing in front of the door to the large Brownstone. She looked around the street. All of them were nice properties. This one had steps that went down to the front entrance, the ones on either side had steps that went up. She wondered why it was different to the others. The officer stepped aside to let her go in, she felt as if she was going down into the depths of hell. As quickly as that thought entered her mind it was gone, pushed out and scorned at. Maria Miller was tough; she lived on her own and didn't believe in ghosts or demons. What she believed in was that there were good and bad people in the world. Unfortunately for her and Frankie they rarely got to see the good as they dealt with the murdering scumbags who didn't care about anyone except themselves. Even so, as she stepped into the entrance of the once grand house, which had been turned into apartments, she felt a cold shiver run down her spine. It was so violent that her whole body shuddered. She heard Frankie's voice as he whispered in her ear.

'You okay?'

She nodded. Two paramedics were coming down the stairs carrying their heavy bags.

'Evening Maria, Frankie. There's nothing we can do for that patient. God bless their soul.'

The paramedic crossed himself.

'How bad is it, Don?'

He made a swiping gesture with his hand across his neck and Maria nodded; they stepped aside to let them leave.

‘We better suit up now,’ Maria said. ‘I was kind of hoping it was a mistake. That it was just a serious assault.’

‘You and your wishful thinking, kid. I suppose we better had.’

Frankie turned to go back to the car and get the protective clothing they needed. Maria waited in the entrance for him. She couldn’t see any forensic evidence, no blood or obvious signs that a killer had come out this way. He came back in, passing her a plastic packet containing a paper suit, gloves, shoe covers and a mask. They both stepped to one side out of the obvious way out and dressed in front of apartment one. Then they went upstairs. There was nothing out of the ordinary on this floor and Maria pointed up. Frankie nodded, so they went to the third floor where there was an officer standing at the foot of the next staircase, his face whiter than the paper suit Maria was wearing. He pointed upwards.

‘Next floor. I hope you have a steel stomach because this isn’t pretty.’

Maria nodded, a gut lined with steel was a requirement for her job. She didn’t ask him what had happened, preferring to take in the scene herself and make her own assumptions. The stairs up to this floor had been brightly lit, and it was warm out in the hallways of the first two floors. She stared up at the uncarpeted, almost black wooden steps which led up to the attic and wondered why it wasn’t as well maintained as the rest of the house. Frankie grabbed her arm. She turned to look at him, his bright blue gloved fingers began to play out rock, paper, scissors. She formed a fist to make a rock at the same time he opened his fingers and he shook his head.

‘You won, it’s your call.’

She tugged up the face mask that was around her neck, covering her nose and mouth. 'I'll go first.'

He shrugged, he wasn't about to complain. Maria began to walk up the wooden stairs that creaked and groaned. She stayed close to the wall in case the killer had grabbed the handrail on their way down. Frankie followed her. She reached the top and, despite the face mask, got a whiff of the tangy, coppery smell that was too familiar. It was overpowering, but she never faltered, crossing the small landing towards the open apartment door. Maria stood at the threshold and stared at the sight which faced her. There were blood splatters all over the painted, antique white walls and beige carpets.

That was one of the reasons she preferred to go first. Once she'd seen what was waiting for her she could cope. Her mind would switch to cop mode and she'd be fine. She always was. The hallway opened into a large open-plan living space, this was also light and airy. It was a nice apartment, Maria stared at the kitchen worktop and tried to figure out what it was that was on there. She tilted her head and heard Frankie mutter, behind her. 'Jesus Christ where's the head? Where's the arms and legs?'

It was then that she realized it was a torso she was staring at, drenched in blood with torn bits of muscle, tendons and bones protruding from where the limbs should be. She stepped closer, her mind trying to process what had happened. She looked at the naked torso with the most beautiful, intricate tattoo of roses and vines which ran from where the thigh should have been up the side and across the body. It snaked across from one side to the other and ended between the two breasts.

Frankie spoke. 'Nice tattoo.'

It was a nice tattoo. It was a quality piece of art done by someone who was very talented. This wasn't your average drunken girl's night out, "let's get matching tattoos done" down a back street in Hell's Kitchen. Maria tore her eyes away from the bloody torso and looked around. She stepped towards the kitchen area where she noticed smears of blood on the huge fridge. Frankie who was still in a trance staring at the body didn't notice her opening the fridge door until he heard her shriek. It was so loud that it made him jump. He looked across at Maria in time to see the missing limbs falling out of the fridge. She barely managed to move back in time, narrowly avoiding being covered in blood and gore. Frankie grabbed her arm, dragging her back. He'd never heard her shriek in all the years they'd worked together. He looked at her face – her eyes were wide in horror at the assortment of appendages that had fallen to the floor next to her feet. Maria whispered. 'Where's her head?'

Chapter One

July 2017

Frankie drummed his fingers on the steering wheel as he stared at the run-down building that had once been the City Hotel but was now abandoned and condemned. Maria, who was trying to decide how many grey hairs had sprouted in her fringe since the last time she'd had it colored, turned to stare at him.

'Give it a rest, I'm bored out of my tree as well.'

He looked at her and scowled. 'Two days we've been hanging around here and for what?'

'You know what. The perp is hiding out in there. You know it, I know it. He has to come out at some point.'

'You think so? What if he doesn't need to? What if he's got lots of supplies and is holed up in there for a month?'

'If he doesn't put in an appearance by the end of…' She stopped mid-sentence and elbowed him. A man wearing a navy hooded sweatshirt with NYPD blazoned across the front of it, and with a matching NYPD baseball cap appeared at a third storey window and stepped out onto the fire escape. With aviator shades covering his eyes, he stood on the top rung of the rusted, metal ladders and surveyed the street. Seemingly happy, he climbed down the steps and began to walk towards 7th Avenue.

'I told you so.'

Frankie shook his head. 'Well, I'll be damned.' He stared down at the black and white photograph of the man they'd been waiting for. He was wanted for the murder of his wife and attempted murder of her lover. Maria didn't gloat, she just smiled at him. 'Follow him as best as you can; when it gets too busy I'll jump out and follow on foot. As soon as I'm sure it's him we'll go for it.'

The man was walking briskly towards 7th Avenue and she wanted him apprehended whilst they were still on Barrow Street. A taxi pulled in front of their car, narrowly missing them. Instinctively Frankie honked the horn and their guy turned around. He stared at Maria then turned and began to run.

'Crap, he's onto us.'

Frankie swerved to the sidewalk and they both jumped out, Maria felt a surge of dread as the newly opened Manhattan Media Corporation loomed into view. The contemporary glass office block was owned by Harrison Williams, who ran a mass media enterprise. The only reason Maria knew this was because she'd read an article about him in the New York Times just a few days ago.

Jackson Quinn realized the cops were gaining on him and spied the revolving door of the swanky offices just in front of him. He darted into it finding himself in the huge glass, marble and oak entrance. Unluckily for Helena White she was about to go on her lunch break. She walked out from behind the reception desk at the same time that Jackson skidded to a halt. Without thinking he pulled the .38 from his waistband and grabbed onto Helena, pointing the gun at her head. She let out a deafening scream as Maria came through the doors first closely followed by Frankie, both of their weapons drawn.

'Drop your gun, Jackson, come on. Nobody needs to get hurt here, just put the gun down and we can sort this out.'

Frankie carried on talking whilst Maria moved to where she could get a clear shot.

'Fuck you. Drop your gun.'

'You know I can't do that whilst you're pointing a gun at that lady's head. Come on, man, you know you don't want this.'

Helena was whimpering. Frankie whispered to Maria. 'Are you thinking what I'm thinking?'

She didn't take her eyes away from Jackson but nodded her head. In the perfect situation, Maria would aim for his chest and shoot to kill. Only she wasn't fond of using her weapon unless it was life or death, which this situation was. Especially for the petrified woman Jackson was holding hostage, she didn't really have a clear shot of his head either. She glanced down at his legs, aimed and then fired twice. Jackson let out a loud howl as Frankie lunged for the woman and dragged her away from the now rendered powerless male on the floor who was screaming like a baby.

'That bitch shot me, she shot me. Get me a medic.'

Maria didn't waste any time and in a matter of seconds had his gun kicked away from him and his wrists cuffed.

'Sorry Jackson, does it hurt real bad?'

'Fuck you bitch.'

Maria smiled at him. 'Really? Jackson Quinn, I'm arresting you on suspicion of homicide. You have the right to remain silent. Anything you say can and will be used against you in a court of law. You have the right to have an attorney present during questioning. If you cannot afford an attorney, one will be appointed for you.'

Sirens filled the street outside and Maria was glad because he was bleeding like a pig all over the new white, pristine, marble floor. Officers streamed in through the doors along with paramedics. Maria stepped aside to let them work on Jackson. A tall, blond-haired man in a pair of Nike shorts and a vest top came running towards her.

‘That was outstanding, thank you, officer. I don’t know what to say. You saved her life.’

He held his hand out and Maria shook it, wondering if he was the security guard who had nipped to the gym on his lunch break.

‘Just doing my job, thanks.’

She turned and walked back to Frankie who was talking to two uniforms. He looked at Maria and grinned. ‘Nice shooting, shame about all the paperwork but at least they’re both alive. Are you okay?’

She rolled her eyes at him. ‘Gee thanks, Frankie, nice of you to ask.’

‘Come on Miss Smarty-pants, let’s go back to the station. Quicker we fill out the forms, the quicker we can call it a day.’

Chapter Two

Greenwich Village, June 1952

The Brownstone situated along West 10th Street was Emilia Carter's favorite place. She laughed as she helped roll out the dough for the fresh bread for breakfast in the morning. She was never happier than helping Missy down in the kitchen. She loved being in the city, away from her suffocating mother and odd brother. Everyone stayed in the sprawling mansion on Staten Island from June to September; everyone except her father who used the town house as a base for when he had business to attend to in the city. Tomorrow was a big day for Emilia. She was meeting Mae for lunch and it still made her stomach churn thinking about it. Not sure what to call her. Her father's lover was probably the most appropriate, they'd met under the most peculiar circumstances a week ago. Emilia had been downstairs before bed, helping Missy again and paused when she'd heard the laughter and music coming from the parlour. She'd looked at Missy who shook her head.

'It's nothing to do with us miss Emilia, maybe you should stay down here. It might be best you don't go up there.'

'Why? Do you know something that I don't?'

Missy shook her head.

Emilia washed her hands in the sink, picking the warm dishcloth off the stove door handle, drying them and went upstairs to investigate. She didn't know who was more shocked, her or her father, as she pushed open the heavy oak doors and found him with a semi-naked woman perched across his knees. Her arms were wrapped around his neck, their lips about to touch. Emilia screamed, and they pulled apart. She turned and ran for the stairs, mortified, her father running behind her. He'd reached out and grabbed her arm, tugging her back.

'Emilia, I'm sorry. I know it's wrong, but she's my best friend. I need you to listen to me. Your mother knows all about Mae and me. She doesn't care, in fact she doesn't care too much about anything. I don't know if you've noticed, but she barely speaks more than two words to me. She makes me sleep in a separate room, but I love her despite how this all looks. She isn't a well woman, you know yourself how she suffers with her nerves.'

Emilia didn't know what to say to him. She loved him dearly. She also loved her mother, who was a nervous woman and not the most affectionate of people. Suddenly she realized that her parents were adults and probably deserved to lead their own lives which had nothing to do with their grown up children. She looked at her father for the first time as a man and not her protector.

'I'm sorry, it was just a shock. It's none of my business. I'm going to bed now.'

'Why don't you come and say hello to Mae, she's an actress. She's starring in a play at the Belasco. We could go and watch it if you like. I know how much you love the theatre.'

Emilia was intrigued; she did love the theatre. Hesitantly, she followed him, all the time wondering if she was betraying her mother by agreeing to speak to the woman who made her father happy. When she walked into the parlour this time the beautiful woman with bleached blonde hair and ruby, red lips was fully clothed. Her back was towards them as she stared out of the huge bay window, onto the leafy, tree-lined street. She turned around to face Emilia and she realized that she wasn't that much older than herself. She crossed the room towards her and was shocked to see the woman draw back into herself and flinch. Emilia was horrified; she thought she was going to hit her. Holding out her hand, she smiled, and the woman's shoulders dropped as she smiled back at her. The pale hand with the same color matching ruby red nails as her lips grasped hers and shook it. Emilia marvelled at how silky soft her skin was.

'Hello you must be Emilia, I'm Mae Evans. I've heard so much about you.'

She smiled at her, wondering exactly what her father could have told her that was interesting. Compared to the beautiful creature standing in front of her she lived a very sheltered life.

'I wish I could say the same about you, Mae, but it's a pleasure to meet you.'

Mae laughed and her whole face lit up. Her green eyes sparkled and Emilia couldn't help but join in. She had the most infectious laugh she'd ever heard; behind them she heard her father let out a huge sigh.

'Phew. Boy… I had visions of you wanting to claw my eyeballs out of their sockets. I'm so glad you're not the angry type. You're very much like Clarke, he has a great sense of humour.'

Emilia turned to her father. 'Yes he does, on occasion. If you'll excuse me I'm going to bed now. This whole thing, well… it's all a bit strange.'

Mae nodded. 'Of course, it is isn't it? Would you like to meet me sometime for lunch? I know a great place near the theatre. It serves up the best clam chowder in midtown.'

Emilia flinched, she couldn't think of anything worse to eat for lunch. Mae began to laugh.

‘Sorry I couldn’t resist. It serves the best pizza. Honey, I couldn’t eat clam chowder if James Stewart served it up.’

Emilia wanted to dislike Mae, but she couldn’t. ‘I’ll have a think about it if you don’t mind. It kind of feels a bit strange if I’m being honest.’

‘I’m sorry, I’m being forward. Of course you can, it is a bit of a mess. If you decide you want to meet me, just let Clarke know, I’m available all week before the show starts. I’ll pick you up at twelve and we can go shopping afterwards. I need some new shoes. Is that okay with you, Clarke?’

Clarke nodded. ‘Emilia can do whatever she wishes, as long as you look after her.’

Emilia frowned at him. ‘I’m twenty two, I think I’m good to go for pizza and shopping, thanks.’

He held his hands up as a peace gesture. ‘Yes you are.’

‘Goodnight, Mae, Pops.’ She left them to it, confused and wondering how she had just become friends with her father’s lover.

Chapter Three

Maria sighed as she signed her name on the last of the forms. She heard some clapping and looked up to see Frankie heading towards her with a huge bouquet of flowers. She wondered if he'd gone mad as he walked straight towards her; she knew he had a bit of a thing for her. A couple of times when they'd been to The Fat Black Pussycat after work and had too many beers he'd stare at her or grab her hand too many times. She always managed to brush it off, as she really liked him, despite the fact that he was ten years older than her and married. She'd told him another time another place and who knew. Thankfully when he was sober he never did anything of the sort, except now. What the hell was this all about? He stood in front of her with a huge smile on his face and held the flowers towards her. A voice shouted: 'Get down on one knee Frankie boy,' to a round of applause.

'What the fuck, Frankie?'

He laughed. 'Nothing to do with me, I'm a married man.' Maria stood up to see if there was a card. There wasn't. She looked at the flowers. They were beautiful, expensive; all white roses, lilies and the most beautiful scented tiny white flowers that she'd never seen before. Her first instinct was to bin them, amid the raucous laughter of her mainly male co-workers. She took them from Frankie, inhaled and gave the rest of department the finger. They would look gorgeous on her coffee table, matching the newly painted walls of her apartment perfectly. For once she did something that surprised everyone and put them on her desk. They'd all been waiting for her to put them in the trash can. Realising she wasn't taking any crap, everyone began to carry on with what they were doing. Frankie perched on the corner of her desk.

'So what do you say we go to the Pussycat for a cocktail or two? Celebrate not getting ourselves and anyone else killed.'

'I don't know, I have a headache.'

'I only asked if you wanted a cocktail, not sex.'

She glared at him. 'Sometimes you amaze me, Frankie, you're such a pig.'

'Guess you're not in the cocktail mood.'

'Take me and my flowers home, I'll think about it on the way.' She winked at him.

Frankie pulled up outside the apartment building where Maria lived on Sullivan Street. Its flaking paint and boarded-up first floor windows had seen better days, so had the back rub shop a couple of doors down.

'This place is a shithole, when are you going to move? I worry about you living here.'

'Beauty is in the eye of the beholder. Yes, it looks like a slum, but the majority of rentals are nice people. I feel safe here, I know all my neighbors. There are no scumbags and we look out for each other. Plus I have Miss Lily's across the road for my morning pastries. What more could a girl ask for? '

He shook his head. 'It's not like you're destitute though, is it? You can afford a better place than this.'

'I'm saving up for my dream apartment and whilst I'm saving this does the job, so stop disrespecting my home. In case you haven't noticed you're not my pops.'

She got out of the car, leaning across the back seat to get the flowers.

‘Who do you think sent those?’

‘No idea and I don’t really care.’

‘Do you want to go to the Pussycat?’

She shook her head. ‘I’ll give it a miss tonight, thanks. I’m going to have a long soak in the bath and an early night. Hey, you should send Christina flowers sometime. Ladies like flowers.’

‘She’d complain I wasted too much money, she’s too ungrateful. I’ll see you tomorrow.’

Maria shook her head and slammed the car door shut. Turning, she walked up the steps to the front doors. He was right, this place looked almost as desolate as the City Hotel they’d been parked outside earlier. One day she would move into a huge apartment with views of Central Park, but for now this was good enough. She heard the familiar sound as her elderly neighbor came out of the elevator and shuffled towards the entrance, her strings of pearls jangling.

‘Good evening, Miss Green, how are you today?’

The woman looked up, squinting in the poorly-lit entrance. She always dressed impeccably. If Maria wasn’t wrong she was wearing a vintage Chanel suit and pumps. What she’d give to go through her wardrobe. It was full of beautiful, vintage designer clothes. Miss Green had told her she’d been a stylist for Vogue back in the day.

‘Ah Maria, good evening. I’m alive thank you, which is always a good thing. Look at you with a bunch of flowers as big as your arms can carry. Who you been keeping from me?’

Maria giggled. ‘No-one, I don’t know who they’re from but they were so beautiful I decided to keep them.’

Miss Green nodded. ‘Wise choice honey. You have a secret admirer. How exciting.’

‘Or the florist got the wrong person.’

‘Tut, tut, don’t be so negative. I’m off to the store, do you need anything? Have you eaten today?’

‘I’m good thank you, I’m going to make a huge bowl of chilli and have a glass or two of wine.’

‘Good, you need it. You work too hard. Goodnight, Maria.’

‘Night, Miss Green.’

Maria called the elevator and was relieved when the groaning doors opened immediately. She was tired, hot and would have cried if she’d had to walk up eight floors.

Chapter Four

He walked along the tree-lined sidewalk shrugging his backpack higher onto his shoulders and keeping as close to the houses as he could. It had been awhile since he'd last visited this particular Brownstone. He had tried to find out if he could rent the empty, top floor apartment. He'd like to live there legally, only the rental company had told him it wasn't safe. It needed major remodelling to make it liveable, so they'd taken his name and cell number in case it became available. It hadn't mattered really, he'd gotten access to it once before, so he could do it again. His battered VW van was parked a couple of blocks away with his worldly belongings inside, and once he'd gained access he would move it nearer. He reached the Brownstone which was situated on the corner. The main entrance was situated on West 10th Street, while the fire escapes could be accessed around the side on Washington Street. If there was no one around, he could climb up to the fire escape and get to the top floor. He'd already been last night and prised the board from the window, placing it against the empty frame from the inside so it still looked secure. There were no buildings which looked onto this part of the street, luckily for him. The bus stop opposite was a bit of a problem, but he'd just need to be cautious and avoid rush hour. He turned the corner into Washington Street which was deserted and climbed up. This was where being taller than most of your high school friends finally paid off. He pulled himself up effortlessly onto the fire escape, and scanned the street to make sure no-one was watching. That was the beauty of being a New Yorker: nine times out of ten nobody gave a crap what you were doing. Everyone was too involved in their own world to give you much attention. He climbed the metal rungs of the ladder quickly, his stomach churning. He'd dreamt about this for three, long years. Scared and immature the last time he'd been here he'd left in a rush and regretted it ever since, but there was something very special about the apartment and he'd had the same dream about it almost every week since that night.

He reached the attic window and pushed the board open wide enough so he could clamber inside. Taking off his backpack he unzipped the side pocket and took the small, but powerful flashlight out. Pushing the board back across the window and making sure there were no gaps he turned around. As there was no light inside the apartment, he blinked a couple of times letting his eyes adjust to the darkness. Then he turned on the flashlight and shone it around; it was just as he remembered. The furniture was covered in sheets, and he wondered if it was the same sofa that he'd sat on with her. He lifted a corner of the dusty sheet. The cracked, brown leather sofa made him smile. He'd spent a magical couple of weeks sleeping on it. He dropped the sheet back down, then walking across to the breakfast bar mesmerised, he shone the light on it. There was a thick film of dust and he traced his gloved finger through it. He closed his eyes picturing every last detail of that night. This apartment was the only place he'd ever stayed in that truly felt like home. Moving away from the open plan kitchen-lounge he walked towards the bedroom door. Wrapping his fingers around the brass knob he marvelled at how cool it was despite the humid temperature outside. Turning it slowly he pushed the door open, remembering that if you opened it too fast it creaked loudly, and he didn't want whoever lived in the flat below realising there was someone upstairs. He stepped into the large, airy bedroom. It had no window, but a huge skylight above the queen-sized bed. He smiled to see the bed was still there. Walking across, he dragged the dust sheet off. There were no covers and he could see the huge, dark brown stain on the left hand side of the mattress. He was shocked that they hadn't taken the mattress away. There had been a lot of blood. As he stepped closer he could see where the CSIs had cut pieces from it to take for forensic sampling. He supposed they couldn't really take a full-sized mattress back to their lab or office. He wasn't really sure where they worked from and he didn't care. Whoever they were they hadn't been clever enough to catch him so they weren't that good.

He shook the sheet several times and lay it down across the mattress. He couldn't wait to lie on it, although there was something he had to do first. Going back into the lounge, he picked up his bag, tugging the zipper open. The glass jar inside was heavy and his shoulders ached from the weight of carrying it around on his back. He smiled at the perfectly preserved head inside it. She was still beautiful and he'd finally been able to bring her home. Carrying it across to the kitchen, he opened the pantry cupboard which had once been full of every imaginable pasta and vegetable you could buy from Wal-Mart. He placed the jar on the middle shelf and stepped back; he'd had to keep her hidden for so long it was nice to have her in a place he could have easy access to. They were going to be very happy here, as they had once before until the time had come to end it. He'd done well and managed to ignore the noises that had begun in his head. At first it was similar to white noise, like static buzzing around his ears. He'd gone to the doctor who'd examined his ears and given him some ear drops, which hadn't worked. It was always far worse at night. He'd lie there in bed with his hands over his ears trying to block the noise out. Then one night he'd realized that no matter how hard he tried it wouldn't go away because it was coming from inside his head. A few nights later the noise turned into whispers, words spoken in an exotic language he didn't understand. It wasn't just one voice either there were several of them, and he felt as if they were having a conversation about him. He'd been scared back then… Hell! He'd been terrified until one of the voices realized he was listening to it and began to whisper to him. Then it all made sense. The others faded away and he didn't hear them as much. This one voice was stronger than them and it told him things he didn't always want to hear, yet it also told him many things that he did long to hear.

Chapter Five

Frankie drove home thinking about Maria, he liked her far more than he should. She was his friend and he was married. It wasn't that he didn't love Christina – he had once upon a time – it was more of a case that she'd fallen out of love with him. The last time he'd had too much to drink and made a pass at Maria she'd made it quite clear where he stood with her and that was okay. He respected her for being straight with him; it still hurt though. In fact, she'd told him to grow a set of balls and do something to sort his shitty sex life out. As he drove past the old church on the corner of Sullivan he noticed the metal sign swinging in the breeze: Marty's Dancing School. When he met Christina she was a dancer at Radio City Music Hall. He used to go dancing with her once a week even though he had two left feet. Once they were married and working long hours to pay the bills the dancing went out of the window. He wondered if he should take her dancing, although he was rusty it had been so long. Maybe if he had some dancing lessons and surprised her with a fancy date at one of the charity balls they held at The Plaza or The Met it might make her see him how she used to. He stopped off at the grocery store and picked up a bunch of pink roses, and instead of the usual six pack he spent ten minutes looking at the wine before picking up a bottle of Chardonnay hoping Christina would like it or that would be twenty bucks down the drain. He knew Maria would approve, she always had a bottle or two in her fridge. He paid and got back in his car, determined to try and rekindle the fire that had long since been extinguished.

He drove down into the parking garage; he only lived a few blocks away from Maria on Hudson Street. His apartment was bigger, with a Starbucks and Prêt a Manger on the ground floor. No massage parlours, no boarded up windows and the rent was a lot more. Christina liked it and that was all that counted. They could have downsized, they didn't need a three bed apartment. The kids they'd longed for had never appeared, but she wouldn't hear of it. She wanted to live in a spacious apartment, so they did. As he got into the elevator he held the wine and the flowers feeling stupid. What if she wasn't in? She got pissed with him when he was late home, and sometimes went out to meet her girlfriends for cocktails. The elevator doors opened and he grinned to see his younger brother Adam standing on the other side.

'Hey man, what you doing? You leaving already?'

Adam laughed. 'Yeah, well I wasn't going to wait around all night for you. Besides Christy is in a shitty mood so I figured I'd leave her to it.'

Frankie frowned; when wasn't Christy in a shitty mood.

'Are you coming back in for a beer?'

Adam shook his head and pointed at the wine and flowers. 'Good luck, I don't want to spoil your surprise. I'll catch up with you at the weekend.'

They swapped places and Adam pressed the ground floor button. Frankie nodded at him then walked down the corridor towards his apartment. He opened the door and sniffed the air which smelt of vanilla and cinnamon. 'Sorry I'm late, honey.' He could hear the taps running and walked down to the bathroom. Christy was standing there in her dressing gown, her face freshly cleansed.

'Nice of you to come home.'

He handed the bunch of roses to her and for the first time she smiled.

'Sorry, you know how crazy work can be.'

'A phone call would be nice, now and again.'

He had phoned her and left a message, she hadn't picked it up. He was too tired to fight with her which was what she was edging for.

'Would you like a glass of wine?' He waved the bottle at her and she nodded. He left her to go and open the bottle. A lipstick stained wine glass was already on the coffee table along with an empty beer bottle. At least she'd offered Adam a drink. He had no idea why she was so angry all the time with him. She knew what his job was like, the long hours. She didn't complain when she went to spend his pay check at the end of the month, did she? He picked up the wine glass and put it into the dishwasher, then dropped the bottle in the trash. Taking two clean glasses from the cupboard he opened the wine and filled them. He took a huge gulp of the wine, it wasn't the best thing he'd tasted, but he'd had worse. Then he downed the rest of it, before refilling the glass and carrying them through to her. She was already in the bath as she took the glass from him.

'So what kind of a day have you had?'

She rolled her eyes at him. 'Well, obviously not as busy as you. Life is pretty boring when you just have an ordinary nine to five job.'

He nodded and left her to it. She was looking for an argument and he didn't have the energy. It would have been nice to come home to something to eat for once. Instead he went back to the kitchen and began to go through the fridge and cupboards to see what he could throw together.

Chapter Six

Greenwich Village, 1952

Emilia checked her reflection one last time. Her long, black hair was the opposite of Mae's shoulder length, platinum blond curls. She pouted her peach colored lips. Although the lipstick had been a birthday present from her brother last year, she'd been too shy to wear it. However, she didn't want to look like a wallflower compared to the exotic Mae. If they were going for lunch and shopping she didn't want to look drab. Her stomach was full of butterflies. She was excited to be doing something so different from the usual baking, reading and wishing her life was better. She also knew that she shouldn't be so happy to be friends with the girl who was her father's lover. It was wrong, and she was as guilty for betraying her mother as much as he was, but she lived in the most amazing city in the world and hadn't really had the chance to explore it. Her brother had arrived this morning, she'd seen him to say good morning to, and then he'd disappeared up to the attic which he'd taken over as his living quarters. He was so quiet; he stared a lot. She didn't like it and had caught him on several occasions watching her. He was strange, but she left him alone to get on with it. She had no idea what he did in the attic. Every time she saw him he had a leather-bound book tucked under his arm. He didn't go anywhere without it. She heard the beep of the cab outside and grabbed her purse off the dresser. She ran to the front door and opened it, to see Mae leaning out of the cab window waving frantically at her. Emilia waved back and ran up the stone steps, pulling open the cab door. Mae smiled at her, she didn't have quite so much make-up on as she had the last time they'd met. Her lips were a pale pink this morning yet were still beautiful. Emilia didn't think she'd ever really taken notice of another woman's mouth before, but Mae's was captivating. She sniffed the air. It smelled wonderful and Mae giggled.

'Chanel No 5, I never leave home without it. Do you like it?

Emilia nodded.

'Good in that case we can call into Saks and pick some up for you. Whilst we're there we can find you a red lipstick. Every girl needs a red lipstick and my neighbor Gina works in the beauty department, she'll find you the perfect shade. You wouldn't believe how many red lipsticks there are to choose from.'

As the cab drove along Fifth Avenue, Emilia had to pinch herself, she'd only ever been along here once before. The thought of going into Saks and buying beauty products made her stomach churn, she'd never done anything like it. Her mother had always frowned upon the women who made up their faces. What would she say if she went home smelling like some exotic creature with ruby red lips and eyelashes as black as coal? Suddenly she didn't care one little bit, she was an adult now. She would do what the heck she pleased.

The cab pulled up outside Saks and she got out while Mae was busy paying the driver and giggling at something he said. A warm arm pushed underneath hers and she was being pulled in the direction of the huge, brass, doors. A doorman pulled open the door for them.

'Well look at you Miss Mae, as pretty as ever. How are you this fine day?'

'Thank you, Fred, you look pretty fine yourself. I'm good, how are you?'

He grinned and tipped his hat to them both.

'All the better for seeing you Miss Mae, have a grand day.'

Emilia smiled at the man, she thanked him as she passed through. She had no idea what she'd been expecting, but when she stepped into the brightly lit store she gasped. It was huge, there were so many different counters, selling so many different things. She leant in close to Mae and whispered.

'How do you find what you need?'

Mae laughed. 'Trust me honey, five minutes in here and you'll know where you want to be.'

Two hours later they were walking out of the store, Mae with her huge shopping bags over one arm. Emilia had one small bag clutched between her fingers, inside was a bottle of Chanel perfume, a red lipstick, face powder and some eye make-up. She stole a glance at her reflection in the shop window and did a double take, Gina had made up her face perfectly. This was certainly not the face of the woman who walked into the store. Mae hadn't stopped chattering the whole time and Emilia loved it; all her reservations about her were gone. She loved how talking to her new friend was so easy, she just wished that Mae wasn't her father's lover. It sort of put a dampener on the whole thing because it was strange, she couldn't get rid of the feeling that she was betraying her mother. Mae hailed another cab and they climbed in. She gave directions to the diner and Emilia was glad, her stomach had begun to growl in the most unladylike manner. She'd been too nervous to eat breakfast earlier and had begun to regret it the louder her stomach protested. As they walked into the diner she inhaled the air which was filled with the smell of pizza dough, garlic and herbs.

'Smells good doesn't it? I told you I knew the perfect spot for lunch. You might not be able to move much after one of Toni's pizzas though, but trust me. It's worth it.'

They took a seat in a booth which looked out onto 42nd Street; people were hurrying by on their way to work, shopping, sightseeing. Mae was chattering to the waitress who stood there listening intently to what she was telling her. Emilia felt a little intrusive, just as Mae was friends with Gina she must be friends with the gum-chewing, young woman. She heard her name mentioned and realized that she was staring at the pair of them.

'What's up, Em, cat got your tongue?'

She shook her head. No-one called her Em, yet it sounded so right coming from Mae.

'Sorry, I was daydreaming.'

The waitress winked at her. 'Now that I am an expert at, I daydream all the time. I'm still waiting for my big acting break. One day I'll be just as famous as Mae and it will be my name on that billboard across the way.'

Mae giggled. 'Shush Susie, I'm not famous. This is Clarke's daughter by the way, she's my new gal pal.'

Susie scrutinised her and she felt the heat as the blush rose up from her neck.

'Nice to meet you Em, say hi to your Pa for me.'

Mae gave their order whilst Emilia was wondering how on earth Susie knew her father, but too afraid to ask. It seemed everyone knew him better than she did.

Chapter Seven

He squatted on the floor, unzipped his bag, then pulled out the antique board that was allegedly made from wood taken from an actual coffin. He'd stolen it from the weird, little occult museum on East 9th Street last month. There were so many tales regarding the Ouija board and most of them were untrue. It was all a matter of how far you were willing to go with it. He wanted to go all the way, he didn't want to summon his Aunt Patsy who'd died of a heart attack two years ago. Why would he? She was a mean old bitch when she was alive. He didn't see that being dead would improve her attitude any. Knowing his luck she'd probably put in an appearance, but if she did she'd soon leave when he summoned who he really wanted. He'd thought long and hard about whether he should even attempt to do this. It was dangerous. He didn't doubt that, but he wanted the power and the energy that only the darkest of demons could give to him. He was more than willing to trade his soul if it meant he got what he wanted. Placing the board on the kitchen counter – the same one he'd left his first offering on – he ran his fingers over the cool marble. How easy the blood had pooled on it. How easy it had cleaned off. It had been three years and he wondered if it had been too long. He'd never expected to have a mental episode after it. The police had picked him up days later and, unable to talk much sense, he'd been given a psychiatric evaluation and thrown in Greystone's Psych Hospital. He'd been amazed the cops had never matched any of the evidence to him. Lucky or unlucky for him the guys who'd caught up with him hadn't wanted too much paperwork so they'd driven him straight to the hospital where he'd been kept indefinitely until he proved he was as normal as he could be. At first he'd been so angry about it and then he realized it was to his advantage. He had somewhere warm and dry to sleep; he got fed, meds and counselling. There was no trace of him to link him back to the murder this way, yet if he'd been left out he'd have been compelled to kill again. He couldn't inside, it would raise too much suspicion. At least this way the heat had completely died down. The Torso Killer had gone to ground as far as they knew. He bet they were hoping he was dead. The apartment had been sealed up luckily for him. No one had wanted to rent it. He'd smiled as he'd listened to the realtor trying to sell him something else, too afraid to admit the reason the apartment wasn't for rent. They might not know about the murders in 1952 that took place inside it, but he did. Whoever the current owner was must be a superstitious person, as they were losing out on rental in a prime area of Manhattan. All things considered it was perfect. If he was quiet and didn't alert the neighbors whenever he visited he should be able to come and go as he pleased. He didn't put the planchette on the board, he wasn't ready. It was never a good idea to leave them laid out together when not being used. He'd seen it with his own eyes once when he'd left it on the board and walked away. It had begun to move all on its own. He didn't want to summon anyone other than the dark forces when he was ready to begin his reign of terror.

Pulling the book of Dark Magic from his bag he placed it next to the board; all he needed was candles. Lots of them, but he would get them later from his van. He didn't bother flicking on the lights, despite the fact it was gloomy and hard to see. He wouldn't risk using them in case any observant neighbors noticed and rang the cops. Just in case, he took the rug and, rolling it up, he lay it across the bottom of the door. That should block out any light from his flashlight or candles. The walls in the lounge had been painted over since his last visit, giving him a blank canvas to start again. In the 1950s when the first murder occurred, the cops had broken down the door and found the entire apartment's walls covered in pentagrams, drawings of winged, horned beasts, and line upon line of Latin. He doubted any of the original drawings still existed, but he would peel back any layers of wallpaper and check under the carpets, just in case. Three sacrifices were needed before the incantation and summoning could begin. He just hoped that the huge gaps between them wouldn't make a difference.

Chapter Eight

Maria decided to walk to the station. It was one of those cooler, fresh mornings that she loved. Summer in the city could be unbearable, she was definitely more of a winter gal. She tugged on her Nikes and slung her purse over her shoulder, she was on a health kick. No more burgers, pizzas or burritos but lattes she couldn't live without. As she turned to check everything was switched off, she spotted the flowers and once more wondered where they'd come from. As she ran down the apartment block steps, she noticed a town car parked opposite – a brand new Mercedes. The only person around here that ever used town cars was Miss Green and she paused, waiting to say good morning to her before she walked away. The rear door opened and out jumped the security guard from Harrison Media, smiling at her. Not sure what was going on, she turned around just in case he turned out to be Miss Green's nephew or something. She smiled at him, then carried on walking not wanting to get into some awkward introduction. She didn't get far before she felt a hand tug at her arm; she moved fast throwing it off and spun around. He was standing directly behind her grinning.

'That's a bit rude. I send you flowers for saving my receptionist's life, then come to visit and you turn your back on me. You could at least say hello.'

Maria looked at him, he was older than she'd guessed yesterday. His eyes were a little crinkly around the edges and his blond hair was peppered with silver strands. 'Excuse me? What do you think you're doing? And how the hell do you know where I live?'

She was already wondering what else their brief encounter had revealed about her to this perfect stranger who she'd never set eyes on before yesterday.

'I know everything.'

'Well, how about I take you to this little precinct I know, we can have coffee and you can explain yourself better.'

She was standing with her arms folded, glaring directly into his eyes.

He laughed. 'Well that's a first. You buy a girl some flowers and come to ask her out to dinner. A simple yes or no would suffice.'

'Look mister, I don't know you. Thank you for the lovely flowers, but I don't care too much that you've gone to the trouble to find out where I live. They have laws against that kind of behavior you know?'

He shook his head. 'Who do you think I am?'

'I have no idea, possibly the world's worst security guard judging by yesterday's showdown. Shouldn't you have been doing your job instead of pissing around on a treadmill?'

He let out a loud laugh. 'I like you, Maria, you're funny. I'm sorry, you have this all wrong. Please let me introduce myself.'

He held out his hand for her to shake. 'Harrison Williams.'

She gripped it as hard as she could. *Holy crap, I hope he's not friends with the Commander.*

'Maria Miller.'

'Yes, I know. I wanted to thank you properly for yesterday. I'm not a stalker, I own a media company. I have people on my payroll who know things and if they don't know then they sure as hell find them out.'

She stared at him, not sure whether to arrest his sorry ass or whether she should be flattered.

'Why don't you let me give you a lift to work, if that's where you're heading? We can talk in the car and you can decide whether or not to come out for dinner this evening.'

'I'm fine thanks, I like to walk. On my own. It helps me to clear my head before the start of a shift.'

His smile disappeared, which made her realize that most people don't say no to him. Well, he would have to learn. She didn't care about his business or how much money he had.

'What about dinner?'

She shook her head. 'I'm sorry, I have no idea what time I'll be finished and I've already made plans to go out for a drink with a friend.'

He smiled. 'Tomorrow?'

She shook her head. 'It was nice meeting you, Mr Williams, have a nice day.' With that she turned and began to take the biggest strides she could to get as far away from him as possible. Her cheeks were burning; she'd never been hit on so openly in all her life. It was crazy – she wasn't going to agree to get in a car with a man she didn't know. Did he not realize she was a homicide detective? How many bodies had she attended of women and men on first dates or picked up in a bar by total strangers. Hell no, it wasn't happening. Her life might not be amazing at the moment, but it didn't mean she wanted it to end. Shaking her head she carried on walking, trying to get rid of the image of Harrison Williams floating around in there. Whether she wanted to admit it or not he was attractive, but so was Frankie – that didn't mean she threw herself at him whenever she could. She hoped today was going to be better than yesterday. For her a good day would consist of no homicides and not having to shoot someone.

Chapter Nine

Frankie was in a rush for work, having got stuck in a jam on Sixth, and was now driving like a maniac to make it to the precinct before Sergeant Addison realized he was late again. By the time he got parked and ran into the department Maria was already there, coffee in hand scrolling through the list of jobs that had come in overnight. He made it to his desk without being caught.

'Nice of you to join us, Frankie.'

'Traffic.'

'Why don't you just walk, or get the subway?'

He frowned at her. 'I'm too lazy to walk and I'm not being crushed against some hairy, sweaty, guy for ten minutes.'

She laughed, but not for long as she heard Addison bellow.

'Miller, Conroy. My office now.'

She looked at Frankie, who shrugged, glad it wasn't just him getting called. They stood up and walked the short distance to his corner office. Ever the gentleman, Frankie let Maria go in first, because then she'd be the one in the line of fire. Addison was an okay boss, but whenever he was angry or excited spittle flew from his lips. Maria tried to keep a safe distance. She looked over her shoulder and glared at Frankie who winked at her.

'Take a seat.'

They both sat down, relieved that Addison was neither angry nor excited. He had a file spread out across his desk, Maria glanced at the technicolor photographs and her stomach dropped to her feet. She recognized the torso and limbs from that night, three years ago.

'We've had a call from a reporter asking all sorts of questions about this case, she wanted to know if we were aware that in the fifties a semi-famous actress was found murdered in the same apartment. Her limbs were hacked from her body and her head was missing. According to this reporter it was never found.'

Maria leant forwards. 'How did we not know this?'

Frankie shook his head. 'How were we supposed to know? It's not like it was a few months ago, I mean that's sixty five years ago.'

Addison shrugged. 'I'm not saying you should have known, hell I had no idea about it and I'm older than the pair of you. I just think it's a bit of a coincidence and I want you to go back over everything you have. Work the case again. I've pulled you off the active on call duties to work it for the next ten days to see what you can come up with.'

Maria leant forwards grabbing hold of the photograph of the entrance to the apartment. Every cop has a case they didn't solve, a killer they couldn't catch. This one had been the one to give her nightmares. She'd wake up in the early hours in a cold sweat, her hands checking to make sure her head was still attached to her body.

'Who is this reporter? How the fuck do they know about the other murder?'

Addison's cheeks began to turn crimson. 'It's my daughter, she's just started working at the Daily News in the archives. She did a thesis on unsolved murders and just happened to stumble upon the original story. She asked me about it and I didn't know. I haven't got the time to look into it and, let's be honest, the Lieutenant would think I'd lost it if I told him why.'

Frankie was staring at the photograph of the limbless body. 'Christ, I was hoping I'd never have to look at this ever again? It gave me nightmares for months.'

Maria looked at him. He'd never told her this. She'd never told him it had been the same for her either, but it had gotten to the pair of them. Much deeper than they could have imagined and now here it was once more. 'Wouldn't you be better asking the cold case review team to take a look?'

Addison shrugged. 'I can't, you know how much use Peters is. He'll laugh his ass off at me when I tell him. I want you two to at least make a start on it. If you can pull something together that could link any of it, I'll pass it on.'

Maria did know what an asshole Peters was and as much as she didn't want to have to pore through the files again she did like the thought of giving it one last shot to find the killer. Whoever it was deserved to be locked up. They deserved much worse than that. To know that whoever it was had been brought to justice would be good enough and make it all worthwhile.

'Yes sir, we'll make a start on it right now. Won't we, Frankie?'

Frankie didn't look as convinced as she sounded, but he nodded his head. Addison scooped up the photographs and put them back into the file.

'These are copies. I Xeroxed everything from the original file.' He pulled open his top drawer and pulled out another file and passed it across to Maria.

'And those are copies of everything Max found in the archives concerning the murder back in 52.'

He wrote a cell number across the front of the file, holding it towards her. 'You need anything else that's Max's number, give her a call.'

Maria took the second file. ‘Thanks.’

‘Oh and can the pair of you keep this to yourselves, I don’t want the rest of the department thinking I’m going soft in my old age.’

Both of them nodded. They stood up and walked out of his office, neither of them saying a word until they reached their desks. Maria looked at Frankie. ‘Coffee?’

‘Of course, you know me baby. I’m anyone’s for a cup of Sam’s delicious, caffeine infused drinks.’

Chapter Ten

Frankie found a parking bay a block down from Sam's Deli and they high-fived each other; if they were leaving the car it had to be in a proper bay. Traffic were prone to tow anything they could get their hands on. Maria grabbed the two files, ready to find a quiet booth, order breakfast and see what they could come up with. For the first time in months she felt glad to be doing something different. To be able to delve even deeper into it, she'd always felt bad that they never recovered the poor girl's head. Or caught the sick fuck who took it away in the first place. As much as it was going to reopen a can of worms inside her own head she was grateful to be given a second chance. She pushed open the heavy door to Sam's which was full of wise New Yorkers eating breakfast and ordering coffee to go. She spied an empty booth at the back, near to the bathrooms and made her way towards it. Frankie stopped to chat with a couple of beat cops who were on their way out, but she didn't recognize them which meant she didn't need to bother with the small talk. Shuffling into the booth, she lay the files down on the table, knowing she wouldn't open them until Marge had taken their order. It wasn't fair to subject nice, normal people to the horrors that they had to deal with. She picked up the menu and began reading, her stomach groaning in appreciation. Despite the fact that she'd had a bowl of granola she was still tempted to have one of Sam's huge bagels stuffed with bacon, eggs, mushrooms, tomatoes and topped with Swiss cheese. Frankie finally sat down opposite her.

'I wasn't hungry until I stepped in here. Why does it smell so damn good?'

'Have you eaten?'

He stuck his tongue out at her. 'Have you?'

'Yes, some granola.'

'I told you, eating that bird food isn't enough. I've had some coffee.'

'And the rest?'

'A couple of eggs, what are you my mother?'

She shook her head, before they could get into an argument Marge appeared like a vision from god.

'You two love birds at it again? What can I get you?'

Maria rhymed off her order, Frankie screwed up his eyes then nodded. 'I'll have the same please, Marge, and two of Sam's lattes please.'

Marge wrote down their order, tucking the pencil back behind her ear. She scooped up the menus and pointed to the files. 'You got something juicy going on in there?'

Maria nodded. 'It's horrific Marge, enough to put you off your food.'

'That good? Why don't you two get a change of department, work something nice? It can't be good for your brain seeing the crap you two look at every day.' She was tapping the side of her head with her pointed, bright red fingernail.

'Someone has to catch them and we're quite good at it.'

Frankie snorted. Marge smiled at him. 'Grow up Frankie.'

She walked away leaving Maria giggling, when she composed herself she wagged her finger at him. 'Yes, grow up Frankie.'

Frankie rolled his eyes. 'So this is a turn up for the books; if we play it right we won't have to deal with any crappy homicides this side of Christmas.'

‘This isn’t some kind of working holiday, it’s serious. We have to start from the beginning, go over everything, pull the evidence and crime scene logs.’

‘I know that, I’m just saying it’s nice. Who’d have thought old Addison would be such a pushover for his kid? I’m pretty shocked, I had him pegged as an asshole.’

‘You peg everyone as an asshole.’

‘Not you.’

‘Good, glad to hear it.’

Maria opened the folder from Max and looked at the assortment of black and white photocopied articles. There was a grainy black and white photograph of the outside of the Brownstone, the caption underneath read, *Family Home turned Slaughterhouse*. She shivered. The house looked in a much better state than it did now. She began to read the article only to be disturbed by Marge carrying a tray with their drinks. She gathered the pieces of paper up, closing the file, not wanting to upset her, and smiled at the older woman who had been serving people here forever.

Chapter Eleven

Greenwich Village 1952

Emilia pushed her plate away – she couldn't eat anymore if she tried. Mae did the same and rubbed her stomach.

'I hope my costume still fastens tonight. Mary will go crazy if it doesn't zip up.'

She began to laugh and Emilia joined in. 'What play are you in and who is Mary?'

'Mary is the wardrobe mistress. It's a musical called *Fanny* about a woman whose childhood love leaves her to go away to sea. After he leaves she discovers she's pregnant and has to marry an older man. I'm not actually the lead, I'm in the chorus. I'm the lead's understudy and stand-in. If she's ill or can't perform then I step in, but don't tell Clarke that. He came to see it the night I was standing in, he was so besotted I didn't have the heart to tell him the truth.'

'Oh, I won't. I'm sure that being the lead's understudy is just as important.'

For the first time Mae's cheeks flushed red. 'Thanks Em, I know you must think I'm a terrible person. Carrying on with your pa and lying to him, but I'm not. I like him and I know that I shouldn't, but he's kind and funny. In a way I wish he wasn't married to your mom.'

She didn't know what to say. She had a sense of duty towards her mother. They weren't close and never had been, her brother had always been her mother's favorite by far. Yet she didn't know this girl well enough to condone her relationship with her father. She didn't know her father well enough and she'd known him all her life. She wanted him to be happy; she really liked Mae. Unable to put how she felt into words she found herself shrugging.

'Sorry Em, this is heavy stuff to lay on you the second time I've met you. I just feel as if I can talk to you way more than anyone else. I've been friends with Gina since high school and we've never felt this close. I shouldn't put you in this position, I hope you're not angry with me?'

'Of course not, Mae, I like you too. I just don't know what to say. It's difficult.'

Mae held her hand up for the cheque and Em began to pull some dollars out of her purse.

'No way kid, this one's on me. I dragged you shopping and to eat enough pizza to feed a small country. It's the least I can do.'

She pulled the money, plus enough for a generous tip from her purse and left it on top of the bill. Standing up, she let out a groan and held her hand out to pull Emilia up. Both girls were smiling at each other. They were friends who shared a secret that made both their lives difficult, but Emilia didn't care. She'd had more fun the last three hours than she'd had in five years. This was how it was supposed to be, shopping, seeing the sights and eating dinner with your girlfriends. Not being shut away in a mausoleum on Staten Island with only your mother and brother for company.

They carried their bags outside into the chilly, autumn air. Em felt Mae's warm arm slip through hers and she smiled. It felt right. That they should be walking arm in arm, or was that reserved for lovers? For a fleeting moment, Em wondered what it would be like to kiss Mae… and then it was gone.

'Should I hail a cab?'

Em shook her head. ‘I need to walk a little, I’m so stuffed. If you need to go and get ready point me in the right direction, I’m sure I’ll find my way home.’

Mae shook her head. ‘I don’t think so. I’m not leaving you to navigate the city on your own. Clarke would kill me. We’ll walk together. I’ll catch a cab back to the theatre.’

Em felt the tight breath she’d been holding release; she would have walked on her own. The only thing was, she’d have been terrified. It wouldn’t have stopped her though as stubbornness was a Carter family trait. They headed away from the crowds of people and back down towards the village.

✪

James watched his sister and her new exotic friend walk towards the house from the attic window. They both looked pretty; his sister looked different. He wasn’t sure what made her look so attractive, maybe it was having a friend and a smile on her face. It made a change to see her smiling and not with her nose stuck in a book. He laughed to himself and turned around to look at the old, cracked, leather book which was open on his bed. It was a bad book, he knew that, and he knew that the best thing to do would be to take it and throw it in the river. Ever since he’d discovered it he had done nothing but think evil thoughts. It was as if it controlled his mind and he knew that was ridiculous, or was it? He’d always had an interest in witchcraft and the occult, he found it fascinating. He wanted to know if the strange creatures that were so carefully illustrated on the pages of the book existed. He kind of believed that they did, but he needed proof. He was going to start working on the ritual to see if he could summon the demon like the book promised. He didn’t need money, his pa had plenty of that. What he did want was the power that the dark forces promised. It said in the book that human sacrifices were needed, three of them. He didn't have a problem with this and in fact he already had them lined up thanks to his sister's new friend. Emilia had always looked down her nose at him, Mae and Missy would be perfect. His problem would be killing them and doing what he had to before his pa found out and killed him. It was ambitious, and it didn't come without risk. His pa wouldn't be too pleased to find his daughter, lover and housekeeper's decapitated and dismembered bodies. It wouldn't matter so long as he didn't find out until he'd summoned his demon. Once he had, he would have enough power to take on an entire army. His angry parents would be of no consequence whatsoever.

Chapter Twelve

Maria was fascinated, this whole thing was a change and something that she welcomed with open arms. Frankie pulled up outside the station to drop her off; he had a dental appointment and she was glad to be free of him for a while. She was going to go back to the apartment and revisit it, speak to the old lady who lived below, if she was still there. She hoped she hadn't died. She remembered her telling her that she'd lived in the same apartment most of her life. Maria jumped out of the car, the folder tucked under her arm. She wanted to make copies of it so she had a file to work on from home. Frankie would scold her if he knew, but this was more her thing. There had been two occasions where she'd almost transferred to the Cold Case Department. The only thing that had stopped her had been Frankie; they made a good team. That and the fact that Lieutenant Peters was a pain in the ass. She ran up to the department where she duplicated everything, before going back to the address. It wasn't as if she needed Frankie to babysit her, she could do this on her own. She was a big girl now.

As she found a gap big enough to park in, she wondered if she should have waited for Frankie. Getting out of the car she crossed the road, walking back down towards the apartment. It stood out amongst all of the others and she wondered if that was because she knew of its disturbing history. Or whether it was because it was so badly neglected. The Brownstones in the village were worth a lot of money, so why had the owners chosen to leave this one to decay? As she reached the stone steps which went down to the front door she stood with her hands on her hips. Was it her or did it give off bad vibes, like it was its own, living, breathing entity? She had no idea how long she'd been staring at it when a car horn beeped behind her, making her jump. She looked around disorientated for a moment and had no idea where she was or what she was staring at. The front door opened and a dreadlocked man came running up the steps, an invisible cloak of cannabis shrouding him. She stepped to one side to let him pass, he looked her up and down. Maria shook her head. She wasn't interested in him and he nodded. He knew she was a cop. He could probably smell it on her like she could smell the recreational drugs on him. He lifted his headphones over his ears and began to walk away but she reached out and grabbed his arm. He turned, glaring at her.

'What you want? I'm minding my own business.'

'Hey, sorry. Yes, you are, I wanted to ask you about the apartments.'

He shook his head. 'You don't want to live here. It's not good for someone like you.'

He turned and walked away and she wondered what the hell that was supposed to mean, so she jogged to catch up to him and this time the look in his eyes told her she was pissing him off big time.

'What do you mean?'

'It's the kind of place you only live if there's nowhere else. That's all.'

'Have you lived here long?'

He put his hands on his hips and she took a step back.

'Ten years. Now you gonna let me get on my way?'

'Yes, sorry. Thanks.'

He turned, striding away from her as fast as he could. She wondered what he meant and walked down the steps, pressing several buzzers in the hope that someone would let her in. She heard the door click and pushed it open, then as she stepped inside the memories of that night three years ago flooded her mind. She felt her body shudder, not sure if it was a replay from the past or the fact that this place truly freaked her out. Until now she'd forgotten how she'd felt when she'd first entered the house. It was creepy as fuck, there was no doubt about it. There was a faint smell of cannabis lingering in the air, mixed with fried onions. They were masking an underlying odour of something damp and rotten, she wondered if the whole block was full of dry rot. There was something wrong with this place. She didn't know what, but it gave her a bad feeling. It was so quiet in here it was eerie. You wouldn't believe it homed at least ten residents. She began to climb the stairs wondering which apartment the guy she'd stopped on the street lived in. As she reached the third floor she stared at the apartment and hoped the woman would still be there. Before she could knock on the heavy, black oak door it opened a crack and she pulled out her badge, holding it up.

'Yes?'

'Good afternoon ma'am, NYPD Homicide. Could I speak to you about the murder three years ago?'

A thin hand reached through the gap in the door and took the badge out of her hand. After a few seconds the door opened and a frailer looking version of the woman she'd interviewed that night stared at her.

'I remember you.'

Maria smiled. 'I remember you too. Could I come inside for a few minutes?'

She thought the door was about to slam shut in her face, but it didn't and the woman stepped back allowing her inside. It was gloomy in the hallway and the first thing she noticed was the number of crucifixes hung on the wall and above each doorway. The woman led her into a spacious living room which had a huge crucifix hanging above the fireplace. Maria tried not to take too much notice of it, religion was a sticky subject for her. The woman pointed to a chair and she sat down, relieved it wasn't facing the enormous cross.

'So, what do you want? I spoke to you when it happened, you never caught him.'

There was no arguing with the woman in front of her, she didn't catch him that was very true.

'I'm afraid we didn't, you're right. Sometimes they get away.'

The woman nodded. 'Sometimes they have a little help.'

Maria frowned, not sure what she meant. 'Have you lived her long, Mrs…?'

The woman began to laugh. 'Miss Carter you can call me Emilia. Yes, I've lived here all my life and that's a very long time.'

'How long?'

'I moved in here permanently when I was twenty-two.'

Maria tried to work out how old Emilia was, failing miserably.

'Sixty five years to be exact. I've been here since I was twenty-two and never left.'

'Wow that's a lot of rent.'

Emilia shook her head. 'I don't pay rent, this house belongs to me.'

Maria was shocked, the woman had never mentioned it the last time she'd spoken to her.

'So, you remember the murder in the fifties?'

Her already watery, dark brown eyes blinked several times.

'Yes I do, as if it was yesterday.'

There was a loud dragging noise on the ceiling above them and Emilia looked up horrified.

'No one lives up there. It's empty, it has been since the night of the murder.'

'Someone must have broken in?'

Emilia shook her head. 'No-one lives there, no-one wants to live there. It's haunted.'

She stated the fact as if she was telling her it was cold outside or rain had been forecast.

'I don't understand. Has anyone been in and checked there isn't anyone squatting up there?'

Emilia nodded. 'More times than you can ever imagine. It's always the same. Scratching, dragging, knocks, bangs, the footsteps are the worst. Heavy, clattering footsteps, but not the kind that you or me would make. Oh no, these sound like hooves, stomping on the wooden floorboards and always at the same time. 3am is when it likes to get busy.'

Maria could feel the hairs on the back of her neck begin to prickle, a feeling of unease spreading over her. Did the woman in front of her have some kind of dementia?

'Right now you're considering if I'm a crazy old bat aren't you? Trust me honey I'm not, I've lived with it all my life. I knew it was a mistake renting the attic apartment out, but the realtors who handle the rentals insisted. They had someone come in and paint all the walls white, sand the floors, clean the windows. It looked good enough, I even went up there to take a peek. I hadn't been up there for over fifty years. I couldn't go inside because no matter what they did to it. I'd never get that image out of my head.'

'What image was that?'

A loud scratching on the ceiling directly above where they were sitting made even Maria jump from her chair. The woman crossed herself and shook her head. 'I don't talk about it and neither should you. I need you to leave now, I don't want to upset it any further. You don't have to live here, I do.'

She stood up and Maria did the same, not sure what was going on as Emilia led her to the front door.

'Thank you.' Unsure what she was thanking her for she passed her a card. 'If you do decide you want to talk, call me. That's my cell. Anytime. Oh, one last thing, who's the guy with the dreadlocks?'

'Mikey.' The woman took the card from her, slamming her apartment door shut.

Maria couldn't ignore the fact that she'd clearly heard someone moving around in the empty apartment above them. She had to check it out whether the old lady wanted her to or not, it was her duty. Turning to make sure she wasn't being watched by Emilia she began to walk up the next flight of steps. Shivering, she felt the goose bumps which had broken out all over her arms. That lady had unnerved her.

As she reached the small landing she wondered why it was so dark up here; even if it was empty it wouldn't cost much to run a single bulb to illuminate the place. A faint whiff of sulphur and rotten eggs filled the air. Maybe there was a gas leak. For the second time in less than an hour she wished she'd waited for Frankie to come back from the dentist before coming here. She stood staring at the door, forcing herself to walk towards it. She had to drag her legs which had turned into lead weights. When she was as close to the door as she could be she turned her head, placing her ear against the wood to listen. The foreboding sense of dread which shrouded her entire body made her knees go weak. Her gut instinct was telling her to get the hell out of there, her stubborn mind ignored it. She squeezed her eyes shut, concentrating. The image of a huge, cloven-hoofed beast filled it. She had a vision of it standing on the other side of the door, imitating her and waiting for her to make her next move. The smell of rotten eggs was emanating through the cracks around the door and she wondered if there was another body in there. She couldn't go in without a warrant, more to the point she didn't know if she was brave enough to go in there with no back up. Her stomach a mass of churning knots, she straightened up and stepped away from the door. If she was going in it was with a couple of officers. *And a priest,* a voice whispered in her ear. She turned away walking briskly to the stairs, and on running back down them she heard a faint scratching. Like razor, sharp talons being dragged across wood. Maria didn't stop, she was well and truly getting out of there. How the fuck Emilia had lived in that house for sixty-five years without losing her mind was a miracle. As she reached the ground floor the guy with the dreadlocks, Mikey, was opening one of the apartment doors. He took one look at her pale face and wide eyes then shook his head.

'I told you this place was full of bad shit.'

Maria nodded, forcing herself to walk out of the door when what she really wanted to do was run as fast as she could and never look back.

Chapter Thirteen

Frankie arrived back at the station with a fat lip, just as Maria pulled up. Smiling at him, he nodded and the pair of them walked up the steps together. He waited until they were alone.

'Do you want to tell me why you look so terrified?'

Maria cursed his perception. 'Do I?'

He nodded. It was pointless lying to him because he'd never shut up.

'I went to pay the old lady a visit at the house.'

'You need to give me more than that. What old lady? Which house?'

'The house on West 10th Street.'

She held her breath, waiting for the lecture about going out alone, being careless. It didn't come, instead he put his hand on her arm.

'What happened?'

She looked around to make sure there was no-one in hearing distance.

'I don't know exactly, but that house is creepy as fuck. I went there to talk to the woman in the apartment below the attic.'

'I remember her, she was a grouchy old bird.'

'Not only did she remember the first murder, she owns the damn building and was there when it happened.'

'Well, maybe we should bring her in for questioning. There can't be that many people alive who remember what happened the first time around.'

Maria was shocked; it hadn't even crossed her mind that the frail woman could be the one responsible for the horrific murders.

'Are you for real? She's almost ninety.'

'Age is just a number, she might be fitter than the pair of us. It's not unheard of.'

'Nah, it's not her. You didn't see the look of fear on her face.'

'Why was she scared?'

'You promise you won't laugh?'

He rolled his eyes.

'There was this dragging and scratching sound on the ceiling above in the empty apartment, it made the hairs on the back of my neck prickle.'

'It's an old house, Maria, it probably has rats the size of alley cats. If the attic doesn't get used for years on end they'll be running riot up there.'

Maria thought about it. This could be very true. Hell, it probably was very true, but her stomach was rolling around like a lead ball. When this happened it normally meant her gut was telling her what to believe. It didn't believe that what she'd heard was a rat. About to tell Frankie this, she changed her mind. She wasn't in the mood for him to march her back there to go and check because he would. She didn't want to set foot inside that house again unless she had to.

'I guess you're right.'

'Of course, I'm right, baby, I always am.'

She stepped forward and slapped his arm. 'Christ, you're so full of shit.' But she couldn't help laughing and felt better. She'd spooked herself and that crazy old woman with her room full of crucifixes hadn't helped. They walked along the corridor to reach the unit which was busy, both went to their desks and sat down. Neither of them spoke as they didn't want the others to know what they were working on.

After an hour Maria looked up to see Frankie who was standing up, tugging on his coat.

'Come on, I've had enough of this place. My face is aching. Let's go to the Cat and talk in there. Maybe we should see if we can get Max to meet us and we can hear everything she has to say.'

She stood up, for once she wanted to go and get a cold beer. Maybe even a cocktail or two and it would be good to meet the girl who had thought the case was important enough to drag it all up and get them reassigned to it.

The Cat had its regular crowd of patrons in there, propping up the bar. Inhaling the aroma of hamburger and fried onions, Maria hadn't realized she was hungry until her stomach let out a loud growl. She walked to the bar signalling for Frankie to take a seat, he was on the phone to Max. He stuck his thumb up at her so she ordered two bottles of Bud and a cheeseburger with fries, onion rings and almost everything else she could think of. Placing a beer in front of Frankie, he nodded.

'My mouth is still swollen, forgive me if I drool.'

She laughed. 'Well there's something you don't hear every day. So what did she say?'

'I haven't lost my charm, she'll be here in thirty minutes.'

'Good, that means I'll have enough time to eat my burger before she comes and puts me off it.'

Frankie groaned. 'I want food, but I can't chew yet.'

'You can have some of mine, your mouth should be working properly by the time they bring it out.'

They sat in silence, sipping their beers waiting for Max to arrive. The bartender, who neither of them had seen before, brought Maria's food over. Frankie stared, his mouth open wide. She grabbed a couple of French fries and pushed them into her mouth.

'What you staring at?'

'I can't believe you're eating without me.'

'Get over it. Here.' She pushed the plate towards him and he picked up the biggest onion ring on the plate.

'Hi, are you Frankie?'

Maria couldn't help it, she let out a giggle. His already swollen face was bulging at the sides, making him look like a hamster stocking up for hibernation. He nodded, pointing at Maria.

'You must be Max, I'm his partner, Maria. Pleased to meet you.' She held out her hand and the woman, who had to only be in her early twenties shook it.

'I've heard a lot about you.'

She shrugged. 'I hope it isn't all bad, your dad doesn't always see the best in me.'

The girl threw her head back and began to laugh, a real hearty, laugh which instantly made Maria like her. When she'd composed herself, she spoke. 'He doesn't always see the best in anyone. But he's not that bad, he could be worse I suppose. At least he's taken me seriously which caught me by surprise. I thought he'd tell me to stop interfering when I showed him the clippings.'

'He did. So seriously that he's given me and hamster boy here a few weeks to reopen the case.'

The girl sat down next to Frankie, Maria picked up the burger and took a huge bite. Frankie picked up his beer.

'So we've heard the condensed version from your old man, now we'd like to hear the full length one.'

Maria held up her hands. 'Please let me finish my food before the gory details come out. Frankie where's your manners? Go and get Max a drink.'

Chapter Fourteen

He opened his eyes and wondered where he was; it was dark and he could feel a firm mattress beneath him. The beads of sweat on his forehead and his pounding heart brought back the memories of the nightmare he'd struggled to wake from. He was in a cave, far below the ground where a fire was burning so hot he had felt the heat from the flames scorching his skin. The cave had been full of dark, wispy shadows that moved and changed shape. He'd thought he recognized the outline of his mother and walked towards it only for it to dissipate. Just like she had been when she was alive: never there for him, not interested in his life, not interested in him. Why would she be there for him now she was dead? There was an old, cracked wooden door and he headed towards it. Needing to get out of the suffocating darkness, he heard the scratching behind him. Loud, claw-like, dragging sounds against the rock face of the cave. For the first time he'd felt terror at what was making the sound. It had scared him so much that it woke him up. He remembered where he was, he was in the apartment. Asleep on the bed where he'd last slept with the beautiful girl, Anya, before he'd killed her. He wondered if Anya was trapped in here, her soul unable to leave because of what he'd done to her. The apartment had been used for satanic rituals and murders, no-one wanted to live in here because of the bad vibes. So what was he doing here? In a rare moment of lucidity, he knew he should leave and get as far away from here as possible. He'd managed to survive three years without being caught for Anya's murder. She'd picked him up in the Russian bar on 52nd Street. He'd been waiting for his date who hadn't turned up and she'd been waiting tables. When she'd finished work she came and sat with him, he'd been mesmerised by her beauty. A sharp pang of guilt stabbed him through his heart. This had been his apartment. He'd brought her back here where they'd spent twenty-four hours making love and drinking vodka. She'd told him about the voices she heard in here. Whispers that she couldn't understand and at first, he'd thought she'd been crazy, but two days later when she'd gone to work and he'd been here alone he'd heard them. Faint at first, hard to understand, they were in a language that he'd never heard before. Once he'd realized he could hear the whispering, it got louder as if it knew it had his attention. He'd heard his name called several times and at one point had thought Anya had returned. Realising that she hadn't, he then proceeded to search the entire apartment only to find nothing. He was alone.

It had been none of his business, he knew that now. He should have walked away and none of this would have happened. He would still have a job, an apartment, Anya would still be alive. He wouldn't be back here where it all began a very long time ago. It was like a sickness, this obsession to come back here. The atmosphere up here was heavy; even in his shorts and t-shirt it felt as if he was cloaked in darkness. This apartment was all he'd thought about whilst in the psych ward. When the police had picked him up he had no ID on him and gave them false details so they wouldn't be able to trace him to the apartment. He'd never been in trouble before, never had his prints taken, the officers thought he was mental, all they'd wanted was to get him off their hands so they could finish their shift. Even though he knew it was wrong he had wanted to be back here. Now that he was, he knew it wasn't going to end well. There would be more deaths. There had to be – it had been written in blood. Whatever it was that had been summoned many years ago was here. Lurking in the shadows, waiting to be called forward into the light to dominate and take over. As scared as he was, he couldn't stop it because it knew his name, it knew every part of him and wouldn't let him go. He was a pawn in this game between good and evil, fighting on the side of the darkness that he knew would consume him and there wasn't anything he could do to stop it.

He dragged himself off the bed, his head groggy. He felt as if he had a hangover from hell. He laughed. That was a pretty apt description. As he walked into the living area he heard the whispering, then shook his head as if it would clear the voices. It didn't, they were there in the background. The smell in here was terrible, rotten eggs and sulphur. It smelt as if someone had been striking matches, he went to check and see if the candles were lit. The wicks were untouched but, something had been in here whilst he was sleeping. A cold shiver ran down the full length of his spine as he wondered whether he would be able to control it when the time came. If it was coming and going as it pleased, did it need him at all?

Chapter Fifteen

Max sat back and took a large gulp of the bottle of Bud she'd been nursing in her left hand. Maria did the same.

Frankie asked. 'Let me get this straight, you think the house has some kind of curse on it?'

She shrugged. 'I don't know if I believe that it's cursed, but there's something wrong with it. There have been two murders in the same apartment. Both women had their limbs cut off and their heads removed. Not to mention the number of suicides and deaths by natural causes.'

Frankie let Maria speak. 'How many other deaths?'

'Seven, well… nine with the murders. You have to admit that's a lot of deaths for one house.'

'You get that with rentals.'

'I know, but they've all been women. Don't you think it's strange?'

'Yes, I do. It's not that I don't believe you, it's just I'm a trained detective who relies on cold, hard, evidence. I'm not very good when it comes to something that's not black and white.'

Frankie joined in. 'It's true, she isn't.'

'Well, what are we going to do about it? I can't leave it, there has to be some connection between the murders.'

'There are sixty-five years between the murders, who would even remember the first?' Maria was trying to keep calm, but the kid was winding her up and she wasn't even sure why.

'What about the old lady you spoke to who owns the building? You said yourself that she knew all about the first one. We need to go back and interview her properly, she must know something. I don't believe that she doesn't.'

Maria glared at Frankie, realising why she was so angry with Max. It was fear. She was scared to go back to the house and she would have to if they wanted to interview her. There was something about the house on West 10th Street that made her blood run cold. Max finished her beer and stood up.

'Sorry, I know I've gone on and got all defensive. I can't help it, I feel as if we have to find out what happened there. Why the women who live in that house die there. It's as if it's gotten under my skin. It's all I think about and I feel as if it's my duty to put their souls to rest because they're not at peace. Whoever has died in that house is stuck there; it's like a form of purgatory.'

She glanced at Frankie who was sitting there with his mouth open. Maria smiled at her. 'It's not often Frankie is left speechless. It was nice to meet you, we'll see what we can find out and be in touch. Is that okay with you?'

'Yes, I guess it is. Thank you both.'

She grabbed her purse and strode towards the exit, not looking back.

Maria stared after her, and then turned to Frankie.

'Well, what do you make of her?'

'I want to say that she's nuts, a complete loser.'

'But you can't, can you, because you think she's on to something.'

He nodded.

'I do too. I'm telling you now, I really don't want to go back to that house.'

'Then what are we going to do? We have to question the old lady, you know that, Maria. She's the only link we have. We go together, in the daylight. Neither of us are to go there alone.'

She stood up. 'I need to go home, I'm tired.'

'Hey, I need to ask you a favour?'

'What?'

'Will you come dancing with me tomorrow night?'

Maria frowned at him. 'Ask Christy.'

'It's for Christy, you told me to put some spark back in my marriage. Well, I figured if I learnt how to dance for real, I could take her to one of the fancy Christmas balls at The Plaza or The Met. Surprise her. What do you say? It's good exercise. You'll be able to burn that burger and fries off you just swallowed whole.'

'Do you have a death wish, Frankie?'

He held his hands up.

'If I need to burn the burger off I'll go for a run, but since this is the first half decent, romantic idea you've ever had I'll go with you. On one condition.'

He grinned. 'What?'

'You don't crush my feet.'

He pretended to look hurt.

'I'm going home Frankie, you should do the same. You better get some beauty sleep.'

She walked to the exit smiling to herself, she was going home for a soak in the bath and refused to think about anything they'd been discussing until tomorrow. She wasn't going to be terrified tonight, not when she was on her own.

Chapter Sixteen

Greenwich Village, 1952

Emilia had never been so excited to go to the theatre, and it helped that Mae was taking the lead tonight. Who would have thought that her friend would be so beautiful and talented? She understood the attraction that her father must feel towards Mae, but she couldn't understand why Mae found him so attractive. He was much older, she supposed he was relatively good looking for his age. James had come down from his room in the attic looking frightful, his face had an unhealthy pallor about it.

'Are you ill James? Do you need a doctor?'

He glared at her. 'No, do you?'

'What do you mean by that remark, why would I need a doctor? It's not me who looks like a patient from a tuberculosis hospital.'

Realising how harsh that was, she spoke in a much softer tone. 'Why don't you come with me to the theatre and watch Mae? I've seen the way you watch her, you like her. It would do you good to get some fresh air and life into your lungs.'

He carried on glaring at her. 'Does it not strike you as strange how you have suddenly become such good friends with the whore who is sleeping with our father? His place is by mother's side, not shacked up with a cheap hooker.'

Emilia crossed the room, raised her hand and slapped him hard across the face, leaving an angry red handprint etched into his skin.

'Why do you have to be so mean? You're just like mom. No wonder pop would rather spend time with Mae. Go back to your creepy attic where you belong, you don't have a decent bone in your body.'

He shook his head at her. 'You'll be sorry, just wait and see.' He stormed out of the room down to the kitchen and Emilia wondered what had just happened. She had never struck anyone before and was wondering if she should apologize to him when the loud beep of the cab sounded outside. Instead she went to the front door and ran up the steps to the sidewalk and the waiting car. She had been given a seat in Mr Lawson's private box to watch the show. If she calmed down by the time she came home she would go and apologize to him. He had always been jealous of her and now it seemed he was jealous of Mae. Which was stupid because he didn't even know her, he hadn't even attempted to speak to her. She got into the cab and pushed all thoughts of her strange brother out of her mind, if he was that bothered about mom he could go back and be with her. She didn't know why he'd come into the city anyway, it wasn't as if he had any business or friends to catch up with. He'd always been such a loner and judging by the way he was carrying on he always would be.

✪

James heard the heavy, oak door slam and ran to the window to watch. His sister was getting far too big for her breeches, but not for long. He would be putting an end to that very soon. How dare she think she could strike him across the face and not pay a penalty? This Mae was having a bad influence on her and the sooner he killed her the better. Mom would thank him for it when she knew what had been going on. She would be more than a little upset to discover her husband was sleeping around so openly. Maybe he should kill him too; take all three of them out in one go. He only needed three bodies. Three was the magic number. Three was the devil's way of throwing his scorn on the holy trinity. He went back upstairs to his attic room, for he had many things to prepare. He took the Ouija board from under his bed and put it on the table. He pulled the drawer out and took the planchette out, his hand trembling as he lifted it to his eye to look through it. Slowly moving around the room, this time there was nothing there. No dark, smoky shadows lingering in the corners. No strange-looking creatures, which considering the anger and hatred that was bubbling inside of him he found surprising. There was a long, drawn-out scratching sound behind him. He swung around. With the planchette still held up to his face, he stumbled backwards on seeing the huge, black, beast standing behind him. His blood turned to iced water in his veins as his heart pumped it around his body faster, turning him into a shivering wreck. The thing had its back to him and for that he was grateful. He wasn't prepared for this yet. He stepped backwards away from it. Banging into the kitchen counter behind him, he dropped the planchette. Frantically searching the floor he panicked. Without it he couldn't see the beast. He didn't know where it was. As he scrabbled on the floor to grab it, he felt the hot, rotten, breath in his face. Looking up there was nothing in front of him; yet he knew different. He could smell it. It was inches from him. James had never felt terror so extreme in his life. He wasn't ready. When he wanted it to appear it would be on his terms, he would be in control. The whole point of this was that the creature would be grateful to him for summoning it from the depths of hell and it would want to do whatever he told it to appease him. It wasn't here on its terms. Every hair on his arms stood on edge as the sharp pain of gut wrenching terror made him double over. The air was charged with static electricity and for a moment he wondered if this was it, was his life about to end? All his planning would be wiped out with one swift blow from the demon standing in front of him. He closed his eyes, forcing his dry mouth to open as he whispered.

'Beast be gone, you will not return until I summon you. You are not to come and go as you please, by the power invested in me as the one who will bring you back I command you to leave. Your time is almost here, we have to be ready or it won't work and you'll be forever stuck half in this world and half in the dark.'

The room felt lighter, the smell had gone and his heart slowed down. Opening his eyes, he lifted the planchette to use as his mirror to the other world. This time he saw nothing through it; no dark shadows and no terrifying beast. For now, it was safe, and the space was his once more. He knew he needed to toughen up if he wanted to do this. How could he command a demon from the depths of hell if he couldn't speak above a whisper?

✪

Emilia gave a standing ovation, she thought Mae had been amazing. She had turned into someone else on the stage who was completely captivating, even more so than her usually exotic self. Making her way from the private box she was met at the side of the stage by a young boy of no more than fourteen. He looked at her and grinned.

'You must be Mae's friend, she sent me to find you.'

He held out his hand. She grasped hold of it, shaking it.

'I'm Billy, you can call me Bill. I work here every night. I'm going to be on that stage soon.'

'Well hello Bill, I'm Emilia. I can't wait to see you up there.'

He laughed. 'Come on, she's waiting for you. She told me not to talk too much.'

He turned and Emilia followed him to the far end of the first floor and a door which led to a stairwell. He ran down to a room with a gold star stuck to the door, she ran down after him. On it someone had written "Mae". Emilia wondered how marvellous it would feel to be like her friend: full of confidence and beautiful. Lifting her hand to knock she paused as a sense of terrible foreboding fell over her, like a black shadow. It clung to her making her feel sick and dizzy. Her knuckles grazed the wood as she fell against it, her legs felt as if they didn't belong to her. The door opened, and she fell into Mae's arms. She let out a scream as Mae caught her and then the room went black.

Chapter Seventeen

Miss Green was shuffling to the elevator when Maria pushed her way through the glass doors of the lobby. Maria caught up with her and did a double take.

'Miss Green, what's the matter?'

She'd never seen the old lady with no make-up or jewellery on, ever. She didn't look at Maria.

'Today isn't a good day.'

Maria felt her heart tear in two. In all the years she'd known her whenever she'd asked her how she was she always replied, 'Today is a good day.' She pushed her arm through hers and pressed the call button.

'Come on, why I don't I make us a nice pot of tea and you can tell me what's wrong?'

Miss Green didn't look at her, she nodded and for the first time in forever it struck Maria just how old and frail she was. There was so much running through her head, she was afraid to find out what was wrong in case it was something that no amount of tea could help. The rickety elevator finally came to a stop on the ground floor, the doors rattled open and they both stepped inside. Maria could feel the burger she'd eaten earlier churning around in her stomach. She pushed the button for their floor and waited for it to judder to a halt. She took hold of Miss Green's elbow and led her down to her apartment where she opened the door for her and followed her in. Maria pointed to the armchair and went to the kitchen counter to switch the kettle on.

'You're a good girl, far too good to be living on your own. You deserve a nice man or woman to keep you warm in bed each night.'

Maria laughed. 'I do. We both do. Although there's a lot to be said for being single. I like being able to eat what I want and watch crappy cable shows all day in my sweats.'

Miss Green looked up, her watery eyes fixed on Maria. 'I do too, but when you get to my age it gets lonely. It's all very well pretending you're happy doing your own thing, but wouldn't you like to have someone waiting for you when you got in from work? You work so hard, doing a terrible job. I can't begin to imagine the horrors of what you must face every day. You are very brave and deserve to be taken care of, find yourself a rich boyfriend.'

Maria laughed, she carried two mugs of tea over and placed them on the table, then she went back and grabbed the half-eaten packet of Oreos from the cupboard and put them on a plate. When Miss Green picked one up and started nibbling on it she smiled, the woman really was a woman after her own heart.

'Thank you, dear, I've just realized how hungry I am.'

'You're welcome. Can I fix you a sandwich?'

She shook her head. 'These are just fine, I'm partial to a chocolate cookie.'

They sat there in silence, both sipping their tea. Maria waiting for the opportunity to ask what was wrong. She didn't have to wait long.

'I bet you think I'm crazy, look at the state of me. I didn't even put my lipstick on before I left the house.'

'You look fabulous with or without it.'

The woman's cheeks turned pink and she laughed.

'You're a sweetheart. I was about to put my make-up on when the letter came, out of the blue, just like that it was pushed under the door. So it must have been hand delivered. I knew it must be something bad and I should have thrown it in the trash like my brain was telling me to.

I didn't. My inquisitive nature got the better of me and now look what a sorry state I'm in.'

Maria sipped her tea, waiting for her to continue. Miss Green pulled a letter out of her purse and passed it to her. She read the single sentence, again and again. Trying to understand what it might mean and couldn't. The words filled her mind.

It's come back

Maria held it out towards Miss Green who shook her head.

'Please would you be a sweetheart and get rid of it for me, I can't bear to think about it.'

'What does it mean? Who sent it?'

The old woman stared at her. 'It means that someone has been dabbling in black magic, messing with things they have no concept of. When I finally fled that house I'd lived in for years, I hoped I'd never have to go back. I saw things with my own two eyes that I never knew existed. Things that I never want to see again. Something that I swore I would never talk about ever again.'

'You can tell me, it might make you feel better to get it off your chest.'

Maria wasn't sure why, but she felt creeped out beyond belief. The hairs on the back of her neck were standing on end and she felt as if a dark cloud had descended over her. She looked around the apartment, surprised to see how dark and gloomy it was in here despite the lights being on. Miss Green shook her head.

'I wouldn't drag you into this, you're much safer kept out of it.'

'I'm a cop, it's my job. I chase the bad guys and the killers every day. Hell, I shoot them if I have to and I don't think twice about it because they're BAD guys. Please let me help you Miss Green, I want to help.'

A single tear fell from the corner of her eye and she shook her head.

'You are a good girl, Maria, God knows this and He will look after you. Don't ever doubt that.'

She pushed herself up from the table. 'Come on, off you go. You have your own life to live and I'm just being a silly, morbid, old fool. I'll have a large brandy and go to bed. Tomorrow is another day. I'll forget about that stupid note and make sure I put my lipstick on.'

She winked at Maria who smiled and stood up. 'Well, I'm only across the hall if you need to talk to me, even if it's in the middle of the night. You just call or give me a knock.'

'Thank you, I will.'

'Promise?'

She shook her head, 'I'll be fine. Thank you for taking the time to listen to a crazy, old bat like me ramble on. I swear even though it sounds it, I'm not senile just yet.'

Maria bent and kissed her cheek. 'I know you're not and I'm serious about calling me.' She walked towards the front door, sensing that Miss Green needed to be on her own.

Maria shut the door behind her and waited to hear the dead bolt turn before heading into her own apartment. No idea what to make of the last fifteen minutes, she kicked off her shoes and turned on all the lights. If she hadn't been creeped out enough before, she was now. Not bothering to turn the TV on she switched the radio on instead as she checked out each room. She felt as if she was being watched, no idea by who or what, but it was enough for her to make sure there was no-one hiding under the bed or in the closets. Changing into her pyjamas and pouring herself a large glass of wine she picked up a notebook from the table. Then sitting crossed legged on the sofa, she began to write down a list of everything weird that had happened to her today. The lively chatter on the radio interspersed with a selection of Lady Gaga songs took away some of her unease. The wine helped as well, as she wrote down what had happened at the house on West 10th then the bizarre conversation with Miss Green. She wondered if there was some connection. How could there be? She hadn't told anyone except Frankie about the house. Miss Green wouldn't know where she'd been or what she'd been doing at work would she? It was all just some weird coincidence, nothing more. She sipped the wine, questioning her beliefs in the paranormal. It wasn't something that she'd ever had to think about before. She didn't believe in stuff like that, being a black and white say-what-you-see kind of girl. *Yeah, but what about saying how you feel, Maria? You know there was something up in that attic apartment. You felt it, you heard it, Christ, you smelt it. Are you going to deny how scared you were? Maybe Miss Green and that house aren't connected, maybe you're the connection?* Her entire body shuddered at the thought. She needed to take her mind off it, needed to relax, or she was never going to sleep. She picked up the phone and waited to see if Frankie answered. It went to voicemail. Downing the rest of the wine she grabbed the throw off the back of the sofa and lay down, an overwhelming feeling of exhaustion making her yawn. Wrapping herself in it she didn't turn any of the lights off and left the radio on. She closed her eyes and hoped that sleep would come fast.

Chapter Eighteen

The hammering on Maria's apartment door was so loud she jumped off the couch confused. Her heart racing, she wondered what was wrong. Her first thought being her neighbor, she ran to the door and peered through the peephole to see Frankie standing there. His shirt buttons undone, sleeves rolled up and his eyes glassy. Relieved it wasn't her neighbor she began to slide back the assortment of bolts and chains, opening the door. She looked at the clock on the wall realising it was almost 2am.

'What the hell, Frankie? You scared the living crap out of me.'

He grinned. 'You rang me and then I couldn't get hold of you. I was worried. Sorry about scaring you. I also need somewhere to stay, I'm locked out.'

She stepped back to let him in and he stumbled past her, the sour smell of bourbon turning her stomach.

'Where have you been? When I left you a couple of hours ago you were on your way home to Christy? How did you get in this state?'

He laughed. 'She's a bitch, you know that don't you. She ripped my head off as soon as I walked through the door. I wanted to strangle her with my bare hands and I've never felt like that before.'

He collapsed onto the sofa. Maria felt scared for Christy, surely he wouldn't have hurt her.

'Where is she? Did you hurt her?'

He started laughing. 'Hurt the ice queen? You got to be kidding me. I wanted to, but I didn't. Come on, Maria, you know me. I'm not the wife beating kind of scumbag we deal with. I left and went back to The Cat.'

She let out a sigh. 'I know you're not.' Turning around she began to fill the percolator up to brew a pot of fresh coffee.

'I need to pee.' She turned to see him stumbling along to the bathroom and let him go. He was going to need an IV of black coffee pumped straight into his veins to sober him up. She remembered that he hadn't eaten and began to make him a sandwich, he needed carbs in his stomach. The noise of the percolator disguised his return. She turned around and screeched to see him standing behind her.

'What the fuck, Frankie.'

'I'm not that ugly.'

She smiled. 'You're not ugly at all.'

'Then why doesn't Christy ever want me?'

He reached out a hand and touched her cheek. 'You're beautiful, Maria, I love you.'

For a moment she was tempted to kiss him; he was very attractive and she liked him a lot – more than she should. Then she came to her senses and pushed his hand away.

'Yeah, you've got beer goggles on. Tell me that when you're sober.'

He lowered his hand, the moment gone. He smiled at her, but it didn't reach his eyes like it normally did. It was the saddest smile she'd ever seen and it broke her heart a little. She passed him the sandwich. 'Eat this, or you're gonna be barfing all day.'

'Thanks. Sorry for waking you up.'

She carried two mugs over, placing his on the coffee table. Nursing hers she sat back down on the armchair. He stuck his thumb up at her as he tried to eat his sandwich without making too much mess. She tried not to watch him, instead she sipped at her coffee wondering if she would be able to get back to sleep. She wasn't angry with him, in fact she was glad of the company. In her dream she'd been about to go back into the house on West 10th and she'd been terrified. He finished his sandwich and she leant across, passing him the mug.

'Good job we're not on an early shift tomorrow.'

He nodded. 'Old Addison has done us a favour. No fresh meat for a while.'

She wasn't sure if she agreed; she had a feeling that this was just the start and they were about to get involved in something she'd never dreamt about in her darkest nightmares. He finished his coffee and kicked his shoes off.

'Can I sleep on here?'

She nodded. 'I'm going to bed, take your pants off or they'll be creased to shit and don't tell me you're not wearing boxers because, if you aren't, leave the damn things on.'

He let out a loud laugh. 'I'm wearing underwear.'

'Good to hear, get some sleep.'

He saluted her, his eyes closing before he'd even laid down. She shook her head and left him to it, going to her bedroom. She closed the door to the sound of his gentle snoring, wondering if she should text Christy and let her know he was okay. Then decided against it. Frankie was a hard-working, decent man and she did treat him like crap. He was too good for her, maybe she needed to realize that and stop taking him for granted. She didn't know how lucky she was to have a husband who loved her so much. Being single had never really bothered Maria, but she didn't know if it was the events of the last few days, or the wine, but she couldn't help wondering how nice it would be to have someone to snuggle up to and take her out on dates. She climbed into her bed, this time turning out the light. She felt safer knowing Frankie was asleep on her couch, even if he was comatose.

Her alarm went off and she reached out to press snooze. Her eyes didn't want to open. No wonder, when she remembered her late night visit and wondered how hungover Frankie was this morning. Forcing herself to get out of bed she walked out of the bedroom to the smell of bacon, crisping under the griddle. She took one look at Frankie who apart from having dark circles under his eyes and a pair of crumpled pants looked better than she did.

'Morning. Sorry about last night, Maria. Was I a complete asshole?'

She shook her head. 'No, not at all.' She wasn't sure whether she was mad or envious of him; if she'd drank that amount of bourbon she'd be in bed for a week feeling sorry for herself.

'I shouldn't have come here, but thank you for letting me in. I appreciate it.'

He passed her a plate of food which she took from him.

'Thank you. Are you not feeling like shit?'

He shook his head. 'Well, apart from a headache and my mouth feeling like it's been licking the men's locker room floor at the station. No, I'm good.'

She shook her head. 'Jeez, if I'd consumed that much I'd be dying. So, have you spoken to Christy?'

'Not yet, I'm going to go home and apologize. Then ask her what the fuck is wrong with her.'

'Don't get angry with her, keep calm. If you two aren't getting on you know you can sleep on the couch here don't you?'

He smiled. 'Thanks Maria, I don't know what I'd do without you.'

‘If you’re going to cook me breakfast every day it’s to my advantage, I’m being completely selfish.’

He crossed the room and bending down he kissed her on the cheek. ‘I’ll see you later, I need a shower, some pain killers and a couple of hours in my bed. We can decide what we’re going to do later.’

He let himself out and she wished that Addison had never given them the cold case to work on.

Chapter Nineteen

Maria left her apartment and crossed the hall to knock on Miss Green's door, she waited to hear the familiar shuffling of her feet along the hallway. After a couple of knocks she released the breath she'd been holding in when she heard her.

'Who is it?'

'Maria, just checking you're okay.'

'I am thank you, I look a frightful state so I'm not going to open the door and scare you.'

Maria chuckled. 'You couldn't look a state if you tried. I'm going out now. Do you need anything?'

'No thank you, I'll see you later, honey.'

'Bye.'

Glad her neighbor hadn't given herself a coronary in the middle of the night she left to go to the public library on 5th Avenue. There was a man sitting on the bottom steps of the apartment building, talking on his cell. She wondered who it was as it wasn't exactly sit on your ass on a marble step kind of day. As she passed him he stood up.

'Maria.'

She turned to him and shook her head as she realized who he was. 'Tell me, Mr Williams, a busy man such as yourself must have better things to do than hang around outside my apartment block?'

She stared at him, her arms crossed waiting for his answer.

'I haven't been here long and to be honest with you, not today, it's my day off.'

She looked around for the fancy town car. There wasn't one. He wasn't dressed in a suit today, he was more casual and he smiled at her.

'Look, all I want is to buy you a coffee, maybe get to know each other a little. You never know, when you have a conversation with me you might not think I'm such an asshole.'

'I never said you were. I said there were laws against this kind of behavior, it's called stalking.'

He held his hands up. 'Sorry, I guess I am a little weird. I sincerely wanted to thank you. I like you and I'm not used to not getting what I want. So I am an asshole, but I'm extremely grateful for what you did the other day. You'll be pleased to know I've hired another security guard. You don't expect that sort of stuff to happen. Hopefully I'll see you around, bye.'

He turned and began walking away, instead of doing what her head was telling her to she followed her heart and ran after him.

'I'm going to the public library to do some research, you can buy me a coffee in there if you want.'

She looked down at his feet and laughed to see his shiny, new Nikes. 'You came prepared today?'

His cheeks turned pink. 'I did.'

'Come on then, you can break your sneakers in.'

They walked towards Washington Square Park. Even though it was winter, it was still busy. Maria liked Central Park, but she loved the atmosphere here. There were always the same faces mingled in with the tourists and some of the buskers were talented. In fact, many a warm, summers night, she'd sit here with a cool drink and a book in her hand, people watching and listening to some performers who were worthy of Broadway. She paused to listen to Marvin playing the piano that he wheeled there himself whenever the mood took him. His bright blond spiky hair always perfect, he nodded at her and she mouthed, 'Morning.' Pulling a ten dollar note from her pocket she felt Harrison's hand on hers.

'Let me.'

She watched as he pulled two fifties out of his pocket and pushed them into the cap on the top of the piano. Marvin's eyes widened and Maria winked at him as he carried on playing and she still put her ten dollar note in. He blew her a kiss and she laughed, then waved and carried on walking.

'That was very kind of you.'

'You're not angry?'

She shook her head. 'No, if you can afford it then it's nice. So long as you're not just showing off for my benefit and besides, Marvin deserves it. He lets Sam – one of the homeless veterans who sleeps in the park – sing along next to him when he's in the mood to sing. Then he gives him some of the money people have given them. He's one of the good guys.'

'He's talented as well.'

'He is, extremely. I've never heard anyone play a rickety old piano like Marvin, sometimes he moves me to tears with his music.'

They carried on walking up Fifth towards the library; it was a fair distance and she wondered if Harrison was regretting his decision to accompany her. She stole a glance at him, he looked happy enough.

'So why aren't you at work today? Is it your rest day?'

She shook her head. 'I wish. Frankie, my partner, turned up drunk in the early hours and slept on my sofa. He's gone home to make it up to his wife and sort himself out, so we're working a late shift.'

Maria wondered if she should have told him about Frankie's business, but if he wanted to be friends with her Frankie was a big part of her life. He needed to know this, not find out later on.

'Frankie is lucky to have you, I take it you're good friends?'

She didn't detect any jealousy or anger in his voice, which was good. He seemed genuinely interested.

'Yes, we are. You have to be able to trust your partner in my job, your life depends on it. He's like an older brother and my best friend rolled into one.'

'That's good to know, I like him already. You have a dangerous job, Maria. What made you decide to become a cop?'

He'd taken her by surprise with his answer about Frankie. She'd thought there might be some Alpha male thing going on even though she belonged to no-one but herself. Although her loyalty would always be to Frankie, she found herself warming to the man next to her. She didn't know Harrison Williams any better than she knew Marvin the busker however he was surprising her and in a pleasant way.

'I like helping people, I don't like seeing nice people having their lives ripped apart for someone else's pleasure. It pays well, and my customer service skills leave a lot to be desired.'

He let out a loud laugh. 'You're also very honest, I like that.' He stared up Fifth as they walked against the crowd of tourists heading down towards the Empire State Building. Maria smiled.

'You don't walk much do you?'

It wasn't a criticism, she walked everywhere because it was cheaper and she hated driving in the madness of the city. The never-ending symphony of car horns drove her insane. If she could afford her own driver then she probably wouldn't be walking either.

'Not really. I play squash, I swim, I'm not into the whole gym culture although there's a pretty decent one at the office. At least that's what the staff say, I don't really go in there.'

The beautiful building of the public library came into view and she thought she heard Harrison sigh with relief. They went up the stone steps and joined the queue to get inside, when it was their turn she smiled at the security guard who stepped forward and hugged her.

'Maria, where have you been?'

She laughed. 'Working.'

'You tell them not to work you too hard, takings are down over at the café.'

'Abe, you are far too cheeky for your own good.' He winked at her and she carried on walking through. Harrison following her to the small café tucked beneath the grand staircase. He was looking around, his mouth open.

'It's beautiful.'

'Please don't tell me that you live in the city and have never visited.'

He shook his head and she rolled her eyes at him. 'What about the Empire State and Rockefeller?'

She watched as his cheeks began to burn for the second time. 'I've been to functions in the Rainbow Room and the NBC studios, I've had meetings in the Empire.'

She tutted. 'You live in this amazing city, with some of the most wonderful buildings and landmarks and you've never visited them, been to the top of them to take in the views?'

'I don't do tourist stuff.' His voice was defensive and she began to laugh.

'I'm not criticizing you, I just can't believe you never been. I love the Top of the Rock, it's my favorite view of the city, plus, you can see the Empire from there.'

'You surprise me, Maria, I thought as a tough New York City cop the last thing you'd want to do is to visit the tourist attractions.'

'Yeah, well, I think it's important to love where you live. I love New York, I love the buildings, the architecture and the history. I feel as if I'm pretty blessed to be here.'

'I've never thought of it like that.'

'But you like the library and that's probably full of more tourists than New Yorkers.'

'Yes, it's stunning. I had no idea.'

She turned so he couldn't see the smile on her face and went to order. The woman behind the small kiosk greeted Maria with the same amount of cheer that the security guard had shown her. She returned with two large coffees and placed one in front of him.

'I took a guess and got you an Americano.'

She couldn't stop the laughter which erupted from her mouth. 'Sorry, it's not funny.'

He began to laugh. 'So what were you coming here for?'

'I need to do some research on a property.'

'Can't you do that at work? Surely you have all sorts of information on the computers.'

'Not this type of research. I actually come here because I have a thing for libraries; I find them soothing, relaxing and I love reading. I spent hours in here as a kid, it was warm and safer than being outside on the streets. What is this anyway? All we've done is talk about me. Are you a stalker?'

'No, I'm not, I'm just not used to not getting what I want. I guess you could say I'm a bit of a spoilt brat.'

'And what is it that you want, Mr Williams?'

He took a sip of his coffee, then looked her in the eye. 'You Maria, only I wasn't expecting it to be so difficult.'

She shrugged. 'Are you saying that you thought I'd throw myself at you because you're the big "I Am"?'

He squirmed and she realized that was exactly what he'd thought.

'Well, now you know that I'm not that kind of girl, to be honest I never have been. Your money doesn't interest me. I've dealt with millionaires who have battered their wives and lovers to within an inch of their lives. I don't care if you're homeless or on the Forbes Rich list, if you treat me with respect I'll be respectful back. You need to know that you can't buy me, I'm not for sale. If I like someone I'll be their friend, that's it.'

He stared at her completely in awe. 'So if I offered you a chauffeur driven car and a penthouse apartment in The Waldorf when the renovations are done you'd turn it down?'

She nodded. 'Don't get me wrong, I'd be crazy not to be tempted. Hell, The Waldorf is my favorite of all the hotels and it broke my heart that they've shut it down. But it would be a no.'

He grinned at her. 'So if I wanted to take you out for a date where would we go?'

'That would be telling, you'd have to work it out for yourself.'

'So, can I take you out on a date?'

‘Why? I’m not in your league, I never will be. There must be a queue of society girls lined up to be the next Mrs Williams.’

It was his turn to laugh. ‘Yep, there probably is. I’m not after a Mrs Williams though, I want a woman I can take on dates, have fun with, and enjoy my life with. I just want to have someone to talk to if I’ve had a shitty day without worrying they’ll sell my story to the New York Times.’

‘I can understand that, I suppose being rich can be a right pain in the ass at times.’

‘More than you know. So what do you say, Maria, if I can come up with a date you’ll enjoy, will you accompany me?’

‘If it’s not something horrific. Don’t bother flying me to the opera in San Francisco, I hate opera. Then yes, I suppose I would.’

He looked at her blankly.

‘*Pretty Woman*. You never seen it?’

He shook his head and she laughed. ‘Forget it, just a joke.’

He finished his coffee and stood up. ‘I have to go, I’m already late for an appointment. May I have your number so I can call you with the details?’

She pulled a notepad and pen from her purse, ripping a sheet of paper out she wrote it down and passed it to him. ‘Nothing too fancy, I don’t like fancy food.’

‘Leave it with me, I like a challenge. Take care, Maria, and thanks for the coffee.’

‘You’re welcome.’

He turned and walked towards the exit. A glimmer of excitement tingled as the butterflies in her stomach got the better of her. It would be nice to have a no-strings-attached relationship, she could go with that. It would do her good to have a bit of fun after work, someone to talk to without having to marry them and be stuck with them for the rest of her life. Frankie would no doubt disagree, but he had his own shitty marriage to sort out. She couldn't wait forever for him to decide to divorce Christy, although after last night it looked as if the cracks were getting too much for him. She loved him, but it would be too much effort juggling work and a relationship for them both. One of them would have to move departments and it wouldn't be her. For now, she would let Harrison Williams take her out for some fun and see where it went from there.

Chapter Twenty

Maria ran her finger along the lines of the antique book – a history of Greenwich Village in the 1950s. There was a chapter about the house and the murder, which she read, horrified. The wealthy family who owned it had lived a nice, happy life until the day it all turned upside down. Max was right, the newspaper articles and the book confirmed that the murders were very similar. So either they had a geriatric serial killer or a copycat, but how would anyone know about the murder in the fifties? Unless they were a bit of a history buff or had been told about it by a relative. The feeling of being watched settled across her and she lifted her head to see if anyone was blatantly staring at her. The room was relatively empty, which was a first for her. There were a couple of students at the far end both working on laptops with headphones pushed into their ears. An older woman was sat a few rows in front of her, but none of them were looking in her direction. Maria turned to take in the magnificent room and see if there was anyone else trying to hide, but there wasn't. A shiver made her entire body shake and she felt a coldness envelop her from behind as if some invisible person was giving her an icy embrace. Slamming the book shut she pushed her chair back, scraping it along the tiled floor, the sound filling the air. She jumped up. Her chest felt as if there was a pair of huge arms pressing against it, suffocating her. For a moment she wondered if she was about to have a heart attack and die. It was hard to breathe, the cold band was pressing so hard against her lungs, squeezing her tight. She did the only thing she could think of and began to pray, if she was going to die on her own, here, she wanted God to acknowledge it. She hadn't been to church for years, even so he wouldn't abandon her, would he?

Finally, the woman in front of her turned around to stare at Maria with the blackest eyes she'd ever seen. Their eyes locked, with Maria unable to speak, pleading with God to help her while the woman stared straight back at her as if she was looking into the depths of her soul. The shrill ringing of her cell phone snapped Maria's attention away, and she felt a surge of relief as she gasped and took in a huge mouthful of air. Her oxygen-deprived lungs were on fire. Grabbing her purse she pulled out her cell and began to walk towards the exit. She had to get out of here, away from the suffocating atmosphere and the woman with the black eyes. Shaking, Maria reached the stairs and ran down them, the entrance to the library was full and she pushed her way to the exit. Abe was nowhere to be seen, not that she'd tell him what had just happened because she didn't know herself. She was either having some kind of medical episode or she had experienced her second strange encounter in as many days. She felt the warmth of the winter sun on her face and she stood to one side for a moment, taking in deep breaths of air. Her chest felt sore, the pressure on it had been so great. Maria decided it might be time to pay a visit to church; it wouldn't hurt to catch the early evening mass at St Joseph's. The feeling of being watched wasn't as intense out in the fresh air, if you could call the traffic fumes that. But she couldn't shake it off and she didn't like it. She began the walk back down 5th to head back to her apartment, feeling again that knot of fear in her heart that she had inadvertently stumbled upon something that she didn't understand, nor did she want to. Supernatural, paranormal, psychic, whatever you wanted to call it, she had never been remotely interested in anything of the sort. Yet how else did you explain what had happened to her? It was crazy and she would be the first to laugh and twirl her finger at the side of her head if Frankie began to tell her this kind of crap. Maybe she was ill. She could have some disease that was fucking with her mind. Before she even considered telling Frankie, she was going to go for a medical. She'd been due one two months ago and cancelled. Maria called the doctor's office to make an appointment.

✪

He'd slept in his van the last two nights because it was too overwhelming inside the apartment. The nightmares were too much and whenever he was in there he felt as if every ounce of his energy was being drained, which it was. He had no doubt about it. The creature – he wasn't going to call it by his real name because he wasn't strong enough to deal with the consequences – was like some energy-draining power source; thriving off his energy; a vampire.

The board was tucked under the front seat, the planchette in his backpack. It was too dangerous but, when he was away from the apartment, he could think much clearer. He was messing around with powerful forces that he had no real concept of, yet he couldn't stop, as much as he wanted to. It was like some addictive drug. When he wasn't in the apartment he had more moments of clarity. The time he spent inside it was unaccounted for, he had no recollection of the last day he'd spent in there and this scared him almost as much as the thought of some beast from the depths of hell breathing down his neck and watching him in the dead of night. He lay there in his sleeping bag in the back of the van, sandwiched between his worldly belongings and wondered if he should forget it all. Burn the board and planchette; forget about the house, the creature, the power, the evil, and drive out of the city. He could head towards Coney Island, find somewhere there to park up. He'd always loved the amusement park, the boardwalk and the beach. Then he remembered it was winter, the park would be closed and it wasn't exactly camp on the beach kind of weather. The voice whispered inside his head, *'You won't have to run ever again. Whatever you want will be yours.'* He nodded. How had it found him? It wouldn't matter where he went, it would follow him. He had no choice but to do as it wished and set it free. He hadn't realized he'd been chewing his nails until he felt the sharp pain of tearing skin. He looked down at the ragged piece of nail and skin, a thin line of blood running down his finger. It was stinging, he shook it. Not sure what he was going to do next he saw a woman on the sidewalk, laughing at someone on the other end of her cell. He recognized her as the cop who'd been going into the house as he'd been coming out. Afraid to move in case he caught her attention, he watched her. She was pretty but looked as if she wouldn't take any crap. For the first time in forever he felt a stirring in his loins. She was his type. It was a shame he wouldn't be hers. He hadn't thought about women and sex since he could remember. His head was always full of blackness, there wasn't much room inside it for the normal kind of thoughts men his age had. The voice whispered inside his mind. *'She will be yours, to do as you please.'* He liked the thought of that. He could take her to the apartment and show her a good time. He got out of the van and began following her, keeping a distance. He needed to know where she lived, it couldn't be too far away from here. As she cut through Washington Square Park and exited onto Thompson Street, he hung back a little. If she was as good a cop as he thought she might realize he was following her. She stopped at the corner of Sullivan Street and headed up towards Miss Lilly's, his stomach was groaning. He never felt like eating in the apartment, but out on the street he'd worked up an appetite. Checking that no one was watching him, he began to stroll up to the bakery. He wanted a fresh bagel and coffee, so he could sit and watch from there. He had a feeling she was close to home, and by the time he reached the doorway of the busy shop she was coming back out. He put his head down and waited for her to pass, then went inside. Watching her through the windows she walked across the street to a rundown apartment block. He was a little surprised if this was where she lived as he'd pictured in a nice apartment over on Hudson. Pulling a crumpled five dollar bill from his pocket he paid for his bagel and coffee then sat on the bench by the window which looked onto the apartment block. His mind was working overtime. Was she visiting or was she working? If she was visiting she'd have had two coffees, yet she only had the one. Maybe she did live here after all, which made it a whole lot easier for him. He scanned the building but could see no security cameras. Not sure about the rest of the street, he'd have to check it out when he left. Miss Lilly's had just become his new place to hang out, and although he didn't have much money to waste, it was cheap enough. He had no rent to pay, so he could linger with a coffee and look like a struggling student. The area was full of them, the New York University was only a short distance. He unwrapped the foil from his bagel and began to take small bites, an expert at making his food last. As long as he was eating and drinking they couldn't ask him to leave. He turned his head, it was busy anyway. Lunchtime rush, no-one was paying him the slightest bit of attention.

Chapter Twenty-One

June 1952

'Em! Em? Can you hear me?' Mae turned around to the kid. 'Don't just stand there, Bill, go get help. What's wrong with her?'

He shrugged, unable to take his eyes off the pretty lady who was now lying flat out on the chaise lounge. Mae pushed him. 'Go, now.'

She turned back to her friend whose face was now the color of alabaster. Mae bent down to listen and see if she was breathing. She was. She then started gently prodding her to get a reaction but there was nothing – she was like sleeping beauty. Breathing, but unconscious. There were tiny beads of perspiration on Emilia's forehead. Billy barged through the door making Mae jump. He had Beatrice the wardrobe mistress in tow. She took one look at the girl on the chair and shook her head.

'She's passed out. Has she been drinking?'

Mae looked at her. 'I don't know, I don't think so. She doesn't smell of booze.'

Beatrice went to the tiny sink in the corner of the room and filled up the small glass that was balanced on the shelf above it. Walking back to the chair she threw it over Emilia's face. Mae gasped. 'I can't believe you did that.'

Beatrice shrugged and pointed at the casualty whose eyelids were now flickering. 'It worked didn't it. Sometimes you gotta be cruel to be kind, kid.'

Mae grabbed a dry washcloth and began to pat Em's wet face. Her eyes opened wide and she stared at Mae confused.

'Where am I? What happened?'

Beatrice spoke first. 'You passed out, kid, have you been drinking?'

Emilia shook her head, then gulped. 'No, I haven't. I feel terrible.'

'Well then, you need to start eating more, skinny is not worth dying for. What if you passed out in front of a bus? Bang, end of story. Look after yourself eh?' With that the older woman turned and walked out leaving them all looking at each other. Emilia pushed herself so she was sitting upright.

'I'm sorry, Mae, I only wanted to tell you how wonderful you were.'

Mae laughed. 'Jeez, you gave me the fright of my life. Look, my hands are shaking.' She held up her hands which were trembling. 'Can you stand? I think we should get you home.'

Emilia tried to stand, her legs were as shaky as Mae's hands. Mae grabbed one arm and shouted to Billy. 'Grab her other arm, we'll walk her out and get a cab.' He did as he was told, gently taking hold of her between them, they marched Emilia out of the backstage entrance. Billy ran to the front and hailed a cab, then ran back and helped Mae walk her to it. Emilia let them help her, she felt so strange she had no idea what was wrong with her. Mae ran around to get in the other side and she pushed the window down. 'Thank you, Billy.'

He nodded a small smile on his lips. 'I hope you feel better soon, Miss.' Then he turned and raced back to the theatre. The cab driver was watching them in the rear view mirror.

'Where to, ladies?'

Mae leant forward. 'West 10th Street, please.'

Emilia placed her head back against the cool leather of the seat, even though it was warm in the cab she was icy cold. Her head felt as if it was all a mess inside; she wanted to go to bed, to curl up in a ball and sleep. She watched as the busy streets passed by in a blur. Mae was chattering away, but she couldn't concentrate, the words didn't make sense. As the cab turned into the street Emilia felt her heart begin to race. Something was wrong and she didn't know what. Mae pointed to the house and the cab pulled over. Mae paid the driver and got out, running around to Emilia's side she threw open the door and leant in to grab her arm.

'I'm okay, I think. You can leave me now. Thank you.'

Mae shook her head. 'No, you're not. You look dreadful and you can't stand on your own two feet without swaying. Clarke wouldn't forgive me if I left you on your own. Hell, you might not even make it down the steps and through the front door.'

They walked arm in arm to the sidewalk and down the steps. Before she could ring the doorbell the front door was opened to a worried looking Missy. 'What's the matter, Miss Emilia?'

'I feel a little funny, I just need to lay down for a while.'

'Should I call the doctor?'

Mae said. 'Yes.' At the same time Emilia said. 'No.'

Missy looked at Emilia. 'No, thank you. I'll see how I am after I've had some sleep.' She turned to Mae. 'Thanks, Mae, I'm fine now.'

'If you're sure.'

Missy nodded. 'She's sure. I'll help her up to bed.'

'Is Clarke home?'

'He went to a dinner a few hours ago and hasn't returned. Do you want to wait for him in the library? He'll be back anytime.'

Mae grinned. 'If you don't mind.' She walked down towards the library. James came running down the stairs, took one look at his sister and decided he should probably be nice for once. 'Are you ill?'

She shrugged.

'Do you need anything?'

Emilia frowned at him, but he did his best to smile and look concerned.

'No. Thank you.'

He walked past her, down to the stairs and caught sight of the gorgeous creature, Mae from behind as she walked into the library. He turned to see Missy helping his sister up to her room where she would no doubt fuss over her for the next half an hour. He had no idea where his father was, but he knew he wasn't in. Maybe he could entertain Mae for a short time, get to know her better and see why she had most of his family under her spell. He strode down the long hallway towards the huge, oak, double doors of the library. A smile spread across his lips that would have terrified his sister had she seen it.

Chapter Twenty-Two

Maria passed Miss Green's apartment and paused, wondering if she should knock to see if she was okay. Her phone vibrated in her pocket, she pulled it out and smiled at Frankie's one word text message: *Outside*. She'd definitely give her a knock when she got back, maybe offer to make her something to eat. She drained the last of her coffee and walked to the lift, feeling a lot better and wondering if she'd had some kind of anxiety attack in the library. When she reached the car, Frankie had his head slumped forward and a loud snore erupted from his mouth.

'You're such a smart ass, I wasn't that long.'

He opened one eye. 'Long enough, so what did you find out?'

She climbed into the car, slamming the door. 'Max was right, those articles were pretty accurate. There was a brutal murder there, July 52. A woman's body was found in the attic, her limbs removed. Her head was nowhere to be found, I don't even know if it ever got recovered.'

'So that would make our killer how old now?'

'At least in his nineties. I'm not so good with math, maybe older.'

'Do we know any ninety-year-old killers?'

She shook her head. 'It's not impossible, you do get those few older people who are still running marathons in their nineties.'

'Why would they leave it so long though? I mean seriously, if that is the case, sixty five years between murders is…'

'A lifetime.'

He nodded.

‘What was the motive?’

‘Don’t laugh at me. Devil worship.’

Frankie turned to stare at her. ‘You’re shitting me?’

‘Nope. Apparently the apartment wasn’t classed as an apartment at the time, it was just a bedroom. Well, it had the full works: Ouija board, satanic symbols and a grand grimoire.’

‘A what?’

‘A book of black magic, used for spells, witchcraft and summoning the devil.’

Maria could feel her cheeks burn; she didn’t really believe in any of this stuff. An image of the woman from the library staring at her filled her mind. *Are you sure about that?*

‘I’m not saying I believe it, I’m just telling you what I read. So what are we going to do now?’

‘Go and get all the files out of the basement on the murder three years ago. See if they ever found an ID for her and her next of kin. Maybe see if they have the original records from the fifties? Who knows… there might be a mouldy box with your devil bible inside it lurking in the depths of the basement.’

Frankie drove off in the direction of the station and Maria wondered if her day could get any stranger. She decided not to tell him about Harrison, he’d only tease her and she wasn’t in the mood for it. She didn’t know how to describe how she felt, but it was tense and foreboding. Like something was wrong only she didn’t know what and couldn’t put her finger on it.

They parked up round the back and went through the rear gate where the steps to the basement were. It was dark, around here. When they reached the bottom Frankie swiped his card, but the door didn’t open. He tried it again,

Maria stepped forward and knocked loudly. A few moments later the door opened and Layla grinned at them.

'Well, if it isn't my two favorite, pain-in-the-ass detectives. What can I do for you?'

Maria grinned. 'We're looking for some case files from three years ago and some from way back in the day.'

Layla stepped aside. 'In that case I'll let you in. Welcome to my humble abode.'

The huge basement had a metal cage blocking the entrance so nobody could get in and help themselves. Layla let herself through the door and sat behind the wire mesh at the counter.

'I'm going to need to see your ID, then you can sign yourselves in.'

Frankie rolled his eyes. 'You're kidding, right?'

She shook her head. 'Sorry, doll, it's new rules. No-one enters the cage unless they've been officially identified. Then I'll escort you to where you need to be, and if no-one else wants me I'll wait with you until you're finished.'

Maria signed them both in, tugged Frankie's badge from his pocket and passed them both over. Layla passed them back.

'Guess you two are the real deal.'

She opened the door and let them in. There were rows that went on forever stacked with boxes full of old case files and evidence. The basement was vast and Maria didn't envy Layla's job of keeping everything in order. As they walked through she shut the door behind them.

'You can't trust half of those motherfuckers upstairs who come in and fuck with the evidence when your back is turned. Well, not on my watch. I've seen *Making a Murderer* and that shit aint going down when I'm in charge.'

Maria laughed. 'No-one would dare, Layla, they're all scared of you.'

Layla dead eyed her. 'Uh huh, good. So what year are you after?'

'1952.'

'For real?'

Maria nodded. 'For real. Do the records go back that far?'

'Yes, they do. I think we have records that go back to 1950. Anything from before then is stored at City Hall.'

Layla walked along the rows of shelving. Frankie let Maria go first and she knew why. He was terrified of the woman in front of them. She wasn't as scary as she made out, but Maria wasn't about to tell Frankie that. The woman had a heart of gold, helping out at the homeless shelter in her spare time. After what seemed like forever she came to a block of shelving, with old, cardboard file boxes on them. The case file, name and number was written in faded, black marker pen. There was a faint hammering on the door. Layla turned to them.

'I'm gonna trust you two to find what you need then come and get it signed out. Don't touch anything else apart from the boxes on this unit.

Frankie nodded. 'Yes, ma'am.'

Layla turned, striding off towards the front entrance.

'Jesus wept, what a place to work.'

'I don't know, the only people she has to deal with are cops. She doesn't have to chase killers and look for bibles written for the devil.'

They began to look at the boxes which were stacked in numerical order making their search straightforward. Maria found the section full of 1952 boxes and felt her heart begin to race. What if the grand grimoire was inside it? The thought of it made her feel sick to her stomach. She'd seen enough horror films to know they were made from human skin and written in blood. Her eyes fell on a box pushed behind another; she moved the first one out of the way and saw the name written on it.

'EVANS / WEST 10TH ST. – 28-06-52'

'Holy shit, it's here. I mean, I didn't actually expect it to be here.' She turned to Frankie. 'Did you?'

He shrugged. 'Suppose not, makes our life a whole lot easier though.'

She grabbed the box and dragged it forward. 'So where we going to take this? I don't want to have to explain to the clowns upstairs what we're doing.'

'I'd say my place, but Christy is still mad at me.'

'We'll take it to mine then. My dinner table can be our temporary office, it's easier anyway. We can get on with it and not have to worry about being called out.'

'Well, if that ain't the first good idea you've had all week.'

She smiled and stepped to the side, 'Big, strong man like you can carry it, you have to come in useful for something.' She left him to grab the box. 'I'll sign it out and deal with Layla.'

Chapter Twenty-Three

Miss Green lay on the bed not quite asleep, but too tired to get up. Every bone in her body ached and she felt every bit her age this morning. For the last sixty five years her life had been pleasant, having been more fortunate than some and she was thankful for that. What she wasn't thankful for was that note that had been pushed under her door whilst she was out shopping yesterday. It had taken a long time for her to block the memories of that horrific night as far from her mind as possible. Then just like that it was back – boom – the images playing on a loop, over and over again. No matter how many times she told herself it wasn't her problem she knew that it was, that she was a part of it and it was her duty to help. *Damn your stupid sense of duty, Missy, you did what you had to and sent it back. This is not your problem. You're an old woman now and it will probably kill you. If that damn demon doesn't then the fear will kill you, your heart won't stand it a second time. Is this how you want to die? Fighting against something that is an aberration of all things good?*

'Shut the fuck up, just shut up.'

She pressed her hands to her ears trying her best to block out the noise from her goddamn, interfering, busybody, internal mind. She turned onto her side, the sun was shining through the crack in the drapes. She could feel it's warmth on her face and it felt so good. She liked the light, the heat, the feeling of safety that the sun brought with it every morning when it rose in the sky. She hated the dark and never went out in it if it could be avoided. The dark was full of shadows that you couldn't see, things that came to life once the sun had set. She knew this from experience, which was why every corner in her apartment had lamps. There were no dark corners in here, she wouldn't let anything hide in her home. Unlike the house on West 10th Street, what lived in the dark there was the thing that most people have nightmares about but forget once they're awake. She had sensed something wrong in the days leading up to that night. Not able to describe it or tell anyone, it was more of a feeling. A sense of terrible foreboding that something wasn't right with the dynamics inside the house, and how do you go about telling someone that? If she'd have voiced her fears, her feelings, to Clarke he could have gone and investigated the attic where James was stopping. If only one of them had gone up there they would have seen the Ouija board, the candles, the book of black magic, the huge pentagram on the wall drawn in blood; whose blood it was she had no idea. He had ripped all the paper off the walls, written all over them. They would have realized there and then they were dealing with a madman, and he could have been taken to the hospital before it got that far; before that beautiful girl was so horribly killed. She shivered, throwing the covers back, and got out of bed. They'd let it get that far without intervening, it was time to go back.

It was an hour since Missy had made the decision to visit the house, she was now sat in the back of a yellow cab which was about to turn into West 10th Street. Her heart was racing and her mouth was dry when the driver stopped at the curb, and she lifted a trembling hand, passing him a ten dollar bill. She thanked him and got out to stand on the sidewalk opposite the house. It's once grand exterior looked tired, in fact it looked as old and decrepit as she felt today. It didn't look anything like it had the last time she'd been here. She knew it had been turned into apartments and wondered how many people had died mysterious deaths or committed suicide in there. Despite it being a warm day the house was dark, there being no sunshine on that side of the street. The window boxes had shrivelled up plants hanging from them. At first she'd read the papers, clipping out any articles about suspicious deaths and putting them in a shoe box. Then she'd stopped buying papers, for her own sanity. She couldn't take the worry, the dread, the guilt. Pulling the gold chain from under her jumper she kissed the crucifix on it and asked God to protect her soul. Taking a deep breath she stepped onto the street and heard the squeal of a car tyres on the tarmac and a loud honk of the horn. She realized that she'd stepped into the street without even looking. Her heart racing, she jumped back, waving at the driver and muttering sorry. In all her years she'd never once stepped into the traffic without looking; the city streets were mean and unforgiving. It was the quickest way to end up dead or racking up a huge hospital bill. Shuddering she crossed herself; it knew she was here and had tried to stop her. It had tried to kill her. That was the moment the stubbornness and strength that Missy had worn proudly on her sleeve in her younger days returned. She stared at the house and whispered.

'*You're scared of me. Well, I'll be damned. You tried to stop me, but it was only a half-hearted attempt. That means you're not strong enough otherwise I'd be lying crushed under that car's wheels. Well fuck you! How dare you. I sent you back once, I'll do it again so whichever dark corner you're hiding in, you better be worrying. I might be much older, but I've still got the stubborn mind of the girl I was last time I was here and you can sense that, you know that I have the power to send you back.*'

This time she held her head up, looked both ways along the street and crossed to the other side. For a fleeting moment she wondered if some huge chunk of masonry was going to fall from the roof and kill her anyway. Then she was down the steps and looking for the buzzer she needed, but before she could press it the huge, glass door opened and she was greeted by a smiling, much older version of the girl she used to dote on.

'You came.'

'I had to, my conscience wouldn't let me turn a blind eye.'

The two women hugged, wrapping their arms around each other and squeezing tight. Emilia whispered.

'It's been far too long, I've missed you.'

'I've missed you too. Who would have thought we'd both still live to tell the tale? We should never have lost touch. You should have sold this godforsaken house and moved away.'

They pulled apart, Emilia lifting her sleeve to wipe the tears that were glistening on her cheeks.

'I know, but I couldn't. I felt as if it was my fault; that I had to stay here and make sure it didn't happen again.'

Missy nodded. She got that. A sense of duty was a powerful thing, especially when you carried it alongside the guilt that came with it. Then she whispered, 'But it did happen again.'

Emilia nodded. 'I had no idea. It's been lingering ever since. I can hear it, I can sense it. Although it's not strong enough yet or we would all know about it.'

Missy grabbed her friend's hand. 'Then this time we'll send it back, for good.'

Chapter Twenty-Four

Mikey sat on his sofa, watching an old black and white movie. He had no idea what it was called or what it was about because for the last ten minutes he'd muted the volume. He could hear the whispering, which wasn't loud and he couldn't make out what the voices were saying. Straining he closed his eyes and concentrated. It didn't sound American. He knew he should really try and find out where it was coming from because it wasn't him. He had no-one else around to be whispering in his ears, he didn't have friends. He kept to himself, went to work, came home, smoked a little pot and watched TV. He stood up and crossed to his kitchen to check the window there was shut, as sometimes noise from the apartment above floated down. Drawing the blind he shook his head, the window was not only shut, it was locked. A loud thud came from the direction of his bedroom. He picked up a carving knife from the block. *If some motherfucker has broken in they're paying with blood.*

Clutching the knife he crept towards his bedroom door, pausing outside to listen. He couldn't hear anything so he threw the door back; a blast of cold air hit him in the face along with the most gut-wrenching, God-awful smell. He gagged, lifting his arm to cover his nose. He couldn't see anything. The room was empty, but he felt it. He felt something, huge, full of anger and blackness charging towards him. For the first time in his life Mikey screamed, a sound so high pitched anyone outside would have sworn it was a woman. He lifted his hands to cover his face as he fell to his knees. He had never felt such unbearable coldness that was now enveloping him. He felt as if he was being slowly, crushed to death. The smell that filled his nostrils was one of decay. Although he'd never smelt rotting flesh before, he felt pretty sure this was what it would smell like. From somewhere inside the building he heard a door slam and women's voices, chattering. He wanted to call out for help, but he couldn't. Whatever it was had squeezed every last bit of air from his lungs, and his eyeballs felt as if they were going to explode from their sockets. '*God, if you're there, forgive me.*' At the mention of forgiveness the pressure was released and he fell to the floor taking in huge, gulps of lovely air. Not sure whether he needed an ambulance, a shot of whiskey or a joint the size of the Empire State Building, he lay there, curled up in a ball on the rough, wooden floorboards, big, wet tears rolling down his cheeks. His heart was hammering so fast he could feel the blood being pumped through his brain as his temple pulsated. Mikey didn't actually know if he was dead or alive. Too afraid to move, he lay there like a freshly caught fish on the deck of a fishing boat, struggling to breathe out of water.

Emilia paused at the bottom of the stairs, turning towards the ground floor apartment that always had the faint smell of cannabis lingering around the front door. Missy followed her friend's eyes, both of them sensing something was wrong. The door opened and out staggered the man who lived there – Mikey. He had a dishcloth wrapped around his hand which was turning deep red, she rushed to him.

'Oh no, are you okay? What's happened?'

He tried to speak, but his eyes were glazed. All he could do was shake his head. Emilia grabbed one arm, Missy the other. They walked him towards his apartment and he shook his head. Emilia frowned at Missy.

‘Well, if you don’t want to go back in there you’re going to have to come up to my place. I can’t have you bleeding everywhere.’ She led him towards the stairs, and they were only three steps up when his door slammed shut. So violently that it made all three of them jump. They walked faster. Emilia let go of his arm to open her front door. She pushed it wide then pushed him and Missy inside before closing the door behind her and locking it. She led Mikey into the spacious, open plan apartment and sat him down at the table. Then she busied herself filling a bowl with cold water, taking a selection of clean dishcloths from the cleaning cupboard that she’d put to one side because they were worn. Then she pulled the first aid kit down from the top shelf of one of the cupboards and sat next to him tenderly unwrapping the heavily, bloodstained cloth from his hand. Both she and Missy gasped to see how deep the gaping wound was that ran the full length of the palm of his hand.

‘Oh dear, I think you might need more than a band aid. We need to get you to the hospital.’

For the first time the man looked Emilia in the eyes and let out a high-pitched laugh. ‘That ain’t going to happen, I pay my rent or I pay the hospital.’

Emilia pressed a cold cloth against the wound, then wrapped some dry ones around it and folded his fingers over it.

‘Keep your arm elevated, I’m not a nurse, but I do know some first aid.’

Missy stood at the sink, watching. ‘Who slammed your door? Is there someone down there we can call to come and help you?’

He shook his head. ‘There’s nobody except me in there.’

'How did you cut your hand?'

He glared at her. 'What are you, the senior citizen's FBI?'

She grinned. 'Who told you?'

For the first time he relaxed and smiled. 'Sorry, I know you're just trying to help and I appreciate it. I'm just a little bit shook up.'

Emilia removed the cloths, rewrapping fresh ones around again. 'Well I'm Emilia and the inquisitive one over there is Missy. You are Mikey if I'm not mistaken.'

'I am.'

'So, Mikey, there is no wind blowing through the building because the front door is shut. Do you want to tell me how your front door slammed shut so hard the whole building shook?'

He lowered his eyes. 'I don't think you really want to know.'

'Well, you can let me be the judge of that. You came out of your apartment looking like—'

Missy interrupted. 'Looking like some fool who had scared himself shitless and sliced his hand open in the process. Am I close?'

'Missy.'

'I'm right, Em; look at the state of him. I've never seen a black man so white and that ain't me being racist because that's not who I am and I never have been.'

Emilia looked at Mikey who was staring across the table at Missy.

'There is something in my apartment, I don't know what the hell it is. It sure isn't human that's for real. Now you can blame it on the pot, I smoke it every day I'm not denying it. But this was no hallucination. Whatever it was, it tried to kill me.'

He looked at them, waiting for them to laugh at him, to call him crazy. Instead both of the women were staring at him in horror and he knew then that he wasn't crazy. He knew that what had happened was as real as he was and they both knew what he was talking about.

Missy came and sat down opposite him. She looked at Emilia. 'It's getting stronger.'

Mikey shook his head. 'Damn, I was hoping you two were crazier than me. I don't know. Maybe we all crazy, this stuff doesn't exist, except for in the movies.'

Emilia spoke. 'It does in this house. I'm sorry, I had no idea it was able to do that.'

'Well, I'd like to know what it was and how it tried to suffocate me when I couldn't see it? I can't get my head around it.

Missy shrugged.

Emilia spoke. 'A very long time ago my brother bought a Ouija board and a book of witchcraft. He decided to sacrifice a young woman and summon a demon.'

Mikey laughed, so loud both women jumped. They waited for him to contain himself. He shook his head.

'I'm sorry, but it's not the usual thing is it? I thought you were going to say it was your dead Aunt's ghost, seeking revenge. Are you for real?'

As he spoke he realized that neither woman was smiling, they were wide eyed. Terrified… and he felt the seriousness of the situation all three of them were in come crashing down on his shoulders.

'Sorry, I'm sorry. That was crass of me. You are for real? It's just kind of hard to believe.'

'Is it? Minutes ago you were telling us that an invisible force had tried to kill you. Did you think it was a load of crap when you were on your knees thinking you were dying?'

'Missy, there's no need to be so rude.' Emilia looked at Mikey. 'Yes, this is all true, I have no reason to lie. You can look it all up, go on Boogle or whatever it is, I'm sure you'll find something about this house on there.'

'Google,' Missy corrected her.

'Then we have a problem.'

Emilia could have hugged the man sitting next to her. He'd lived here for years and she'd never said anything more than good day to him. He wasn't going to leave them alone to fight it. Missy didn't stop herself, she stood up. Walked around to Mikey and wrapped her arms around him, whispering, 'Thank you,' into his ear, they would take all the help they could get.

Chapter Twenty-Five

June 1952

Mae was trailing her finger along a row of leather-bound books. She loved to read almost as much as she loved to act. The door opened and she turned to see a handsome, younger version of Clarke standing there.

'Well, hello. You must be James, I'm a friend of your Pa's. I don't believe we've been formally introduced.'

She crossed the room, holding out her hand which he took. Instead of shaking it he lifted it to his mouth, brushing his lips so softly over the back of her hand that it sent a shudder down her spine. He stared at her, his huge, dark almost black eyes drawing her in. She felt a sudden rush as her foolish heart began to pump the blood around her body faster. Her stomach swooshed and she felt a sudden rush of warm heat fill her panties. She let out a small gasp, the feelings taking her completely by surprise. James raised his eyebrow, aware of the effect he was having on the beautiful woman standing in front of him and enjoying every second.

She laughed, but her voice quivered. 'Well, James, it's very nice to meet you.' She tried to pull her hand away from him, needing to get some space between them. He didn't let go. Instead he ran his finger along it, the pressure in her panties made her squeeze her thighs together. She had never felt such arousal. She wanted to throw herself at him and beg him to make love to her there and then, and he knew it. He was enjoying watching her squirm, her mind emptied of all rational thoughts. She wanted this man, inside of her and that was all that mattered. He leant forward, his mouth pressing against hers. He kissed her with such passion that she felt her knees go weak. Pulling apart he took hold of her hand, pressing it against the hard bulge in the front of his trousers. She ran her tongue along her bright red lips. He grabbed her hand, pulling her.

'Not here, upstairs. I don't want to be disturbed, I want to lick and bite every single part of you.'

Mae smiled. The thought was almost too much to bear and she followed him along the hallway towards the back of the house. He led her to a staircase that she'd never seen before and realized it must be the staff stairs. She didn't care. He could take her here on the bare, wooden staircase and she'd have let him. He rushed upstairs, lifting his finger to his lips. She kicked off her shoes so they wouldn't clatter on the wooden steps. Damn this was wrong, cheating on Clarke with his son. She didn't care. She wanted to lie on his bed and be fucked. She would deal with the aftermath later, right now she wanted James. Inside her, biting, sucking and doing anything he desired. She let him pull her up the stairs. Unable to shake the trance like state she was in, they reached the tiny attic staircase. They went up and he opened the door.

The room was in darkness, candles were burning on the table in the middle of the room and it was much colder up here than the rest of the house. He pulled her inside, closing and locking the door behind him.

'I don't want anyone disturbing us, I want you so much.'

He kissed her again, crushing his mouth against hers and she leant into him. He scooped her up, into his arms. Carrying her into the bedroom, kicking the door open with his foot. Mae's nose wrinkled, there was a terrible smell in here. Then she was on the soft bed and he was removing her stockings. A loud thud from the corner of the room made her jump.

'What's that? Who's there?'

He laughed. 'No-one, it's just you and me, baby. Close your eyes and relax, I'm going to eat you up.'

The smell of rotting garbage was overpowering, suddenly every bit of passion and lust that she'd been feeling moments before disappeared. Something or someone else was in this room. She pushed him off.

'I don't like it in here, it smells really bad.'

James stared down at her. The face she'd thought was dashing moments ago looked nothing like it now and for the first time in her life Mae felt the cold, hard, reality of fear bearing down on her. She needed to get out of the dark, foul room. Back down into the warmth and the light, she wanted Clarke. He always made her feel safe and she'd been about to betray his love and trust in the most shameful way that she could think of.

'You don't mean that do you?'

Her mouth was dry and her stomach began to churn, every lustful feeling from moments ago had turned into disgust. She twisted herself away from him and stood up. Not even bothering about her stockings or shoes she backed away from him, towards the door. He started to laugh and she made a break for the door, it wouldn't open. With what little light there was she couldn't make out any locks, twisting the door knob and tugging as hard as she could it didn't budge. James was still laughing.

'Let me out or I'll tell your Pa.'

He laughed even louder and began to clap. 'Now how are you going to do that, you cheap whore? He's not in and you're locked in this room with the two of us for company. I'm afraid you're not going anywhere, ever again.'

She knew there was someone else in here. Mae opened her mouth to scream, but nothing came out. A hand clamped across her mouth so tight that she couldn't breathe. She tried to bite down on it, but she couldn't. She struggled against the rope which had been looped around her neck. Clawing at his hands trying to make him to loosen his grip. Silver specks began to float across her eyes and then the room went black.

Chapter Twenty-Six

Frankie downed the last of his coffee, pushed the file he was reading away and stretched. 'I'm going to have to call it a day, I want to go home and shower before our dancing lesson.'

Maria looked at him in wide-eyed horror. 'Crap, is that tonight?'

'Don't tell me you forgot.'

'I'm so sorry, Frankie, I did. I have other plans now.' She didn't know if she could tell him about the text she'd got an hour ago from Harrison, especially now he was looking at her like a four year old looks when he's told he can't have a candy bar.

'Oh, it's okay. I guess I can go on my own tonight.'

'Are you sure? I'll be there next week, I promise.'

He nodded. She waited for him to ask, although she didn't want him to ask because she didn't want to have to lie to him. She'd never lied to him, but she had no idea how he'd take being blown off for a rich man. He stood up, grabbing his jacket from the back of the chair.

'Thanks for the coffee and the food. I'll catch you tomorrow.'

'Have fun at your dancing class.'

He didn't laugh, he smiled, waved his hand at her and walked out of the door, leaving her feeling bad for letting him down. He shut the door a little louder than he usually did.

Maria whispered. 'Shit, Frankie I'm not your wife. You don't need to be so pissed with me.'

She looked at the contents of the box that were spread across her table; there had been no Satanic bible which she'd been kind of glad about. She wasn't sure she wanted anything like that in her house, who knew what kind of stuff it might attract. The pictures were gruesome, black and white stills. The house was gorgeous from the outside: window boxes filled with flowers, the glass on the windows and doors gleaming it was so clean. Who would have guessed what horrors it held inside? The inside had been photographed and it was decadent to say the least: crystal chandeliers, polished wooden floors, gleaming brass door knobs, huge vases filled with fresh flowers. She would have loved to have visited it back then. There was nothing to show anything was amiss on any of these photographs. The ground, first and second, floors were immaculate. It was only when the photographer reached the attic that the tone of the photographs changed dramatically. The heavy, wooden door was pushed open to reveal a glimpse of the pooling blood on the floor. As he'd stepped inside and began to photograph, Maria wondered if he'd gasped, shocked by the horror of what he was capturing through his lens. The attic walls had writing all over them, symbols that she didn't recognize and many dark patches of blood. When the photographer had captured the surroundings, he'd focused on the body. Maria couldn't look at it any longer, she shuffled the pictures together. Placing them and the typed-up police reports back into the box, next to the brown paper bags of the victims, heavily bloodstained clothes, she then put the lid on the box and picked it up. Carrying it to the closet she placed it on the floor, not wanting to be reminded about it every time she saw it. The fact that it had happened so long ago didn't matter. The horror was still as fresh to Maria. This had been brutal. An act of pure evil. She wanted to know what the writing and symbols on the walls said. This meant she was going to have to track down either a bookshop or a professor who might know something about Satanic symbols and demonology because this was way beyond her realm of knowledge. Frankie had pretended he knew a little. She didn't want to discourage him, but she knew this was way out of both of their leagues. They needed to find a professional who could explain it to them in layman's terms. What it looked like was some kind of ritual killing, and at the time they'd locked the perp up as a lunatic in the nearest mental institution. It didn't look as if anyone had bothered to find out what he was doing and why? There were no notes explaining what any of it had meant. They hadn't cared. They had a body and they had their killer. That was all that mattered. Plus he was from a wealthy family, so they would have no doubt paid to have had him taken care of. The lack of newspaper reports surprised her; there were some, but in her opinion, only minimal coverage. She'd never heard about it and she'd been born and bred in New York along with her entire family.

She walked into the bathroom and began to fill the tub for a nice soak to wash away the horrors. Going back into the kitchen she opened the fridge, taking out an almost empty, cold bottle of Pinot Grigio. She poured its contents into a wine glass and took a sip. Kicking off her shoes she sat down on the sofa, curling her legs underneath her. Today had been one hell of a crazy day. She suddenly remembered Miss Green, she hadn't checked on her. Taking a huge mouthful of wine she forced herself to stand up, placing the glass on the table. She padded across to the front door, opened it and stepped into the hallway. Leaving the apartment door ajar, she crept down to Miss Green's and knocked on the door, waiting to hear her shuffling along the carpeted hallway. There was no sound. Maria stepped forward and pressed her ear against the door. There was no noise. She rapped again, much louder. This was a cop knock that she usually reserved for work, the 'no shit answer the fucking door' knock. Still no reply, 'Hello are you there? It's Maria.' A hand touched her shoulder. 'Holy shit.' She screeched so loudly that Miss Green jumped more than she did.

'Jesus, Maria, you're giving me a coronary over here. What's wrong with you?'

Maria laughed. 'Geez, I'm so sorry. I've been trying to catch hold of you all day. Are you okay?'

For a split second Maria could tell that the old lady standing in front of her was not okay and would probably never be okay again. Then the reserved, polite and smiling Miss Green took over and she nodded her head.

'I've been to visit a very old friend today, a long overdue visit if I'm honest. Oh, and yes dear I'm fine. Just a little bit tired, it's been emotional.'

'If you're sure, you know if there's anything I can do I will. You just have to ask.'

Her friend leant up and kissed her cheek. 'I know you will lovely, thank you.'

'Oh shoot, my bath. I have to go, I have a date.'

The smile that spread across Miss Green's face lit her up. 'Well then, don't be wasting your time talking to an old broad like me. Go and get yourself all beautiful, I hope he's the one who's been sending you those gorgeous flowers.'

'He is, it's nothing serious. We're just friends, sort of.'

'That's how it should be. Now go – shoo – get ready. Tomorrow we'll have a nice pot of tea and you can tell me how it went. I'll be waiting for the full details so don't go disappointing me, Maria. Life's too short to spend it on your own.'

Maria laughed and rushed back into her apartment, locking the door she ran into the bathroom and turned off the taps. The bath was almost full, she'd have to watch she didn't flood the apartment below when she got into it.

Chapter Twenty-Seven

Frankie parked in the underground garage, he was home much earlier than normal when he was working a late shift. He wanted a shower before he went dancing, so was hoping that Christy wasn't home yet. He spotted her car, but that didn't mean she was home. Like Maria she often walked to work. He opened the door and walked inside holding his breath. If there was the slightest chance of Christy finding out what he was up to it wouldn't work. This was going to be his last attempt to put some life back into their very stale marriage. He wasn't going to stay with her if she didn't care, he had feelings for Maria that ran far deeper than any he'd ever had for his wife. It was wrong, but they made such a great couple. The apartment was empty, he checked each room. The spare room was much tidier than the last time he'd been in it. The bed was made up with what looked like expensive, cotton bedding. He crossed to the bed, stroking the covers. This was nice, much nicer than what was on their bed and he wondered why on earth she'd gone to so much bother. Had she said they were having visitors and he'd not heard? That was always a possibility; he did have a habit of switching off when she was talking. Loosening his tie and undoing the buttons on his shirt he walked into the kitchen to get a cold beer. If he was going dancing on his own he was going to need a bit of a helping hand with his nerves from Mr Sam Adams. A loud buzzing noise behind him made him turn around to see Christy's phone vibrating on the kitchen counter. Not really thinking he picked it up even though he wasn't into the habit of reading the messages on her phone. He saw Adam's picture flash across the screen and he wondered why his brother was texting his wife. Sliding the screen across he was surprised she didn't have a pass code on it. Then again, she was even worse with technology than he was. He read the message twice, not quite sure if he was reading it right.

'Can't wait to finish work so I can bury my head between your legs and taste your honey. xx'

Frankie felt a rush of white, hot rage fill his chest as he read it again. All this time he was thinking of doing things to make it better when she was fucking around behind his back. With his brother. The dirty, rotten, cheating bastards. Pushing the phone into his pocket he downed his beer and pulled another one out of the cooler. He was pacing up and down the apartment. He wasn't perfect. Yes, he'd tried it on with Maria the other night, but she'd put him in his place and he didn't think he'd have had the balls to go through with it. But this… She'd been sleeping with Adam under the expensive bed sheets in the spare room. He stormed in there, ripping the covers off the bed. He pulled the pillow cases off and crumpled them all up into a ball which he then began to jump all over. The anger began to subside and he realized that he was tired, of all the bullshit, of this crappy marriage. He grabbed another beer and took it to the couch where he sat down. He was numb. Too numb to turn the television on, he lifted the beer to his lips and sipped. Waiting for her to come home.

✪

The broken buzzer for Maria's apartment vibrated and she checked her watch, he was on time. Eight pm, he'd told her he'd be downstairs waiting for her. That's providing it was Harrison and not Frankie or anyone else. She checked her reflection in the mirror and smiled, tucking a stray strand of hair back into the chignon she'd carefully pinned up.

Spritzing herself one last time in Chanel Crystal she grabbed her purse off the side and tried to push the butterflies in her stomach back down. She went to the elevator, pressing the call button, praying that it was working. She didn't want to walk down the stairs and get all sweaty before she'd even seen him. The cranky doors opened and she stepped inside, briefly wondering if Frankie had made it to the dance class. She felt bad for letting him down, but she was entitled to a little fun as well. What Frankie should be doing was taking Christy with him, not her. When the elevator opened and she stepped out she did a double take at Harrison Williams who was dressed in a pair of navy trousers, with a white shirt not quite fastened at the top. Her breath caught in the back of her throat, his hair was styled just a little too perfectly to have been done by himself. He was standing with his mouth open.

'Mr Williams, didn't your momma teach you it was rude to stare?'

He clamped his mouth shut and nodded his head. As she reached him she got a whiff of his aftershave. It was seductive, but not overpowering. She took hold of his arm, linking hers through his.

'Maria, you look beautiful.'

She threw back her head and laughed. 'You'd be amazed what a full face of make-up can do for a girl. So where are we going?'

'It's a surprise. I can tell you it's definitely not the opera.'

She looked at him and smiled. 'Good, because I hate it.'

They walked out of the buildings doors to the waiting limousine and he held up his hands.

‘I tried to get a town car, but I left it too late. I had no choice.’

‘We could always walk.’

He looked down at her heels. ‘No, the car is a must. I’m far too lazy to walk where we’re going.’

‘I suppose I can make an allowance, just this one time.’

The driver was out of the car and holding the door open before they reached the bottom step. She slid into it and felt the cool leather seat press against the back of her legs. Harrison got in next to her, as she spotted an open bottle of champagne and two glasses. One of them was already half full.

‘Sorry, nerves. I was scared you might have changed your mind so I had a glass to calm me down.’

Maria looked at him to see if he was being sarcastic and realized he was being serious. He topped up his glass then filled the other, handing it to her. She took it from him and whispered, ‘Thank you.’ He smiled at her.

‘Phew, that was easier than I’d imagined for the last two hours. I’d convinced myself you were going to give me a hard time.’

‘I’m not always a bitch.’

‘Oh crap, that’s not what I meant at all.’

She laughed. ‘Well, not all the time.’ Sitting back she watched as the limousine turned onto Sixth Avenue and began to drive into Midtown. This was nice, she’d never been in a limousine drinking expensive champagne, ever. Then and there she decided not to give him a hard time tonight; if he was as nervous as she was then she’d go easy on him. For some reason she’d thought that he’d be cocky, self-assured and full of himself. It was refreshing to discover that he wasn’t. It wasn’t really his fault if he had more money than she could ever dream about. She was going to be a lady if it killed her, for this was one of life's magical, rare moments which came along. If there was nothing more to it, she wanted to be able to remember the night she was wined and dined by Harrison Williams. To be able to store the memory in the part of her brain where she kept her happy thoughts, her special memories to look back on one day. If her mom could see her now she'd probably pee her pants. She pictured the scene from one of her favorite films: *Arthur*. The one when Liza Minnelli was telling her dad about Arthur.

'I take it this bum will be calling you.'

'Dad, he's a millionaire.'

'You have my permission to marry him.'

That would be her mom, she wouldn't care who Harrison Williams was. His bank balance would be enough. Thank God she wasn't that shallow and she hoped that he knew that. Harrison began to ask her about the library and she tried her best to answer in a normal voice. She couldn't tell him what had happened after he'd left, she'd sound like one of the crazies locked away at Greystone's.

'It was interesting, I found a little of what I was looking for.'

'Good, that's great. You know I have an office full of researchers, so if you were to let me know I could get them to look up anything you want. It would save you the time and effort… that's if you were too busy. I know you like the Public Library, it's your happy place.'

Maria was too afraid to tell him that she was now terrified to visit and spend time there alone, in case it happened to her again. She didn't want to die on the cold, tiled floor of the New York Public Library no matter how much she loved it.

The car turned onto West 49th Street, stopping outside the front of the Observation Deck entrance for the Rockefeller Building. Maria looked at Harrison who shrugged.

'You said nothing too fancy and after your lecture about not visiting the town's iconic buildings I thought you might appreciate this.'

She began to laugh, so much that tears filled the corner of her eyes. Shaking her head she downed the rest of her champagne which was far too nice to waste. Then the door opened and she was being helped out by the driver who was grinning at her. She thanked him and waited for Harrison to climb out. Smoothing down her dress she wondered if she should have worn a pair of jeans. Hell, if she'd known they were coming here she would have worn a pair of jeans and Converse. Harrison led her towards the doors where there was a sign on them apologizing that it was closed for the rest of the evening. She pointed to it.

'Aw that's such a shame, but I'll give you ten out of ten for being original.'

'Come on, they might let us squeeze in if we're nice to them.' He pushed open one of the heavy glass doors where the doorman came rushing over. His cheeks, burning.

'Sir, I'm sorry. We're shut for the rest of the evening. We'll be open again tomorrow morning at eight am.'

'Do you think if we paid a little extra you could squeeze us in, I've waited ages to come here and I wanted to impress my friend.'

The doorman looked across at Maria, smiling.

'Oh, I'm sorry, sir. Yes, I think we might be able to squeeze you in on the last elevator up.'

Harrison shook his hand. 'Good man, thanks.'

Maria watched as Harrison slipped a folded note into the guy's hand. She had no idea how much it was, but they were led straight to the first elevator.

'Have a good evening sir, welcome to the Top of the Rock.'

The doors shut and Maria looked at him. 'Well I'll be damned, did you already buy tickets?'

He nodded. 'I got my assistant to pre-book them this afternoon.'

She smiled at him. 'I don't suppose we'll have much time, I definitely should have worn my sneakers. I hope the queue isn't too long.'

They got out of the elevator to an empty floor where the only people were the security guards, leaning against the wall chatting. They waved them straight through. She leant towards his ear and whispered.

'Wow, how much did you tip that guy?'

He laughed. 'Probably not enough.'

They were stopped by the photographer. Harrison shook his head and Maria looked at him.

'Come on, don't be a spoil sport. I'll buy the souvenirs. Please.'

She jumped onto the bench with a black and white back drop of New York City behind them. Harrison rolled his eyes but sat next to her. The woman with the camera laughed.

'Right you two love birds, give me a thumbs up. That's great, now cross your arms. Uhuh, now give him a push and show him who's boss.'

The camera flashed and both of them laughed. The young girl standing next to the photographer passed Maria a ticket. They walked arm in arm to the next bank of elevators where they were put into another car.

‘I can’t believe it’s so empty, I mean it’s never this quiet. I’ve been as soon as the doors open and there’s people waiting in line. Even late at night it’s fairly busy.’

He smiled at her and shrugged. ‘I don’t really like heights, so I wouldn’t know.’

Maria looked at him. ‘Is that why you’ve never been before, is it some well-kept secret?’

‘No, I’m just stating a fact. I’m not petrified of them, I mean I don’t have to cling onto the walls or whoever I’m with to make me feel brave.’

‘Oh, that’s a shame. I was hoping you’d want to cling on to me.’

He laughed, the doors slid back revealing another empty corridor and they stepped out. Maria whispered, ‘At least we don’t have to wait ages in line for the photographs.’ She led them to the heavy, glass doors which opened out onto the observation deck. They were the only two people out there. Maria looked around; it was the two of them and a couple of security guards. He hovered near to the wall and she grinned at him, slipping her hand into his.

‘Come on, tough guy, you need to move away from the wall to make the most of the views.’ She led him around the entire observation deck and to the stairs to the next level. He laughed. ‘Do we need to? I can see everything just fine from here.’

She shook her head. ‘We’re here now, you have to.’

He followed her up and watched her as she pressed her face against the toughened safety, screens.

‘Don’t tell me you aren’t sorry you came. Look at our city. It sparkles and shimmers under the moonlight. It’s beautiful, a city full of hopes and dreams. A city brimming with romance and character, so much history.’

'Even though you deal with the criminals and see it under a different light, you still love it?'

She pointed at the Empire State Building, 'What's not to love. Every place, every person has their dark, dirty secrets. You have to see through the darkness to appreciate the light.'

'There's one more floor isn't there?'

'I'm afraid so. Do you really not like it?'

This time he took her hand. 'Of course I do, come on.'

He led her up the steps to the next floor and she let out a small gasp. Hundreds of candles lit the way to the far end where there was a table with two chairs. Flickering candles were blowing with the warm breeze. It was one of those mild nights, where the heat was almost as intense as in broad daylight. On the white tablecloth was an ice bucket with a bottle of champagne resting in it, next to two crystal champagne flutes. He led her towards it.

'Now, I've done the tourist thing, so you have to do the dining thing. I hope this meets with your approval.'

She began to laugh. 'Well, it's certainly different. It's beautiful. Thank you.'

'Oh, and don't worry, you said you didn't like fancy food. I've had the Rainbow Room prepare us some cheeseburgers and fries.'

He winked at her and Maria felt as if her heart was about to explode. She kept looking around to see if there were cameras, if she was being filmed for some crazy TV show that he was producing. All she could see were the two grinning security guards.

'Am I being filmed, you know for some reality show?'

He looked genuinely shocked. 'Of course not, I wanted to let you have a nice, almost normal evening.'

Maria took the glass of champagne that he passed to her and she took a sip, turning around, allowing her mind to take a mental snapshot of the magical scene before her, one of those special memories that she wanted to lock away forever.

'Thank you, I don't know what to say.'

He leant forward and kissed her tenderly on the lips. 'Then don't say anything.'

Chapter Twenty-Eight

By the time Christy came home, Frankie's burning rage had turned into simmering fury. She waltzed in as if nothing was wrong in her yoga pants and crop top. He stared at her; she had a good figure for her age. She took one look at him and her pretty face turned ugly. 'Why are you home and are you drunk?' He shrugged as he began to clap his hands together, 'Bravo Christy, you had me. You really did.'

Confusion in her eyes she didn't know what he was talking about which angered him even more.

'What Frankie, what did I do?'

He pulled her phone out of his pocket, waving it at her. 'Did you forget something? Is that what you came back for? You cheating, lying bitch.' He stood up, a little unsteady and thrust it into the palm of her hand. She read Adam's message, at least she had the decency to squirm as her cheeks began to burn.

'Don't insult me by telling me it's not what I think, I don't want to know any details. How long it's been going on. What I want is for you to pack your bags and get the fuck out. Go stay with Adam in his nice, cramped, studio apartment in Queens. See how much you enjoy fucking him when you have to live with him. All this time I was trying to make it better and you were sleeping with my brother.'

'How dare you judge me, I know you've been screwing Maria. You fawn over her like a puppy dog with those big eyes. You make me sick, you hypocritical bastard.'

She grabbed an empty coffee cup and launched it through the air, any other day Frankie would have ducked in time. The beer sloshing around in his brain made his reactions a lot slower and it smacked him full force on the corner of his eyebrow. A gash opened up and blood began streaming down his cheek.

'Oh shit, Frankie. I'm so sorry I didn't mean to hit you.'

He stumbled back and fell onto the sofa, Christy grabbed a dish cloth off the counter and rushed to him. Pressing it against the cut, to try and stem the flow of blood.

'It's going to need stitches, I'll drive you to the emergency room.'

He shook his head, pushing her away. 'I've never slept with her, ever.'

Adam who had walked in through the open door thinking Christy had left it ajar for him, took in the sight before him and muttered, *'Oh fuck.'*

Frankie looked at him. 'Take her and get out of my life, you piece of shit. This is how you repay me, all the years I've looked out for you.'

Adam held up his hands, 'Whoa, Frankie. What's going on, you've got it all wrong.'

Christy turned to him, glaring. 'He knows Adam.' She turned back to Frankie.

'I'm sorry, please let me get you to the hospital.'

He shook his head. 'Yes, Adam, I know. Just get the hell out of my sight before I get her arrested for battery.'

Her face turned even paler than it already was, he took hold of the cloth that she'd been pressing against his head and she let go. She hissed at Adam. 'Go wait in the car, I need to stop with you for a few days.'

If there was any justice in all of this it was the look of horror that crossed Adam's face at the thought of having to let Christy stop at his bachelor pad where he screwed every woman he met. Frankie began to laugh.

'She's all yours now bro, no more sloppy seconds for you.'

Adam turned and walked out, back to his car, the dawning realization that his free ride had just ended in the most spectacular way.

Frankie could hear the drawers and wardrobe doors being open and slammed shut. She was never going to fit all her stuff into an overnight bag and suitcase. Good, he'd take it all to Goodwill, that would serve her right. She appeared looking a lot less flawless than when she'd walked in fifteen minutes ago.

'I've got some stuff; I'll let you get sorted out. I'm giving you a couple of days and then I'm coming back so we can talk about it. About this, about our stuff.'

She was waving her hands around, he didn't care. He could see two of her. Damn! She must have thrown that cup with some force because he was concussed.

'Get the fuck out, Christy.'

She opened her mouth about to have the last word then closed it again. Turning she pulled the case behind her and hoisted the overnight bag over her shoulder. He watched her go, just like that. She didn't slam the door like he'd expected her to, instead she closed it softly. He pushed himself off the sofa and immediately felt a surge of stale alcohol and bile fill his mouth. His head was smarting like a bitch so he did the only thing he could think of and stumbled into the bedroom leaving a trail of bloody handprints and smears on the walls behind him. His bed looked huge now he knew he was going to be sleeping in it alone. Kicking off his shoes, he clambered onto the white, cotton bedding and closed his eyes. Trying to stop the room from spinning, he wondered if he should call Maria, get her to come and stick his head back together, but he'd left his cell in the kitchen and he wasn't getting up again. He had no idea if the front door was locked and he didn't care. If anyone broke in they could take the lot, none of it mattered now. Squeezing his eyes shut he willed the room to stop spinning and began to drift into a semi-conscious drunken slumber.

Chapter Twenty-Nine

June 1952

James towered over the bloodied mess that minutes ago had been his father's lover and his sister's new best friend. He couldn't see the demon, but he could sense him. It was there. He needed two more sacrifices to summon it fully. Something that he was more than willing to carry out, although he hadn't particularly enjoyed killing Mae. It had been necessary. He could feel her wet, sticky blood on his hands and face. He could see it dripping from the meat cleaver onto the wooden floorboards. He dipped his fingers in the spreading, pool of blood. Then he drew the biggest pentagram onto the bedroom wall he could. So absorbed in what he was doing he never heard the commotion from downstairs. After finishing what he was doing, he decided the best way to dispose of her was to remove her arms and legs. He wanted to keep her head. Even though the terrified look in her eyes took away some of her beauty, she was still pretty. He lifted the meat cleaver and hacked until he had her head. Lifting it up he stared at her. Kissing her soft lips one last time, he knew he was going to have to put her in a jar and pickle her if he wanted to preserve it. Wrapping it up in pages of the *New York Times* to absorb some of the blood and fluid leaking from it. He put it inside the thick, leather, Gladstone bag. He went downstairs knowing he had to hide it somewhere they would never find it if they came looking. As he came out of the spare room which was used for storage he heard his father. He was drunk judging by the noise he was making. Fear making his heart beat too fast he turned and ran back to the attic, knowing he had to get rid of her body before she was discovered. As he reached the top step he heard his father holler. 'Mae, where are you? Damn you, don't make me come looking. You promised you'd be here when I came home.'

Emilia's door opened and she came out onto the hallway, struggling to walk on her own two legs. She felt so disorientated. 'Pa, what's the matter? Mae is here, she's in the library.'

She heard his heavy feet as he thundered up the stairs. 'She's not there, where did she go?' He looked at his daughter's pale face. 'What's the matter Em, are you ill?'

She shrugged. 'I don't know, I feel as if my head doesn't belong to my body. Mae might have got a cab and gone home. Missy helped me to bed, I left her downstairs.' The room began to spin and Emilia felt her legs give way as she lurched towards him. Reaching out she grasped hold of the handrail and recoiled. There was something sticky on it, lifting her hand up to take a look her eyes widened in horror and she let out a gasp.

'Oh my, is that… is that blood?'

Clarke stared at the red liquid coating his daughters hand, he grabbed her wrist pulling it towards him. Lifting it to his nose, he sniffed. 'Blood.'

Emilia screamed and Missy came running up the stairs. Clarke stared in morbid fascination at the blood dripping from her fingers. Missy took one look and screeched.

'Miss Emilia what have you done?'

She shook her head and whispered. 'It's not mine.'

Clarke stared up the narrow staircase that led up to the attic. He turned to Missy.

'I need you to call the police, now. Tell them it's an emergency. That much blood, someone is hurt. Real bad.'

Missy let go of Emilia and ran down the hallway to the master bedroom where there was a telephone. Clarke rushed upstairs, twisting the door knob hard. It wouldn't move, it was locked from the inside. He slammed the palm of his hand against the heavy, oak door.

'James open the door. Are you hurt? Let me in this minute. I command you.'

He was greeted by silence, he hammered on the door with his fist. He could hear some noise from inside the attic. He stepped back and ran at the door as best as he could in what little space there was. His shoulder hit the door and pain shot through his entire body, but it didn't move.

'Open the goddamn door now, James.'

Emilia and Missy were watching him from below, there was a loud thud and a growl which made Emilia whimper. She looked at Missy and whispered, 'What was that?'

Missy crossed herself. 'Dear Lord, I have no idea.'

Clarke ran back towards them. 'Someone's in there with him. Did you call the cops?'

Missy nodded, they heard the sirens as the cars turned into the street. She ran downstairs to open the door and let them in. There was a stampede of heavy boots as the four cops ran up to where Clarke was standing. He pointed at the blood.

'I can't find my friend, Mae. My son James is in the attic. Someone is bleeding real bad. There's someone inside and they won't open the door.'

The oldest of the men nodded. 'Sir, I'm going to ask you to step aside. Do we have your permission to gain access?'

'I don't care if you break down the damn door, do what you want.'

He went and stood with Emilia and Missy, putting his arms around them both. A sinking feeling that no matter what they found on the other side of that door, his life was going to be irrevocably changed. The cop who had spoken hammered on the door.

'Police! Open the door now. I'm going to give you to the count of three and then I'm going to shoot the lock off.'

There was only silence. The cop pulled his gun from his holster and aimed for the lock on the door.

'One, two, three.' He fired four rounds into the door handle then the burly guy next to him kicked the door. It splintered and gave way. As the door opened, the sight that greeted the hardened, city cops was one that would stay with them for the rest of their lives. The walls of the attic were covered in an assortment of symbols, daubed in red paint. It was the strong, metallic, sickly smell which made them realize that it was in fact blood and not paint. On the kitchen counter was a gory mess. Guns drawn, the cops stepped into the room, trying to decide what it was they were looking at until one of them retched. 'It's a body, there's no head.' Clarke who had come running up the stairs behind them took one look at the tangled mess of bloodied body parts and let out an anguished cry. Wrapped around the delicate wrist that he had held so many times was the twenty-two carat, diamond encrusted bracelet he'd bought Mae for her birthday. A piercing scream filled the air and Emilia felt herself being pulled away by Missy. The cops who had all drawn their guns began to search the attic. Kicking the bedroom door in they found James standing on the bed. Naked and covered in blood, he threw his head back and began to laugh. The sound echoed around the walls. Three of the cops dived towards him. He didn't put up a fight, there was no point. For now it was over, they could do what they wanted to him. He'd made a start, he'd done the hard work. It would help him to get free; it needed him now as much as he needed it. They cuffed his hands behind his back. Clarke ran in and, drawing back his fist, he hit his son in the jaw as hard as he could.

'You son of a bitch! What did you do to her? My beautiful Mae.'

The older cop grabbed Clarke, pulling him away. 'He'll get plenty of that where he's going.'

'Where is he going?'

James who was rubbing the side of his face began to scream at the top of his voice. 'He's coming, he's coming, he's coming and you can't stop him. He's been summoned.'

The cop shook his head. 'Greystone's Psychiatric Hospital. He's nuts.'

Chapter Thirty

Maria opened her eyes then squinted, the sun was streaming through the blinds which she'd forgotten to close before she climbed into bed. She smiled as she remembered last night. It had been wonderful. When they'd finished eating he'd led her down to the Rainbow Room where they'd drunk cocktails and danced to the most amazing singer she'd ever heard. She had no idea who she was, but she needed to find out. Harrison had been a perfect gentleman, dropping her off at her apartment and escorting her to the front door. He'd kissed her and going against every rule she abided by, she'd asked if he wanted to come in. He'd declined and said he would love to, but he didn't want to pressure her into anything. She hadn't felt hurt, in fact she'd felt relieved. She was more than a little drunk and didn't want to end the night in some drunken fumble she might regret the next morning. Now it was the next morning she was regretting not dragging him in, it had been so long since she'd woken up next to someone it would have been nice to have someone to talk to. Her cell began to ring, and she grabbed it from under her pillow. There was no mistaking the voice on the other end.

'Maria, can you do me a favour?'

She held her breath wondering what the hell Christy was doing phoning her, as they weren't exactly friends.

'If I can.'

'Can you go check on Frankie? He was drunk when I got home. We had an argument and he threw me out. I don't want to see him, but he's not answering his cell.'

Maria sat up. 'He did what?'

‘Look I’m late for work already, I can’t go and check, and he won’t let me in anyway. Please Maria, just make sure he’s okay and let me know.’

Tucking the phone under her ear she began to pull on her sweats, pushing her feet into her sneakers. She ran to the bathroom, all sorts of images running through her mind. Why was he drunk? Why did he throw her out? Why wasn’t he answering his cell?

‘I’ll let you know.’ She ended the call and rang Frankie. *Shit, you better not have done anything stupid, Frankie.* It went to voicemail. ‘Frankie, answer your damn phone, ring me as soon as you get this.’ There was no reasoning behind the panic in her voice, he’d never had suicidal tendencies or talked about it. But she’d been to enough suicides, the majority of them men his age, who had decided they’d had enough of the crap life threw at them.

She brushed her teeth and took a large glug of mouthwash, swirling it around her mouth before spitting it out. Rinsing her face, she still had traces of last night’s make-up on, but she didn’t care. Tying her hair up she ran towards the door, willing her cell to ring so she could hear his hungover voice – deep and gravelly as if he’d been smoking too much. She ran towards the elevator. As the doors opened she heard Miss Green shout, ‘Morning Maria, don’t forget to come and tell me how your date went.’

She turned and waved at her as she stepped inside. ‘I won’t. It was great.’

The judder as the doors slammed shut vibrated the elevator and she heard a muffled reply. Jabbing the ground floor button, she prayed that the heap of junk wouldn’t choose this exact moment to decide to break down in between floors. It didn’t and before too long it opened, she ran out through the glass doors and onto the street. 'Damn you Frankie, I hate running.' She muttered to herself as she began to make her legs pump faster. It was the quickest way to get to his apartment, a cab would get stuck in traffic. She began to run up Sullivan Street, not even giving Miss Lilly's a second glance. If she had she would have seen the man, perched on a stool in the window. Nursing a coffee and watching her every move.

Maria ran onto Bleeker Street, glad that it wasn't too busy and even more relieved that it was flat all the way to Frankie's apartment. She was a little out of breath and her throat was dry, she'd not even taken a sip of water yet after all the alcohol she'd consumed last night. Finally, she reached Eighth Avenue, ran across dodging the cars and onto Hudson. She could see his fancy apartment block looming in the distance and pumped her legs even harder. Pushing through the front doors she managed to squeeze into the elevator just before the doors slid shut. Panting she turned to the elderly couple who were watching her, she smiled. 'Morning.' They nodded, and the lady smiled back. She turned away from them, her legs felt like jelly and her stomach was rolling from side to side. When the elevator stopped on Frankie's floor she stepped out and ran down the hall to his door. Lifting her hand to rap on the door she realized that it wasn't even shut. She pushed it open and stepped inside.

'Frankie, Frankie.' She was greeted by silence, the first thing she noticed was the bloodied smears on the walls and she let out a gasp. She began to pray for the second time in as many days. *Please God, let him be okay.* She was aware that this might be a potential crime scene, at the same time her heart was hammering in her chest because this was her best friend. She didn't know how she would cope if anything bad had happened. She followed the blood along the hallway to the master, the door was shut. Pushing it open she saw him lying on the bed, with blood all over the pillows and lamp.

'Frankie.' she screeched and ran towards him. Reaching out she poked him in the shoulder and his eyes flew open. This time she screamed and jumped backwards.

'Holy shit, Maria, what are you trying to do give me a heart attack?'

She stepped forward and slapped his shoulder. 'Why the fuck didn't you answer your phone? And what happened to you? You're bleeding, there's blood everywhere.'

'You should be a cop, has anyone ever suggested that?'

'And you shouldn't be such a smart ass. Christy rang, she said you were drunk and threw her out.'

He pushed himself up onto his elbows and groaned. 'My head hurts.'

Maria looked at the crusted, bloody, black gash on his forehead. 'I can see why your head hurts, is that your brain I can see?'

'Are you serious, you can see my brain?'

She started laughing. 'Okay, maybe that was a slight exaggeration.'

He threw his legs out of the bed and pushed himself up. His head hurt and he wasn't sure if it was because of the hangover or the cut. He held his hand out and she grabbed it, tugging him to his feet.

'Jeez, Frankie. This place looks like a crime scene. What happened?'

'Go make me something to eat while I wash up and I'll tell you all the gory details.'

She shrugged. 'Do I have a choice?'

'No food, no gossip.'

She turned leaving the room and Frankie to sort himself out, she went into the well-stocked kitchen and began to pull out bacon and eggs from the fridge. She busied herself making them both breakfast, and when he finally came in he looked and smelt much better. The gash above his eyebrow was angry and open, but his clothes were fresh. A trickle of blood was seeping from the wound and she pulled a cloth out of the drawer, rolling it up she passed it to him.

'You're leaking, press this against it. You need stitches.'

He shook his head. 'No ER, I'm not explaining to some kid playing at doctors that my wife got me good.'

'Where's your first aid kit?'

'Bathroom, top shelf in the cabinet.'

Maria passed him his plate of bacon and eggs then went to retrieve the medical box. Placing it on the table she pulled out some gauze pads and tape.

'You haven't got any strips, we'll stick one of these on and stop off to pick some up. So what happened?'

She stood there with her hands on her hips and her face stern, Frankie looked up from his food. He let out the biggest sigh she'd ever heard.

'She's screwing around with my brother, I found a message on her cell.'

'No way. Adam?'

He nodded. 'Yep, she accused me of…' He went quiet, not sure if he should tell her the next part of his story.

'What? What did she accuse you of?'

'Of sleeping with you.'

Maria spat the mouthful of coffee she'd just taken a sip of all over. 'Sorry, sorry. That's crazy, why does she think that?'

‘I don’t know, it doesn’t matter. She’s the one screwing around and then she threw a coffee cup at me.’

‘You could have her picked up, put her in the cooler for a few hours.’

‘No way, I’d never live it down.’

He had a point, the guys would be rubbing it in for the next three years.

‘So, what are you going to do?’

He shrugged. ‘No idea.’

Chapter Thirty-One

He'd watched her come racing out of her apartment as if she was running for her life. Which was interesting because the last three days she hadn't broken more than a brisk walk. He'd taken up a twice daily lookout in Miss Lilly's, watching her come and go at the most unusual times. Something was wrong, he'd never seen her look so serious or scared and he wondered what had gotten her into such a mess. He downed the last of his coffee which was now cold, he'd been nursing it that long. He crossed the road and walked up the apartment steps, expecting the front door to be locked. It wasn't, it was open for anyone to walk in and out. He stepped into the gloomy entrance and blinked a couple of times, his eyes adjusting to the darkness. He walked across to the row of mail boxes and stared at the names, none of them meant a thing to him. He could discount all the Mr and Mrs, she didn't wear a ring and she'd only ever taken that cop she worked with in with her. That left eight possible mailboxes, all of them had first and second names except for one with MILLER in black capitals. He stared at them, which one would a NYC cop use. His eyes were drawn back to the box with Miller and he nodded. He would place a ten dollar bet that was her, the box next to that said Miss Green. If he could figure out who she was he might be able to work out which was hers. The elevator doors opened, and he picked up a brown, paper package. Turning the address label over, out of sight. He stared at the old woman who came out, she was dressed all in black with a large floppy hat and an oversize pair of Chanel sunglasses. He stared at her and she stared back.

'Can I help you?'

‘I’m looking for Miller, she needs to sign for this.’

‘Eighth floor, apartment twenty three.’

‘Thank you, ma’am.’

He headed towards the elevators. Miss Green on a good day would have challenged him and asked him why he couldn’t read the address on the parcel. Today her mind was in another place and she carried on out of the front doors onto the street, not giving him a second thought. The old elevator took forever to reach the eighth floor. When the doors finally opened, he let out a sigh of relief. He walked along to apartment twenty three. The hallway was dark, a couple of bulbs had blown which was good. Hers was the last apartment on the right and quite some distance from the elevators which could be problematic. If he tried to ambush here it would be unlikely he would make it out without anyone intercepting him. It was risky. He walked up to her door and looked around, but there were no surveillance cameras that he could see, and he didn’t think this place provided high tech, covert cameras. The elevator was older than he was, the whole building needed a serious cash injection. The hallway was deserted so he pulled his sleeve down and tried the handle. To his surprise he realized the door wasn’t actually shut, it was resting against the frame. Pushing it gently he tried to peer through the gap. It was quiet, there was no tv or music playing. ‘Hello, anyone home? I have a package delivery for Miller.’ The silence that greeted him made his stomach clench with excitement. Checking the corridor to make sure he was still alone he pushed the door wider and stepped inside. The thought of being inside a cop’s apartment as attractive as her made his legs quiver and his belly roll. It would be a challenge and it was very dangerous, he had no doubt about it, but it would make the result much sweeter, and that he could risk. The demon would appreciate all his hard work in making the final sacrifice the most significant. He didn't know what it was, but since he'd focussed all his energy on making it happen he felt different. He felt stronger, in control. The voices in his head were still there only they were encouraging him. At first he'd been worried they were mocking him, but they were agreeing with his ideas, egging him on. He had the planchette tucked safely in his back pack, wrapped in a cloth. He didn't dare leave it at the house in the apartment, just in case someone went in there and found it. The time was getting nearer, he just needed to make sure he could get her into the house without getting caught.

Chapter Thirty-Two

Miss Green hailed a cab. She had a yearning to go to church. Not just any church, she wanted to go to Saint Patrick's Cathedral on Fifth Avenue. She felt as if she needed to confess her sins in the Godliest place she knew, not that she had committed many. Chocolate, wine and expensive clothes were probably her worst vices. Who was she to turn down a designer handbag? She had nothing else to spend her money on and she did have lots of money. Her days as a housekeeper for Clarke Carter had ended when he'd died and left her a lot of money for being a loyal employee and family friend. She'd stayed on after what had happened to Mae, while the family had been thrown into turmoil and shock after her violent murder and she'd been the one to pick up the pieces. It had been a terrible time; the newspaper reports had been shocking. Mrs Carter had stayed at the house on Staten Island, she never came back to the House on West 10th Street. Clarke had told her over coffee one evening that she referred to it as Hell House, a den of inequity that had torn apart her entire family. Emilia had stayed there, she felt a duty towards her father and she felt as if she'd be deserting Mae if she left. It was her fault her friend was dead. If she hadn't taken ill, if Mae had never befriended her, she might still be alive and that had been a huge burden for her to bear. Missy had tried her best to help Emilia, she had a soft spot for her, she always had, but Emilia didn't want any help. She'd wanted to be left alone to wallow in her grief, like her father. Clarke blamed himself, although he couldn't have known that James was so mentally disturbed that he would kill anyone in cold blood in the attic.

The house had never been the same after that night; it scared Missy and she wouldn't step foot on the attic staircase. There was always an uncomfortable feeling of being watched. The smell was the worst; from nowhere the halls or certain rooms would fill with the disgusting smell of what she could only describe as rotting garbage. It would fill a room then seconds later be gone. The house was always so dark, despite the bulbs being regularly changed and it was always full of black shadows. The long hallways had filled her with dread, the light which had once filled the house no longer illuminated all the corners of the rooms. It always fell short so you couldn't tell if anyone or anything was lurking there. It was worse when the house was empty, on the rare occasion that Emilia or Clarke left she would hear the scratching and dragging sounds. Only once did she summon up the courage to go up to the attic alone; the ice-cold fear that had filled her veins had been enough to send her running back down to her room where she threw herself on the floor and prayed harder than she'd ever done before. She felt as if whatever it was that was there was taunting them. Time had no meaning for whatever thing James had summoned all those years ago. The murder three years ago had been almost identical to Mae's yet nothing since. Who even knew about Mae? Emilia was the only Clarke family member left, James had died in the hospital. He'd hung himself from the back of door with a bed sheet. Clarke and his estranged wife had both died within months of each other. The only fear she had was that someone or something had been summoned to the house to carry on with whatever the ritual was. How did that happen? The only thing she could think of was that the monster that lived in the attic was strong enough to draw people in. That meant that there had been a shift, and it was dangerous for them all. Emilia needed to leave the house for her own safety but what about all the other tenants who lived there? Did that mean their lives were in danger?

The cab stopped on the corner of Fifth and East 50th to let her out. She stood and stared up at the beautiful Neo-Gothic styled building. It was breath-taking. It stood there, serene and proud, taking up an entire city block it was so huge. She walked up the steps and didn't even give Saks a second glance, which was a first for her. Never one to say no to an impromptu shopping trip, she spent many hours browsing in the department store. Today she had more pressing things on her mind, like how a couple of old gals could send one of Satan's soldiers back to the depths of hell, when neither of them were trained in religious studies, knew exactly what it was they were dealing with or even had the slightest clue. Maybe she could recruit a priest whilst she was here. If she got a sympathetic one in confession he might feel duty bound to help. *Or you could speak to one and ask for their help, Missy. Is there any point in faffing around? Just ask, Father I need you to come fight the forces of evil in my friend's house on West 10th Street. It won't take long, maybe an hour and if you don't die trying I'll make you a lovely pot of tea and the best chocolate chip cookies you've ever tasted. As long as you don't tell him it's been lingering around, gathering strength since the fifties you should be good to go. What's the worst that can happen?* The worst she knew was a sympathetic glance, a prayer and not being taken seriously. She stepped into the cool foyer and smiled at the guard checking purses, but she didn't have one, so he waved her through. What kind of world was this that you couldn't go to church without the fear of some madman coming in with a gun and shooting dead the parishioners?

The church was warm, comforting and busy with tourists all walking around the edges of the pews. Looking at the beautiful marble statues, altars and stained glass windows. There was a mass in full flow so she made her way to the gift shop, it wouldn't hurt to buy some rosary beads and St Michael medals just in case they needed them. She waited behind the queue of loud Korean women asking a bazillion questions about how much this and that was. Missy tried not to roll her eyes, as it was people like this who probably kept the Cathedral open. She picked up a couple of rosaries and turned to see what was happening at the mass. It was then she noticed the guy from the house – Mikey – the one who had been scared to death the other day. He was now dressed as a security guard and was on purse-checking duty. He must have sensed her staring at him because he looked across at her, not recognising her until she elevated her hand and waved. He smiled and waved back. *Well I'll be damned, he has a job. A decent job at that, I had him down as a bum.* She tutted at herself.

'Yes ma'am, can I help you?'

'These please.'

She passed the beads and medals over, along with fifty dollars. The woman turned, passing her a bag and some change.

'Put it in the donation box, do you know that guard over there? Has he been working here long?'

'Who you pointing at? Mikey or Sasha?'

'The man.'

She nodded her head. 'Mikey, yep he's been here a few years. Why?'

'No reason, he looks familiar that's all.'

The woman shrugged, then turned to serve the next person along. Missy clutched hold of the paper bag containing her things as if it was an expensive brooch off the Chanel counter and headed towards Mikey.

'You didn't say you worked here.'

He frowned at her. 'No, I didn't. I can't see that it's particularly relevant.'

She felt her cheeks begin to flush. 'I'm sorry, it isn't. I'm being nosy.'

'What brings you here? I can't say that I've seen you here before.'

'That damn house brings me here.' She looked up to the high ceiling, crossing herself. 'It scares me stupid, I just wanted to come and speak to a priest. Maybe confess my sins, ask for some help. I don't know really. It felt right, I'm glad that I did.'

'Good, this is a special place. If you need to confess there is no finer place in this city to do it.'

'How were you last night?'

He looked around to see if anyone was listening to their conversation. There was a lull in the flow of tourists and Sasha was running the line for the few who were trickling in.

'Scared, I don't feel real comfortable talking about it here. If you get what I mean.'

Nodding her head, she did. It didn't seem right talking about such abomination in a house of worship. 'I'm sorry, you're working and I'm keeping you. I'll see you around, Mikey.'

'Yes, you will.'

She walked off towards the confessionals to wait for the priest to finish the mass. Not sure if it was going to help any but determined to do it anyway.

Chapter Thirty-Three

October 1952

Emilia stayed in her room a lot, venturing out for food and drinks. She hadn't spoken more than a few sentences to anyone since that night. She blamed herself and she knew that her father blamed himself. She felt as if Mae was always going to be here, her soul trapped because of the horrific way she'd died at the hands of her brother. How was it even possible? James was locked up in Greystone's Psychiatric Hospital for the rest of his life or so she hoped because how could they ever let him out of there? Nice, respectable people didn't murder innocent women. As she lay in bed each evening she would strain and see if she could hear Mae's voice calling to her. She didn't quite know what she was going to do if she did. The thought of it was too much to comprehend. The police had found one of those stupid Ouija boards up there that was all the fashion. She'd heard people say they could speak to dead relatives through them and as far as she knew they hadn't taken it away. Why would they? It was of no use to them. Missy had also told her there were lots of symbols painted on the walls. Emilia desperately wanted to speak to Mae, she needed to tell her she was sorry. She needed to hear that she forgave her and wasn't angry with her. As she lay on her bed she realized that she needed the board, if she could use it then she might be able to speak to Mae. She'd only known her a short time, but she missed her. They'd made such a strong connection it was as if they had known each other forever. A loud sob erupted from her mouth. She'd wanted to be best friends with Mae forever, grow old together. She stood up, pulling on a pair of slacks and a black jumper because she was shivering. She'd decided what she was going to do. Walking downstairs she went to the library to see if her father was there, but it was empty. The house seemed empty, so she checked the other rooms. There was no sign of him, then she went downstairs to the kitchen which was Missy's favorite room. The woman was dressed in her overcoat with a hat, scarf and gloves.

'Well look at you, it's nice to see you up and dressed, Miss Emilia. Would you like me to fix you something to eat?'

Emilia shook her head. 'Where are you going?'

'Church, I need to go and say some prayers. Do you want to come with me?'

She fixed Emilia with her piercing, green eyes.

'No, thank you. I'm not in the mood for church. Have you seen my father?'

'He left about an hour ago, he's gone to meet some business associates at The Waldorf. Would you rather I stayed here with you?'

Emilia shook her head vigorously. 'No, I'm good. Thank you.'

Missy crossed the room and, pulling her close, she wrapped her arms around her. 'You need to start living your life Emilia, none of this is your fault. The only person to blame is your brother and he's paying the price for what he did.'

She forced herself to smile. 'Thank you. Say a prayer for me.'

Missy laughed. 'I'll be praying for us all.'

She walked out of the kitchen and Emilia sat down at the long table. She lifted her hands and hadn't realized how much they were shaking until she tried to clasp them together.

She waited for the heavy, oak front door to slam. It did, despite the house being warm and being dressed for winter. She shuddered. For the first time ever she was alone in the house and not locked in the safety of her bedroom. Rifling through the kitchen drawers she pulled out a huge, butcher's knife. It felt heavy in her tiny hand, but it also felt good, reassuring. Even though she knew her brother was locked in a secure unit, in a padded cell where he'd never be able to hurt anyone else, she still didn't want to go up into the attic without something to protect herself. What if he escaped? It happened. She'd seen headlines in the *New York Times* before about killers who'd been locked up and escaped, going back to their favorite place to kill again. She went upstairs to the drawing room, needing a slug of something strong to calm her nerves. On the large dresser were several crystal decanters most of them full of brown liquid, plus one full of clear liquid which she picked up and tugged off the stopper. Lifting it to her nose she inhaled. It had a faint smell of alcohol, but it wasn't as potent as the assortment of whisky and brandy in the others. Lifting it to her mouth she tipped her head back and took a huge mouthful and swallowed. It made her choke so much she let go of the knife which hit the wooden floor with a heavy clatter. Coughing and spluttering she used her arm to wipe her streaming eyes with her sleeve. Her throat was burning.

When she eventually regained control of herself she grinned. The vodka was warming her insides all the way down to her belly, she liked it. This time she took a glass and poured a generous measure out, popping the stopper back into the bottle she took small sips of the liquid. It was like a magic potion; her shoulders which were tensed relaxed and she felt much calmer than she had in months. Why had nobody told her this magic potion would do the trick and make her feel better? Bending down to pick up the knife, she grabbed the decanter with the other hand and carried it upstairs to her bedroom. She was keeping this. If her father dared to tell her off she would tell him that if he hadn't decided to fuck around with a girl not much older than his own daughter then they wouldn't be in this stinking mess. Emilia gasped. Who had said that? Not her. She didn't talk like that… ever. Then she smiled as she looked in the mirror, realising that it had been her and with the help of her new found liquid form of courage she did indeed speak like that.

Leaving her bedroom she went up the next flight of stairs. There were so many rooms, all of them wasted. Her father slept on this floor, she slept on the one below and Missy slept in a self-contained apartment in the basement near to the kitchen. James had chosen the attic as his bedroom. It had always been creepy, she didn't like attics. She didn't like basements either, but at least the one in this house was used as a kitchen and not empty. They'd been like four ghosts that passed in the night, rarely speaking to each other. It had been bad before Mae's murder, now it was even worse. She walked along the hallway to the far end where the servants' stairs were and the narrow staircase that led to the attic. She wasn't sure if it was her eyes playing tricks, but this part of the house seemed much darker than the rest. As she neared the foot of the attic stairs the bulbs in the chandelier began to flicker, she looked up. It stopped, flared bright and then there came a loud pop and a shower of hot glass exploded all over her. She screamed and jumped back, brushing the broken glass from her hair. Her heart racing she didn't notice the trickle of blood running down her left cheek where a sliver of glass had left a fine slice in her delicate skin. She'd need to tell her pa to sort the lights out, she'd almost died of fright there and then. Feeling stupid for screaming she began to laugh. Damn, if this wasn't so crazy she'd be crying like a baby. Stepping over the pieces of glass she began to climb the steps with the urge to speak to Mae stronger than ever. As she got to the top there was that awful smell, of rotting garbage. The door was shut and she expected it to be locked – a part of her wanted it to be locked so she didn't have to go in there. Maybe this was a stupid idea. Why did it smell so bad? Was that what death smelt like? Is that what her beautiful, Chanel wearing friend now smelt like? Her stomach felt queasy. As she reached out and touched the door knob a wave of fear rushed through her veins. She wondered if she should have brought a flashlight or if the lights were working. Gripping the knife tight in her left hand she twisted the knob and pushed the door open so hard it flew back and slammed against the wall. She felt along the wall for the light switch, pushing it down to illuminate the room, and stepped inside.

Chapter Thirty-Four

Maria waited for Frankie, he was much slower this morning than usual and she wasn't sure whether he had concussion or a hangover. Probably both. He took forever getting out of the car as she held the heavy door of Sam's Deli open. She didn't tease him when he reached her, instead she smiled and let him lead the way to their usual booth tucked away at the back of the diner.

'Are you hungry?'

He nodded. 'I'm always hungry; gut is a bit off today though.'

They waited for Marge to bring the coffee pot over. When she did, stared at the mess on Frankie's face.

'Someone try and knock some sense into you?'

'Something like that.'

'Well, I sure hope you gave them something back, honey, they've ruined your good looks.'

Maria laughed, Frankie smiled at her.

'You think so? I was thinking it made me look more rugged.'

'If that's your brain leaking through that dressing you're in big trouble, buster, you need every cell you have.'

He gave her the finger and she walked away laughing.

'So what are we going to do? Did Max say she could get here?'

'I'm here.' Max squeezed into the booth next to Maria. 'You're in luck, I wasn't far away when you called. I've come across some more stuff in the archives that might interest you.'

Frankie arched an eyebrow at her. 'Is that so? That was lucky because at this current moment in time we're stumped as to why. We need a motive. What's the motive for two women being murdered in cold blood and their limbs ripped from their bodies?'

'I think its devil worship at its highest level.'

Maria looked at her. 'What do you mean? Its highest level, what other level is there?'

'The thing is I found some articles about how popular devil worship was back in the sixties and seventies, but it was simmering away in the fifties. I can't help wonder if the first murder in 1952 was some sort of catalyst.'

Frankie was staring at his coffee cup, his brow furrowed. He looked at the two women opposite.

'Whoever is doing it must have some knowledge and be into the occult. So I think the murders are sacrificial offerings to summon the Devil. We need to start looking where devil worshipper's hang out.'

Maria nodded. 'Yes, I think you're right. How would they know what to do?'

Max leant on the table. 'He must have an instruction manual; there are all sorts of books out there.'

'Like a spell book or a book of devil worship?' Maria began typing into Google. She looked up. 'Holy crap you can buy a Satanic Bible on Amazon.'

'So it could be anyone, damn it.'

Max frowned. 'No, I think whoever is doing this has more than a second hand copy of a book off Amazon. I mean if you could summon demons for ten dollars wouldn't we all be at it?'

Frankie shuddered. 'Why the hell would anyone want to do anything like that?'

'It's about power, most of the bad crap that happens in this world is because some egotistical bastard is on a power trip.'

'I think you're right, Max, it is about power. So James Carter wanted to summon the Devil in the fifties only he didn't do a very good job of it.'

'No Frankie, I think he did a half decent job. There's something about that house on West 10th that freaks me out. It has a bad atmosphere. It smells bad inside and I swear to God I heard hooves clattering around on the wooden floorboards of the attic when I was speaking to the old lady. If he didn't do it properly then whatever he did summon is trapped, half in this world, half in hell.'

'So this punk three years ago was trying to finish the job?'

She nodded. 'Only it didn't work. Why wouldn't it work? Christ, I can't believe we're actually talking about this stuff. Your dad would have a coronary if he heard us.'

Max spoke. 'He'd think we were all crazy, but I think I know why it didn't work, or at least not properly, because wouldn't we know if a demon had been unleashed onto the streets of New York?'

Frankie laughed. 'Not necessarily, have you seen some of the crazies walking the streets?'

'I think he needs another sacrifice. It's all to do with the power of three. The mocking of the Holy Trinity is prevalent when there is a demonic presence. Have you ever watched those ghost shows on cable? You can guarantee there will be three knocks, three bangs, when anyone gets scratched it's normally three red marks that are visible on the skin. Why wouldn't it work when summoning a demon?'

Both Maria and Frankie stared at her, mouths open and eyes wide. He turned to Maria. 'You ever get the feeling we might be out of our depth on this one?'

She pictured herself in the library, something cold and strong squeezing the life out of her. 'It's getting stronger.'

'What, you're a psychic now are you?'

'Get screwed, Frankie. When I went to the library I had this creeping sensation I was being watched and then suddenly I couldn't breathe. Something was squeezing the air out of my lungs and I thought I was going to die. I was so cold and scared.'

Frankie, about to say something sarcastic, realized how white her complexion was, instead his hand reached out and squeezed hers.

Max looked at them both. 'If it was able to do that it's stronger and it knows that you're onto it. It must be worried that you were gonna work it out and stop it.'

It was Frankie who spoke. 'If it's worried we're onto it that means we can do something about it. We can stop it before it gets any stronger.'

'How?'

'I don't know…., what do they always do on the TV?' He directed his question at Max.

'They call in a priest.'

'That's it. We go to the church, grab a priest and get them to go to the house and send it back to where it came from.'

Max began to laugh. 'Easy, peasy. Why didn't I think of that?'

He shrugged then pointed to his head. 'You either got it or you don't.'

Chapter Thirty-Five

As they left the diner and waved goodbye to Max, Maria got the feeling they were being watched. She turned around and scanned the street, the cars and the pedestrians. Nobody stood out. There were very few people around, only the ones that were too busy talking into their headphones to give a damn about her. Still she couldn't shake the feeling and a part of her wondered if it had anything to do with the thing at the house. She was too scared to call it by its name in case it somehow gave it strength.

'We need to go to the station, I want to get some stuff out of my desk drawer.'

'You need to go maybe, but I don't. I'll wait outside in the car for you.'

They got into his car and he drove to the Precinct, parking up front instead of in the car park. Maria got out, walked the short distance, and went in through the front doors. She did her best not to make eye contact with any of the people hanging around. It always ended badly: she'd get caught up in some search for an old lady's cat; stuck in the middle of a domestic; be screamed at by some angry person who was off their meds. About to push through the doors that led her out back she paused.

'Please, you have to help. I've just come back after being home to Russia and I can't find her. It's been three years since anyone last saw her. This is very important.'

She turned to stare at the tall woman leaning against the counter.

‘Look ma’am, like I told you before. Take the form and fill in the report, I’ll get someone to come and speak to you.’

‘How long will this take?’

The officer shrugged. ‘Honey, if you haven’t seen her for three years and have only just realized your friend is missing it’s not what we would call a high priority. She could be married and living in Florida, or maybe she doesn’t want you to find her.’

The woman muttered a whole sentence of Russian that Maria was convinced included lots of expletives and stormed back to the chair with the clip board. She crossed the room towards the woman and held out her hand.

‘I’m Detective Miller, perhaps I can take your details and get this sorted out a little quicker for you.’

The woman looked Maria up and down, then stood up, taking her hand.

‘Petra Orlov.’

Maria led her towards an empty interview room. ‘How come you are only just reporting your friend missing?’

Petra shrugged. ‘We had a falling out, I went back home. Broke my phone, lost her numbers.’

‘What about Facebook, email? Did you not speak to her again after your argument?’

The woman’s blue eyes began to fill with tears as she shook her head.

‘I went home, family problems. I didn’t think about Anya very much if I’m honest. I was angry with her; my mother was dying, and my father couldn’t cope.’

‘I’m sorry to hear that. So you’ve come back and you decided to look her up only you can’t find her?’

Petra nodded. ‘We both worked at The Russian Bar on 52nd, I felt bad. I left her on her own, I wanted to go and make it right. Only they haven't seen or heard from her since the day after I left.'

Maria felt every nerve in her body tense up. When something was about to happen she got the most intense feeling in her gut. Was she about to be able to identify their Jane Doe from West 10th St?

'When did you leave?'

'The second of December.'

Maria wanted to punch the air and shout yes as loud as she could. This might be the break they were looking for. If they could identify the victim and trace her last movements, they might be able to place her with her killer, who could then explain to them what the fuck was going on with that house. Instead of jumping up and yelling, Maria smiled at her.

'I'm going to take as many details from you as you can give me. I know it's been a while, but the more information you can give me about Anya the better chance I have of finding her. Do you have a photograph of Anya? Does she have any tattoos or scars?'

Petra nodded and began to dig into her purse. 'Yes, a big one, roses across the side of her body. Thank you, yes of course. Where do you want me to start?'

✪

Forty minutes later Maria was heading back to the car where Frankie was snoring so loud she could hear it from twenty feet away. She felt bad, he looked terrible. His normal tanned complexion was pale, his face was a mess and he was exhausted, probably suffering from a delayed hangover as well. He needed to go home and sleep. She opened the door which made him jump. He sat up, wiping his mouth with his sleeve.

'Was I drooling?'

‘No, sorry. I didn’t realize you were asleep. Look there isn’t much we can do right now. I’ll go and see a priest at the local church and ask them if they can come to the house with us tomorrow. There’s probably all sorts of crap you have to go through to even get them to do that. Why don’t you go home, get some rest and you’ll be feeling brighter tomorrow?’

‘I’m okay, I’ll go with you.’

‘No Frankie, you’re not. I have a headache just looking at your face and I can’t be bothered. Let me take you home, we’ll call it a day. Start fresh in the morning.’

She didn’t look at his face in case she’d upset him.

‘You don’t mind? You won’t be mad at me?’

‘Hey, of course I don’t. Addison has given us free reign for a couple of weeks. We’d be fools not to go a little bit easy on ourselves. One evening isn’t going to hurt, we can make up for it tomorrow.’

He turned the key in the ignition and pulled out. ‘Yeah, you’re right. What the hell, a few hours off will do us both some good.’

She smiled to herself. ‘Actually I’m going to get out and walk, I want to go shopping.’

He stared at her. ‘Are you ill? You hate shopping?’

She laughed. ‘No, I need some new clothes. I fancy having a stroll down Fifth and doing some window shopping. I need to do something different, take my mind off this case.’

‘I’ll drop you off.’

She opened the car door. ‘No, you won’t, you’ll get stuck in Midtown traffic. It’s quicker for me to walk, you get yourself home. If you need me call me, I mean it.’

He nodded. She slammed the door shut, waited for him to drive away then hailed a cab. One pulled over and she jumped in.

'The Russian Bar on 52nd please.'

Whether it was still open she had no idea, but it was worth a shot. Pulling the photo out of her pocket she stared at it; although not the clearest of pictures, it showed a beautiful, young woman laughing with Petra. Their arms draped around each other, shot glasses in hand, raised towards the photographer. Maria was almost sure that Anya was their Jane Doe, even if the bloodied, headless corpse looked nothing like the image in her hand. After all this time they had something to go on, they were one step closer to identifying her. Which also meant they were one step closer to finding her killer.

Chapter Thirty-Six

Missy waited patiently for the priest to finish his last confessional; there had only been four and she'd been one of them. When he stepped out of the box she was surprised to see just how young he was, she'd been expecting an older guy. She stood up from the hard, wooden pew she was perched on and called out.

'Father, have you a minute?'

He looked at her and she wondered if his instinct was telling him to say no, but he smiled at her showing a set of brilliant, white teeth that any Hollywood movie star would be proud to own and headed in her direction.

'Of course, how can I help?'

For a split second she felt guilty, she was about to involve this young man in something so horrible and detrimental that it might just put him off the priesthood for life. What choice did she have?

'Thank you for the confession, it's right what they say. It is good for your soul.'

He laughed. 'Well, as long as I helped. That's what it's all about.'

'You might regret ever meeting me today, but I need your help. It's about a matter of life and death and I have no idea who else to ask.'

'Well, now…'

'Miss Green, but please call me Missy.'

'Well then, Missy, how can I be of service?'

'Is there somewhere we can talk, away from the tourists and photographers?'

'I was just going to grab myself my morning Starbucks, you're welcome to join me.'

She would rather not have to drink in one of those overpriced coffee shops, but she knew this might be her only chance.

'If you don't mind an old crone, cramping your style I'd love to.'

'Great, follow me, I know a short cut.'

He led her out of the Cathedral across the road and into the Rockefeller Concourse. Missy was fit for her age, but he was a gentleman and kept to her pace. Before too long the steamed up windows of a coffee shop appeared in sight. He held the door open and gestured for her to take a seat. She shook her head. 'You take a seat, I'll grab the drinks. As long as you don't want some fancy crap I can't pronounce.'

He laughed. 'No, just a plain Cappuccino with an extra shot. Don't worry, they know what I like, just point to me when you get to the till.'

Missy did just that when the kid behind the counter asked her name she pointed to the priest, realising she didn't know his name, and the kid said, 'You with Father Michaels?' She nodded.

'We got his drink down, what would you like ma'am?'

'Coffee, just a regular coffee please with milk.'

She handed over the money and waited for the drinks. It was like a cattle market. The queue was almost out of the door. She felt a hand on her shoulder.

'You sit down, I'll bring them over.' She smiled at the kid who looked not much older than eighteen and thanked him, her perception of the staff in the overpriced shops changing dramatically.

As she sat on the leather bench in the corner, the priest smiled at her.

'Well, this is my first time in one of these shops. I was a Starbucks virgin until sixty seconds ago.'

Father Michaels began to laugh a lot louder than she'd anticipated and she immediately felt at ease, for he seemed a good man with a normal sense of humour.

'Wow, I take it you've lived in the city a few years and you've never visited?'

'I have a wonderful delicatessen opposite my apartment, why would I give my money to this?'

'Well, I admire your honesty and your loyalty. So how can I help you, Missy?'

She felt her stomach lurch at the very thought of talking about it in public, in a coffee shop to a priest. It just didn't sit right.

'I'm going to sound like I belong in a psych unit and you're probably going to wonder if you should call the cops or the EMS. I need you to trust that I'm one hundred percent sane and also that I'm telling the truth. I wish I could have been long gone before it happened again, but for some strange reason God either has a wicked sense of humour or he needed me to keep an eye on it. Either way I'm screwed and a little scared.'

He leant towards her, his eyes fixed on her. 'I'm listening.'

She nodded. 'Do you believe that evil exists?'

He smiled. 'Missy, I'm not sure if you've noticed the dog collar or not. I'm a priest, my whole career depends upon the existence of evil.'

She laughed. 'Yes, I guess it does. I'll put it another way, do you believe that a person can summon a demon?'

He nodded. 'Yes, I do. I know that they can for a fact.'

'You do? Good because this is not some bullshit I'm about to tell you. This is one hundred percent a true story.'

‘Then you better tell me.’

Chapter Thirty-Seven

October 1952

She didn't understand how it could smell so bad, the blood had been cleaned up by a professional team who had come in. There was a faded, pentagram on the wall. It looked as if they had tried to scrub it clean and failed miserably. Emilia knew it had been Mae's blood. In a way that was all there was to remind her. She forced herself to cross the room, so she was standing in front of it. Reaching out and placing the palm of her trembling hand against it she sobbed. *Oh Mae, I'm so sorry. Are you still here or did you go to a better place? I really hope you did.* She leant her forehead against the cool wall and closed her eyes. Willing an image of her beautiful friend to come into her mind, she tried to concentrate, emptying her head of all thoughts until all she could see inside her head was white. It was then that she heard the growl – a low, guttural sound so close to her it made the tiny hairs inside her ear tingle. Her eyes flew open and she felt the hot, foul-smelling breath of something breathing down her neck. Emilia had never felt fear like it. Afraid to turn around and see what was behind her she froze to the spot and began to pray like she'd never prayed before. Mae wouldn't growl at her. This was something bad, really bad. Clenching the knife in her fist she counted to three and spun around, expecting James to be standing behind her, wild eyed and crazy. She swung the knife and it sliced through the air. How could that be? She could smell it. Hell, she could feel it and she'd heard it. She could sense the danger, the raw animal enmity. Yet the room was empty or at least it was to her naked eye, then she spotted the Ouija Board and planchette underneath the coffee table. Her mouth dry and heart pounding, she lunged for it, grabbing them both before turning and running to the door. For a fleeting moment she imagined whatever beast or animal it was blocking the doorway and her exit. Then she was through it stumbling onto the landing. For what good it was she slammed the door shut behind her then ran downstairs to her bedroom where she flung the door shut, locking it. Her legs trembled so much she found herself collapsing onto the bed. Her heart thudded so loudly in her chest it deafened her. Dropping the board and planchette on the bed next to her, she placed the knife on the nightstand. She wished more than anything that she wasn't alone in the house. Did whatever it was know that she was? *What did you do, James? What have you done to our home?* Sitting on the bed, her knees drawn up to her chest, she wrapped her arms around them and hugged herself. The knife lay within reach if she needed it, but what good was a knife against something that you couldn't see? If by some miracle she didn't die of fright before the morning she was going to insist on visiting James. She would find out exactly what he'd done tomorrow and find out how to deal with it. Having a clear plan of action made her feel a little better, when after fifteen minutes no gargantuan beast from the depths of hell had broken her door down she began to relax a little. There was no doubt about it, her brother had been messing with things that were way out of his control. Well, there was no way she was going to spend the rest of her life paying for his mistakes. First thing she would visit her father's friend at St Patricks and ask him for his help. Then she would go to Greystone's and demand that James tell her how to put things right. The atmosphere in this house wasn't just one of grief and despair, it was one of pure fear and evil.

Emilia opened her eyes and blinked. How had she fallen asleep? She had waited, locked in her bedroom for either her father or Missy to come home. The sun was shining through the crack in the curtains. She looked at the clock, it was almost seven. She was on top of her covers, fully dressed. The Ouija board and planchette were on the floor, she must have knocked them off. The knife was still where she'd left it and she was still alive which was an unexpected blessing. She had never realized how precious life was until she lost Mae. She got herself up, washed and dressed then unlocked her bedroom door. She tucked the knife under her pillow, not knowing what good it would do against the thing that was hiding in the attic. It made her feel better, not like some helpless damsel in distress. She hadn't realized just how tough she was until last night when she was faced with the fear of being attacked. She knew she wouldn't go down without a fight. Whoever or whatever was up there would have to give its best shot to kill her. Hindsight was a wonderful thing, she had no idea how James had got Mae upstairs, but she hadn't known at the time that she was walking up to her death. She was aware that the dynamics in this house had changed and not for the better, so stepping out onto the landing she wasn't sure what to expect. The smell of rotting garbage still lingered, much fainter than last night. She went downstairs to the kitchen, the smell of fresh pancake batter filled the air and her stomach let out a loud groan. She went into the kitchen to see the biggest stack of pancakes she'd ever seen.

'Are you hungry, Missy?'

'Yes, I am. I also have a visitor coming for breakfast.' Missy turned around the grin across her face turning into a screech as she dropped the spatula she was holding.

'Shoot, Miss Emilia, what happened to you?'

Emilia frowned and turned to stare at her reflection in the kitchen window, she did a double take. Was that even her? Her face was pale and there were the biggest dark circles under her eyes she'd ever seen. Her hair was stuck up and she looked dreadful. Turning to Missy she whispered, 'I don't know.'

'Well, you need to sit down, eat something and have a think about it because you look like a walking corpse.'

'Missy, do you believe in…' She tried to find the right words, but they were stuck in her throat. It was as if she couldn't bring herself to speak them aloud in case what she was terrified of would be brought to life because of it. Missy sat opposite her, her hand reached out and clasped Emilia's.

'Do I believe in ghosts, demons? I'd never had much call to consider it, but these past few months I have. A lot. And if you want the honest answer it's yes, something is hiding upstairs in the attic. I haven't seen it, but I've felt it. I didn't want to bother you or Clarke, but it's getting stronger and I'm scared for us all.'

There was a loud knock at the front door which made them both startle. Missy stood up, rushing to answer it. Emilia forked three pancakes from the stack, put them on a plate and carried them back to the table where she drizzled maple syrup all over them. She had a feeling she needed to keep her strength up. She heard muffled voices then two pairs of footsteps coming down the stairs. When she looked up she felt a huge wave of relief to see a priest standing behind Missy. He crossed the room and shook her hand.

'Charles Morgan, pleased to meet you.'

'Emilia Carter.' She gripped his hand much harder than she meant to. It was huge, warm and felt safe. She didn't want to let it go. Missy pointed to a chair and he pulled it out and sat down. He began to talk about the weather, the upcoming masses and a choir concert he was helping to organize while Missy made a pot of coffee and placed it on the table along with the stack of pancakes. Emilia was eating whilst listening to him; he had one of those easy voices to listen to and it wouldn't have mattered if he was talking Italian to her. He made her feel safe and she hadn't felt like that in this house since the day before Mae's murder. She noticed how his hand kept moving up to the starched, white, collar he wore around his neck. His fingers kept pushing inside it as if it was too tight and he was trying to loosen it. Emilia was fascinated by it because he didn't even know that he was doing it. His cheeks were turning pinker by the minute as if he was in the middle of a sauna and not their draughty kitchen. There was a fine film of sweat on his brow and he pulled a handkerchief from his pocket to dab at his forehead. The whole time she couldn't stop staring at him, Missy joined them at the table.

'What's the matter, Father? You look ill?'

He stared at her as if he couldn't understand what she was saying. Emilia giggled, it was rude of her and she knew that. It was just the craziness of the moment, both of them stared at her and she stopped as abruptly as she'd started. 'Sorry, I don't know why I'm even laughing because none of this is the least bit funny. In fact, I'm terrified because there is something evil in this house that no-one can see. Except for James, I think maybe that he could. I think the only reason it's here is because of him. He's such a sick boy he killed my best friend, chopped her head off like he was doing something normal then summoned a demon. Why would he want to do that, Father? I mean it's not your everyday behavior is it?'

Charles picked up his tea and began to sip it, mopping his brow at the same time.

'I don't know why he did it or how he did it, but he's done something bad. I felt fine before I set foot in this house and now I feel as if there's a tight band squeezing the life out of my chest. Something is trying to suffocate me only I won't let it. Whatever evil he has summoned is strong. I'll give it that, but it's not as strong as God. I'm a servant of God and he has given me his blessing to fight Satan and his legion to keep his children safe. That's what I'm here to do. We can't talk here though, I need to get outside, into the fresh air. That smell of rotting flesh, how long has it filled the air inside the house?'

Emilia nodded, glad he could smell it too. 'It was never prevalent until after Mae's murder, now it lingers in the air. It comes and goes, sometimes it's so powerful it makes me gag. Otherwise I can barely smell it.'

He stood up 'I didn't come prepared. I wouldn't leave and give in so quickly, but I have nothing on me to protect any of you and I won't deal with it if there's a slight chance you could be in danger.'

Missy spoke, 'Are we in danger?'

He looked around the room as if making sure no-one had crept in to eavesdrop on their conversation whilst their backs were turned. 'Yes, you are. Anyone who chooses to live in this house is in danger. Can't you feel it, hovering in the background like some disease? It's nauseating, cunning and strong, but it can be dealt with. I need to speak to the Archbishop and take some advice and then I'll be in touch with you, Missy. If you need to talk anytime then come to the church, I'm always around and if not, someone will get a message to me. He crossed the room and made the sign of the cross on both of their foreheads with his thumb. Then placing both hands on top of their heads he began to recite a prayer in Latin. Emilia closed her eyes. The warmth of his hand on her head made her feel safe and at peace for the first time since that night. Why, when her life was beginning to get interesting, did it all have to be taken away so brutally? She was so glad to have had the pleasure of Mae in her life for what short time they'd spent together. She had been like a breath of fresh air to this house and she hoped that Mae had enjoyed her last days as much as she had. Of course she would give anything to turn back the clock and change it. Even if it meant her pop never having an affair with Mae and her forging such a close friendship. If she could stop it all before it happened she would, treasuring the knowledge that she'd known how swell it was to find a friend so special. She felt the pressure removed from her head and opened her eyes to see that Missy was holding a paper towel in her hand. She waved it at her and it was only then she realized that her cheeks were damp and she'd been crying.

Chapter Thirty-Eight

The taxi pulled to the sidewalk, she paid her money and got out. The bar was all in darkness and she pressed her face against the glass. Cupping her hand against her forehead to block out the light, she saw movement in the far corner and hammered on the glass. Pulling her ID from her pocket she pressed it against the plate glass window so whoever was inside would see her badge. The door opened enough for her to squeeze in and she found herself standing in front of the biggest, man she'd ever seen. His arms crossed against his chest he nodded at her.

'NYPD Detective Miller. I need to ask you or anyone else who works here some questions about a girl who may have gone missing December 2014.'

He didn't say a word, she pulled the photograph from her pocket and passed it to him. He studied it and she wondered how long he was going to take when he muttered.

'Anya.'

'Yes, Anya. Do you know her?'

He pointed to a bar stool. 'Please, sit down.'

She did and he went behind the bar. In her entire life Maria had never seen so many types of vodka. There were bottles of every color and flavor you could imagine lined up against the glass mirror on the oak bar. He unscrewed the cap off one and poured out a large measure, handing it to her. She took it, not wanting to insult him and stared at it. He poured himself one, downed it then poured another. Turning to look at her she noticed his eyes were brimmed with tears and she wondered how close they had been. Lifting the shot glass to her lips she took a sip and immediately regretted it as she began to cough and splutter as it burnt all the way down her throat.

'Sipping is no good, you need to tip your head back and swallow it all. Yes, I know Anya. Very well, she worked here six nights a week. Never missed a shift, one night she picked up some guy and they got drunk in the corner together.'

He pointed to a booth. 'She never came back, it broke my heart. I liked her, she was a good worker. A kind girl, easy on the eye.'

'Did you report it to the police?'

He laughed. 'What was there to report? She shacked up with some guy who bought her drinks all night. He made her happy, it's life.'

'Could you describe the guy she was with?'

He stood up and went back behind the bar where he began to search around under the counter, muttering in Russian under his breath. He shouted, 'Da.' Then turned around and came back to where she was sitting, clutching a piece of paper in his hand. He passed it to her and she looked at a grainy black and white still of Anya with a man. It wasn't the best quality, but it was something.

'That's him, I don't know why I took the picture from the system. I didn't like him, something about him was off. I have a nose for that kind of thing. Do you know where Anya is?'

Maria couldn't tell him she was almost one hundred percent sure she was dead. 'No, someone reported her missing this morning and I'm following up what little leads we have. Can I keep this? I'll return it as soon as I can. Does she have any tattoos or birthmarks?'

He nodded at her. 'Yes, she has roses and vine tattoo from her leg to her…' He pointed to his chest. 'I should have called it in? Yes?'

She didn't want to make him feel any worse than he already did. 'You weren't to know. Thank you for your help.'

She lifted the shot glass and downed the rest of the vodka. He smiled and saluted her. Standing up she walked towards the door.

'Hey, if you find her tell her Viktor wants to say hello.'

'I will.'

She tugged the heavy door open and stepped out into the bright sunlight, which was so light she had to blink several times. So their Jane Doe was Anya Petri. The tattoo would be a huge step in a positive identification. Poor Viktor carried a bit of a flame for the beautiful girl. Who wouldn't? She was stunning. The feeling that things were coming together along with the shot of strong vodka made her smile for the first time today. She couldn't wait to tell Frankie, but it wouldn't be today. Tomorrow she would come back and show the photographs of the tattoo to Viktor, she would probably bring Frankie with her when she broke that news. She had no idea how the huge guy would take it. Right now she needed to go back to the station to look up Anya Petri, see if there was anything on the system about her, along with Petra and Viktor. Who wasn't to say they weren't all involved in an organized crime group or had something to do with her murder? Her phone beeped and she smiled as she read the text.

Busy tonight or do you fancy grabbing a bite to eat? You choose where and when. Harrison x

She did fancy going out for supper, it would take her mind off today. A twinge in her stomach reminded her something was wrong, and suddenly picturing Frankie's bruised and bloody face wiped the smile off her face. She felt bad, almost as if she was cheating on him. *Come on Maria how can you cheat on a guy who isn't your lover? He's your friend and partner. That's it.* Before she could change her mind she began typing back.

Love to, Black Tap on Broome @ 8pm. x

Tomorrow she would tell Frankie about Harrison, she might feel better. Confession is supposed to be good for the soul. He wouldn't be mad at her, he'd be happy. She was worrying over nothing then she could cheer him up with the news that they finally had an ID for their vic. Tomorrow they would find out where she lived before she went missing and see if they could find anything to match to her DNA. If she had family living here it would be easier, but it didn't matter though. She knew it in her gut that it was Anya and that was all that mattered.

She thought about getting the subway, but it was too hot to be stuck down there. Normally she'd walk, but she wanted to get as much information off the system as she could before going home for a shower. She looked like a tramp in her sweats, not her usual work attire. Hailing her second cab of the day she asked him to drop her at the station. Her head was spinning and she could feel the beginnings of a migraine in the back of her eyes. She massaged her temples. Frankie had given her a heart attack this morning. All in all, today had been one stressful mess. She was looking forward to a couple of drinks and some food with Harrison. All week she'd been fantasizing about one of the Black Tap's freak shakes because they made the best damn milkshakes in the city. After her run to Frankie's apartment this morning she'd earnt one. Slipping into the station no one gave her a second glance which was fine by her. The department was unusually quiet. She sat down at her desk and began typing in the passwords to get access to the system to run the checks she needed. She could hear Addison shouting down the phone inside his office, even with the door shut. She wanted to get out of here before he dragged her in for an update, he'd want to know where Frankie was and she wasn't about to drop him in it. Sending everything to the printer she slipped from her desk and went the long way around to collect her paperwork so she wouldn't have to pass his office window. Waiting for the ancient printer to spit out her papers she crossed her fingers behind her back that he wouldn't see her and yell for her to go speak to him. The paper stopped coming out and she scooped the pages up, shoving them into a cardboard file. Tucking it under her arm she left, running down the stairs. Leaving by the rear exit so she didn't have to talk to anyone, she began the walk to her apartment. The thought of a cold shower giving her a good enough reason to keep walking, despite the uncomfortable heat and the tiredness spreading through her bones.

When she finally reached her apartment block she let out a small whoop. She was hot, smelly and needed a glass of wine or a candy bar to boost her energy, probably both. Relieved to be in the cool foyer she leant against the wall as she called the elevator, it was quiet in here. Compared to the hustle out on the streets, she'd cut through the park which was busy. It was always busy, just how she liked it. Maybe after they'd eaten they could sit in the park and watch the world go by. It would be perfect if Marvin was playing tonight, even better if Sam was singing along. When she walked out of the elevator on her floor she saw Miss Green come out of her apartment and did a double take. She was dressed as impeccably as ever, but she looked as if she had aged twenty years since yesterday.

'Maria, I'm glad you're here. You left your front door open, what were you thinking? I came home a couple of hours ago and it was wide open. I called out, but there was no answer. I had a quick look inside, it didn't look as if you'd been broken in to. So I shut it behind me, I hope you have your key?'

Maria felt every nerve-ending in her body spark to life as the adrenalin began to rush through her veins. She didn't want to scare her neighbor who quite frankly already looked terrified.

'Thank you, I'm so sorry. I rushed out this morning and can't have shut it properly.' This was true, so panicked about Frankie she had literally run out and couldn't remember whether she'd shut the door behind her. Still alarm bells were ringing. She smiled at her as she stepped into the elevator.

'I do hope everything's okay, honey. I'll catch you later; you still owe me some gossip.'

Maria laughed, waiting what felt like an age before the elevator doors finally closed. Pulling her gun from the holster she wondered if she should call one of the cops from the station to come down and check her apartment. Her not very big apartment which she could clear in two minutes. Deciding against it she put the key in the lock and pushed open the door. Lifting the gun, she stepped inside.

Chapter Thirty-Nine

Maria paused for a moment, pushing the door wide open so she had a clear view of the hall. Reaching in she flicked the light switch waiting for the flickering light to stay on long enough to illuminate the apartment. She stepped in, moving from room to room. Opening one door after the other, she checked under the bed in the closets and behind the curtains. Nothing looked out of place, there wasn't anything missing. Saving the bathroom until last she had a fleeting moment of fear, wondering if there was anyone hiding in the tub behind the shower curtain. Grabbing it and ripping it to one side she let out a sigh of relief. In her panic about Frankie she must have left the door ajar, there was no other explanation how it could be wide open. Turning around she saw that the toilet seat was up and felt the hairs on the back of her neck prickle. Stepping closer she stared into the bowl which was clean. She never left the seat up and always shouted at Frankie whenever he did, so how was it up now? Had she lifted it up to clean it? She knew she hadn't, but she'd checked the apartment. She went into the bedroom to check her drawers, pulling them out one by one she couldn't see anything amiss. She sat down on the bed and wondered if she should call it in? Get CSI out to dust for prints. She could hear Addison's voice now. 'Tell me again why you need CSI, Miller? Because you left your front door open and nothing has been disturbed except your toilet seat?' Fuck that, he'd think she was going crazy. She did another check of every room. It didn't make sense, unless someone had come in and used the john while they had the opportunity. She went back to the bathroom and took a photo of the offending toilet seat.

Then shuddered, she didn't know who had used it. Pulling on a pair of rubber gloves she set about immersing the bowl, seat and every other part of it in a bleach bath. It was so strong she felt as if the hairs in her nose had been burnt off by the chemical. Satisfied it was clean she stripped off the gloves and dropped them in the waste basket. *Are you losing it, you might have spent twenty minutes cleaning a toilet that only you've used.* She laughed at the possibility. Feeling better she turned on the shower and stripped off, she needed to get ready to meet Harrison. At least she didn't have far to go, The Black Tap was only three blocks away.

✪

He sat there cross legged not daring to breathe, it was amazing how she hadn't checked the crawl space in the closet. It was tucked away at the back, behind the rack of coats. He was lucky that he had found it, but he'd known there would be someplace in the apartment to hide. It was tiny, and he could only just fit inside. He had managed to stretch his legs enough that he didn't get cramp, but he didn't know how long he'd be in here for. He hoped it wasn't too long. However, he was furious with himself as the only thing he'd done was pee. Habit had made him lift the seat and he hadn't even considered whether he'd left the seat up or down. He wouldn't make that mistake again, he'd make sure of it. If she left the apartment he would make his escape through the window next to the fire escape. He should have got out when he had the chance, but he'd wanted to see her relaxed. Stupidly he'd left the door open, but that was how he'd found it and he didn't want to arouse her suspicions too much. She could have come back at any moment, as soon as he'd found his snug hiding place he'd crawled inside. The warmth and the dark had made him feel safe and he'd drifted off, awaking to the sound of someone throwing open doors and slamming around. At first he'd felt disorientated wondering where he was and then the closet door had been thrown open and he'd smelled her perfume, it was Chanel. It all came back to him, he was taking a huge risk. One that was worth it in every sense, even if she dragged him out and shot him at least he'd die looking into her eyes. Finally, he heard the shower turn off. It had taken every ounce of his self-control not to sneak out and take a peek. He didn't know what he'd do if he saw her naked body. He wasn't a sexual predator. Anya had slept with him of her own accord, but he didn't know if the sight of a naked woman whose apartment he was hiding in would be too much for him to bear. So he stayed where he was, pins and needles beginning in his feet and legs. He shifted slightly, hoping that she was going to go back out soon or he'd have to risk it all. The closet door opened again and he got a stronger smell of the perfume, she must be going out. He could see her bare ankles, the heels she was wearing not too high. Just enough to accentuate her slender calves and he felt himself getting hard. He couldn't see how short her dress was. He didn't think she would be the kind to wear a short skirt; she would go for a knee length dress. Something black; he didn't care to be honest. He knew she would look good in anything and he couldn't wait to get her back to the apartment. The beast was getting restless; it had been waiting for an eternity to be set free. When it was, he would have the power to attract any woman he wanted – women like Maria would flock to him and be ready to satisfy his every need. This city wouldn't know what had happened and he would be there for the ride.

She left her apartment, this time checking the door was shut tight. She had to push down the butterflies which were fluttering in her stomach. She felt nervous about seeing Harrison, but she felt more nervous about coming home late at night to an empty apartment. Checking her watch she was a little late, but that was a woman's prerogative. As she reached the door a little breathless she waved at Harrison who had somehow managed to grab the window seat. She walked into the restaurant and her stomach groaned at the smell of burgers and fries with the underlying smell of sweet vanilla. There was a table behind them full of students all sipping at the most amazing strawberry pink, candy floss creations in a glass she'd ever seen. Harrison stood up, he opened his arms and his lips brushed against her cheek.

'You look and smell even better than those milkshakes.'

Maria giggled. 'I'll take that as a compliment because right now those milkshakes are the best things I've ever laid my eyes on. They smell amazing.'

She sat down in the window seat opposite him, he looked a little bit uncomfortable surrounded by laughing teenage girls.

'Sorry, I didn't realize it would be so busy or so loud.'

'Don't be sorry, I had to stop myself from drooling at the food when it was taken to that table over there.'

The waiter appeared and Maria rhymed off her order without looking at the menu. Harrison looked at him. 'I'll have the same please.'

He took their menus and disappeared. Maria was staring into space and he waved his hand in front of her face. 'Are you okay?'

'Sorry, it's been a long day. Yes, I'm okay.'

'Do you want to talk about it?'

Instinctively she shook her head, always the one to act tough. Her eyes betrayed her though and she felt stupid when they began to tear up.

'Hey, talk to me. It's what friends do and I'd like to think I'm your friend, that you value me enough to be able to tell me what's bothering you.'

Picking up a napkin she dabbed at the corner of her eye and laughed. 'I don't know what's wrong with me. I'm so sorry, I guess I'm tired.'

She looked at his face and realized that she wanted to talk to him, to tell him all about her fucked up day. The worry of finding her apartment door open and her fear of someone being inside, before she knew it she was pouring out the day's events to him. Only pausing when the waiter brought their milkshakes over, she smiled wondering how she was going to tackle drinking it.

'Did you call the cops, Maria?'

She laughed. 'I am the cops, no I didn't.'

'Why not?'

'I couldn't be sure if I'd left the door open and the toilet seat up. I was so scared about Frankie I ran out of there. My head was all over the place, I'm probably being paranoid.'

'Well, you're not going home tonight. When we leave here we're going to my apartment. I have a spare room you can stop in. Tomorrow I'll go with you to yours and we'll check it out, I have a friend who can fit a camera on your front door and extra security measures. I want you to be safe.'

He reached out and stroked her cheek, for the first time in a long time she knew that this was what she wanted. She didn't want to be alone tonight; she wanted to spend the night with him. Preferably in his bed, with his arms wrapped around her feeling safe and loved.

'Would you not mind?'

He laughed. 'For a moment I was expecting you to give me a whole load of crap about not needing a man to keep you safe. I can think of nothing that I would like more, it would be my pleasure.'

'Thank you, that's great.' She wondered what Frankie was doing and how he would react when he found out she'd stopped at Harrison's. Then she realized that it didn't matter what the hell he thought about it because this was her life and she was tired of being lonely.

Chapter Forty

October 1952

Emilia bid goodnight to Missy. They hadn't spoken much after the priest had left, both afraid that the monster who was half living in this world and half in the underworld could hear them. They didn't want to let it know what they were planning to do. She hoped that Father Morgan could help them, but if he went to the Archbishop he had to make him believe him. How long was that going to take? She wanted this resolved now. She wanted her home back the way it was: warm, peaceful and as happy as a home could be under these terrible circumstances. What had happened to James? She didn't understand why he had done this; it didn't make any sense. As she went upstairs to bed she couldn't get the image of Mae out of her head. She wanted so badly to speak to her and ask her forgiveness. She went into her room and shut the door, turned the key in the lock and looked at the Ouija board. What did she have to lose? It was a stupid child's game; nothing more. James was mentally unbalanced, he did what he did out of pure hatred and jealousy. She picked up the board, placing it on the bed and took the planchette from the drawer where she'd hidden it. Not sure if there was some sort of protocol to using one of these things she lit the candles on her dresser and turned off the lights. She placed the planchette on the board, not realising her hands were trembling until it began shaking. Now what? She didn't know what the hell to do with it. Did it move of its own accord? She waited, staring at the board willing it to move with all her might. She pictured Mae's smiling face and waited. Nothing moved, nothing happened. Tutting she stood up and walked across to blow out the candles. The sound was faint, like a scraping fingernail against a chalkboard and she felt the hairs on the back of her neck stand on end. She turned back to the bed where the planchette was edging its way across the board. A screech escaped her lips as her hand flew to her mouth. How? How was that happening? Her feet froze to the floor. She willed herself to go back to it, but a voice in her head was whispering *Get rid of it, burn it, throw it out of the window. Whatever you do don't try and communicate with it.* The planchette moved to the H then I, E,M,M. *'Hi Emm.'* She gasped, running back to the bed she sat on it, careful not to disturb the board. 'Mae, are you there? Oh Mae, I'm so sorry, I miss you.'

The pointer began to spell out more words and Emilia grabbed a journal and pencil off the desk.

I,M,I,S,S ,Y,O,U.

Emilia stared at the words and let out a sob. 'I miss you to Mae, I'm sorry. Where are you?'

H,E,R,E, R,U,N.

She scribbled down the words hererun, where was hererun? She'd never heard of it, did she mean heaven? God she hoped so because if anyone deserved to be in heaven it was her. There was a loud knock to the left of her and she whipped her head round to see where it had come from and who had made it. There was no-one or nothing there, she turned back to the board when an even louder thud made the floor vibrate. It sounded as if someone had jumped onto the wooden floorboards, a foul stench filled the air making her gag. Where was that coming from? There was movement in the corner of the room once more, yet she couldn't see anyone. Picking up the planchette she lifted it to her face to study it. Unable to work out how this simple, teardrop shaped piece of wood with a piece of glass in the middle could move on its own. Holding it to her left eye she peered through the glass wondering if it was like the magnifying glass her pops had on the library desk. The room loomed larger through the lens, the walls seemed much closer, covered by a dark shadow which moved. She lowered the planchette. She couldn't see anything. There was a scrabbling noise behind her. Turning her head she lifted it again and closed one eye, whispering, 'Mae is that you? Where are you, I can't see you.' Movement again. There was something there. An overpowering smell of rotting garbage seeped into her nose and she dropped the planchette on the board. It began to move again.

I,T,S,H,E,R,E,R,U,N

Itshererun, she breathed out a white plume of smoky breath. She cried out, 'Where is hererun, I don't understand Mae. The candles flickered wildly then the flames extinguished, just as she had split the words up. ITS HERE RUN. A growl, low and guttural, filled the air and Emilia threw the board off the bed. The words were screaming in her mind: 'It's here, run.' She ran for the bedroom door, throwing herself through it. She screamed at the top of her voice and ran down the staircase as fast as she could, Missy came running out of her room. Emilia grabbed her hand.

'We have to leave now. There's something in my room.'

Missy stared up the staircase wondering what it could be while Emilia began to pull the woman as hard as she could. Before she could tear her gaze away from the top of the stairs she saw a huge, black cloud begin to form into two, cloven-hoofed feet.

'Missy, move now!'

Missy let the girl tug her towards the front door, and they ran out onto the sidewalk. The door slammed in the wind behind them. Emilia kept on tugging Missy's hand until they were running across the street to the opposite side. Emilia looked up to see a black, shadowy figure at the second floor window, it was her bedroom window it was staring out of. They hammered on Mrs Smith's front door, screaming to be let in. The poor woman opened the door to a pair of screaming banshees, wild eyed, their faces stricken with horror. Mr Smith appeared with a gun, thinking they were being chased. Mrs Smith slammed the front door shut.

'Child, what on earth is wrong with you?'

Emilia couldn't speak, her voice was hoarse. Missy looked at their neighbors who looked as petrified as they did. Composing herself, she whispered.

'There's something in the house.''

'Like what? You mean there's an intruder, someone has broken in?'

Emilia shook her head. 'No, I don't know what it is. It's a monster.'

'Honey, the only monsters in this world are the bad people who do bad things to good people. Like your…'

Mrs Smith stopped talking, a faint redness creeping up her neck.

Emilia looked at her. 'Like my brother, you're right. He is a monster. This isn't a human being I'm talking about. I was using the Ouija board to speak to Mae, but something else was there. It smelt bad, it made the room freezing cold, and it growled louder than a grizzly bear.'

Mr Smith was talking to a police officer on the phone. Mrs Smith led them into the drawing room, closing the door behind them.

'Honey, you shouldn't be playing around with one of those boards, they're evil and bring forth spirits that have no place in this world. I read that your brother used one as well as painting satanic symbols all over the walls. I think he may have summoned more than your dead aunt from Milwaukee.'

Missy looked at the woman and Emilia felt her knees give way as she slumped onto the couch. She was relieved that Mrs Smith believed her, it meant that she wasn't going crazy.

'What do we do about it because it's getting stronger and it's taking over the house?'

Mrs Smith checked to see her husband wasn't listening. Then leant forward and whispered.

'I can help you to get rid of it, but it won't be easy. We mustn't let David know either because after the last time I chased an evil spirit he made me promise I wouldn't ever do anything like it ever again. You are lucky you hammered on my door because Mrs Fitch is a good Christian woman who would have shut the curtains and turned her television louder.' She winked at them.

'Why did he make you promise?'

'It nearly killed me, honey, but I survived. Damn it, I knew there was more to this than your brother flipping his lid. He's been meddling in stuff he had no right to meddle in. Have you called in a priest?'

'Yes.'

'What did he say?'

'He got sick and had to leave; he rushed out of the house and said he had to speak to the Archbishop.'

Mrs Smith chewed her bottom lip. 'That will take a long time and the church although it survives by preaching to its flock about the fight between good and evil, well, it has kind of a hard time actually believing that those kind of evil spirits truly exist. Some priests are good and will help, others won't. Do you think he'll help because it would make it better if we had a man of God standing with us?'

Emilia didn't like the way this conversation was going. What did she mean by 'standing with us'?

'I don't know, I thought I could trust him, but he ran away.'

'Fear can do that to anyone, sometimes what you need to do is stand your ground and fight it head on. These demons, entities, whatever you want to call it. They feed off fear, they invoke it especially for their own pleasure.'

Emilia stole a glance at Missy who was looking paler by the minute, this whole situation had gone from nought to one hundred in the space of an hour. She had spoken no more than a few words to the short, round woman standing in front of her for the last couple of years. Yet here she was giving them shelter and talking about fighting a demon with them. Any moment now someone was going to shake her awake from this nightmare. How relieved would she be to discover it had all been a horrible dream and that Mae was at this moment in time taking her final bow on the theatre stage. That James was back on Staten Island and the House on West 10th Street wasn't the current home of some beast from the depths of hell.

'I don't suggest we deal with it tonight, they like the dark and gather more strength. Daylight is their enemy, so we will gather what we need tomorrow morning including your priest. I will wave Mr Smith off to work with his lunchbox just like I do every day and then we will prepare to do battle. Is this agreeable by you?'

Emilia nodded. 'Yes, thank you. I don't expect you to put yourself at any risk though, Mrs Smith.'

'I can no longer live across the road from a house full of evil and ignore it than I can a starving child begging on the corner of 5th. It's my calling; my mom had it and so did her mom. Mr Smith doesn't understand it, he thinks it's all a bit of game. I've been cleansing houses and speaking to dead people since I was eight years old. I do God's work, not all spirits are bad. Some are lost, or lonely, some are shocked and don't understand that they're dead. A guiding hand and a soothing voice can send them on to where they need to go. Most of the time they're thankful to be able to speak to someone who can still hear them. Some of them are a bit grumpy. You get used to it, I like to think that I do God's work on earth for him. A bit like a shepherd, only instead of a flock of sheep I gather lost souls.'

Emilia stared at the woman wondering if she was being serious and decided that she was. Mrs Smith smiled at her and she saw a flicker of golden light in the iris of her chocolate, brown eyes. It was warm, loving and for the first time since Mae's horrible death she felt safe, in this room with the friendly woman standing in front of her, smiling. Emilia nodded, she understood that somehow, she had been led to this house. Out of all the Brownstones in the street she ran to this one, a safe haven from the horror that had taken up residence in her home.

Chapter Forty-One

Frankie opened one eye and groaned when he moved his head. It hurt like a bitch. It was throbbing and he wondered if Christy had chipped his skull when she'd thrown the oversized coffee cup at his head. For all he knew he had swelling on the brain, it sure as hell felt like it. He wondered if Maria was up yet, he didn't want to spend the morning feeling sorry for himself. He'd rather be up working and trying to find the killer before Addison hauled them off the case and gave it to the cold-case team. It would be pretty fine if they solved it, prove just how good Miller and Conroy were. It sounded good. Miller and Conroy could be one of those fancy detective series on the television. The modern equivalent of *Cagney and Lacey* or *Starsky and Hutch*. He sat up feeling a little dizzy. For the second time in less than five minutes he wondered if he had some kind of permanent brain damage. When he'd showered and dressed he put some bagels under the grill and called Maria. She sounded even groggier than he did.

'Urgh, what time is it?'

He looked up at the oversized kitchen clock Christy had insisted they had to have from Macy's that he fucking hated. It was like looking up at Grand Central's huge clock which looked great on the side of a building, but not in his freaking kitchen.

'Eight.'

'What do you want?'

'Oh, that's real charming, I was going to ask you over for breakfast. I thought we could get an early start.'

'I'm not home, hang on.'

Her voice went muffled and he knew she'd clamped her hand over the mouthpiece. What was worse she was talking to someone else and he felt his stomach drop. She came back on the line.

'I can be at yours in an hour, I need to go home first.'

'Where are you?'

There was a pause and he knew it really wasn't any of his business where she was, Maria was also probably thinking the same.

'At The Plaza.'

He began to laugh. 'Yeah right, you spent the night at The Plaza.'

'Why is that so hard to believe?'

He laughed even harder. 'Because you'd never pay Plaza rates for a room, Miss tight-ass.'

'Fuck you Frankie, I'll see you at nine.'

She ended the call, she was being serious. *Holy shit, Maria, who did you screw to get a night there?* A bitter taste filled his mouth, he knew exactly who she'd spend the night with. Harrison Williams probably had a whole goddamn suite at the fucking Plaza. He clenched his fist, he wanted to smack the smug fuck in his mouth and knock his row of perfect white teeth out. For the next twenty minutes he slammed around his apartment until he calmed down. He knew he had no right to feel so angry because Maria had gone out on a date. What she did in her own time was nothing to do with him. They worked together, they were partners. That was it, they weren't lovers. They'd never slept together. The voice in his head whispered, *Yes, but you wanted to didn't you? Now Christy has been screwing around, you're a single guy and after years of being single the woman you've been in love with for years has found herself a very rich lover. So where does that leave you, Frankie? Out in the fucking cold, that's where.* This time it was him who picked up one of the stupid cups, another thing Christy had spent a small fortune on. The clock began to chime and he launched it at it, ducking at the almighty crash and as shards of glass flew everywhere. He stood tall and looked at the mess. Jeez, it was going to take him an hour to clean it up, but for the first time since he'd woken up he smiled. He would put the clock and pieces of broken glass in a paper grocery sack and mail it to Adam's house as a housewarming gift.

✪

Maria smiled as Harrison fiddled with his tie. 'So do you always bring your dates here? Is this like your own personal suite?'

He shook his head. 'My mom's in town, she's on her twice yearly visit with her entourage of friends. I booked this suite for her, but she insisted on stopping with me. I love her, but, Christ, she drives me mad. I didn't want to subject you to a grilling by her and the two ugly stepsisters.'

She laughed. 'I could have handled your mom.'

'Oh, I have no doubt about that, however I really like you and I don't want her putting you off agreeing to another date with me. Which you would, I'm sure you would.'

Maria got out of the bed, slipping on the fluffy white robe emblazoned with the hotel's logo. She crossed the room and began to fasten his tie for him. He let her and she enjoyed being so close to him, he smelt of mint and lemon shower gel.

'I need to shower and go home, I have work. Thank you for last night, I enjoyed it.'

She turned to walk away and he tugged her back, pulling her face towards his he crushed his lips against hers and she felt her stomach begin to churn. As much as she wanted to go back to bed with him she had to go to work. She pulled away, her cheeks flushed.

'Sorry, I do have to go. Could I have a lift please?'

He laughed. 'I don't know what shocks me more – you asking for a lift or the fact that you stayed the night.'

She shook her head. 'Yeah, well it must have been the milkshake overload. All that sugar made me lose control of my senses.' She turned and walked into the huge bathroom. He shouted after her.

'I have to go, I'll have the car drop me off and come back for you. Is that okay?'

'Perfect, thank you.'

Maria turned the shower on, she never heard him leave. She had a lot to do today, even though facing Frankie was going to be difficult she wanted to get it out in the open. She didn't know how long this 'thing' with Harrison might last, but she sure as hell wanted to enjoy it. And she couldn't if she was sneaking around behind Frankie's back.

✪

As she got in the elevator she smiled at the elderly couple who were bickering over what to eat for breakfast. She couldn't help wondering how long they'd been married. She felt a little overdressed for this time of day, but what the hell. They weren't to know she'd only stayed overnight to sleep with her date. She felt a little bit like Vivienne from *Pretty Woman* and was relieved to reach the lobby. As she walked out of the entrance doors and down the red carpeted steps she saw Harrison's driver jump out of a stretch limousine. He opened the door and nodded as she slid inside the car and he shut it behind her. Not quite believing her ride was so luxurious she stared out of the window watching the hordes of New Yorkers on their way to work. She would make it up to Frankie and buy him lunch, and she wanted to do everything possible to identify the man on the still, last seen with Anya. It was going to be a long day, but it was what she loved. The car stopped outside her apartment and she leant forward. 'Don't get out, I can manage. Thank you.' The driver shook his head.

'Ma'am it's a long, boring day driving around. If I get out I can stretch my legs.' He was out of the car and round to her side before she could object. He opened the door and she stepped out.

'Thank you, what's your name?'

'Benjamin.'

'Thanks, Benjamin.'

'You're very welcome, ma'am, I hope to see you again soon.' He tipped his hat at her and she laughed. She walked up the steps to the building and wondered if she would see him again. Or now she'd given in so easy to Harrison Williams would he even be interested in her. It didn't really matter, she'd had a good time and that was what counted. She went into the dark apartment building, the elevator took her up to her floor and she got out. She'd forgotten about yesterday and her door being left open, all she could think about was finding Anya's killer. Opening her front door she inhaled and wrinkled her nose, it smelt terrible. Had she left food or milk out? She didn't think so, yet it smelled like rotten garbage. Closing the door behind her she kicked off her heels and went to the kitchen in search of the foul stench. It was so cold in here, she must have left the air con on super high. A shudder racked her entire body as she checked the bin and cupboards to see where the smell was coming from. The noise of the cupboards and drawers opening and slamming shut disguised the creak of the closet door as it slowly opened. There wasn't anything obvious, although tugging open the fridge door it didn't light up, the power had gone. All her food must have gone off. Annoyed, she checked the plug and saw it had been pulled out of the socket. *What the fuck! How did that happen?* Furious, she plugged it back in, the light illuminating the inside of the cooler. As she opened the door wide she opened her mouth to scream, on the shelf was a decomposing head. It was black and green, two eyes were staring at her. Open wide in horror, the smell was coming from the head. She cupped her hand over her mouth and nose. Panic filled her chest. Where was her phone? Realising she'd left her purse in the car she turned to run out of the apartment to Miss Green's and slammed straight into the man who was standing behind her watching. Opening her mouth to scream his fist shot out and he punched her so hard in the side of the head her vision blurred. Stumbling, she grabbed the nearest thing to her which was a glass vase and threw it at him, he ducked as it whistled past his head, smashing against the wall sending shards of glass everywhere. He lunged for her and she side-swiped him, unsteady on her feet she was almost past him when he stuck his foot out and she fell forwards. Trying her best not to go down, she knew if she did he'd be at an advantage and she almost didn't until he threw himself at her and they both landed on the carpet with a heavy thud. Maria felt her breath whoosh from her body as he straddled her back. Opening her mouth to scream the sound was cut off by the tautness of the rope wrapped around her neck. She gagged as she choked. He pulled tighter until she saw flecks of silver floating around in her eyes and then everything went black.

Chapter Forty-Two

Miss Green paused. Had that loud thump and crash come from Maria's apartment? Not nosy in the least, but more concerned, she pressed her ear against the wall. She couldn't hear anything, and if Maria had hurt herself she'd be shouting for help. It had occurred to her that if she had asked her Maria would have come to help them. The last thing she wanted though was to put her in any danger, she already walked that line every single day. Gathering what she needed she slung the heavy purse over her shoulder and turned to look around her apartment. She couldn't complain, she'd had a long, happy life. It was far more than Mae Evans had and she felt truly blessed that God had seen fit to let her do so. If she died today then so be it, she was going to die sometime – that was one thing there was no escaping from. She placed the smooth, ivory envelope on the sideboard and walked out of the front door, closing it behind her. She decided to take a town car to West 10th, she could afford to splurge. As it stopped outside she leant forward and tipped the driver, he looked down and shook his head.

'I can't take this, ma'am.'

'Yes, you can. Thank you.'

She got out and stared across the road at the house that had belonged to Mr and Mrs Smith. What she would give to have Mrs Smith fighting their corner once more. Only she was now older than Mrs Smith had been the first time around. Missy wondered if Mrs Smith was watching over her now, since that dreadful day she'd never really felt alone, even when she was. This thing, beast, demon, monster whatever it was called had inflicted far too much suffering on innocent, unwitting victims. It was time to end it for good.

The house stood tall and proud cloaked in a veil of shadows. Had it always been so dark? She didn't think that it had; she remembered the days the sun was so bright it would burn through the windows. The heat would be far too hot, making the rooms stuffy and unbearable until she'd thrown them open to let the air flow through. No, the house hadn't always been one of black shadows, cold draughts and foul smells. It had been a happy, warm, loving home, her home, her happy place until that night. None of them had ever felt safe again in there, she hadn't been able to wait to move out. The day she left she'd been guilt ridden because Emilia had insisted on staying on, even after Clarke's death when she could have gone back to the family home on Staten Island to be with her mother. How had she spent the last sixty five years living in the grasp of such evil? It was something Missy didn't think she'd ever be able to comprehend. She turned around realizing she was standing at the foot of the steps to Mrs Smith's Brownstone. She reached out and touched the gatepost, which was warm and her hand felt as if it was heating up. This house was the polar opposite of Emilia's, it emanated light and peace from every brick. Placing both hands on the bricks she felt as if she was absorbing some of the goodness. She whispered, 'Mrs Smith, I don't know if you're here. It feels as if you are, please send us your strength. You helped us to send it back once, please help me again. I don't know if I'm strong enough to do it on my own.'

'Good morning, Miss Green.'

The voice – so loud and unexpected – made her jump, and she turned around to see Father Anthony standing there smiling at her. He was dressed in a pair of faded jeans, with a short-sleeved, black clerical shirt. His pristine white collar so bright she wondered if he'd worn a new one just for the occasion. This made her smile. He was going to need more than that if he was to go in the house with her.

'Father, you scared the life out of me.'

'Sorry, I didn't know how deep in thought you were until you jumped that high off the ground. You'd have cleared a hurdle.'

She laughed. 'At my age that would be quite something. What are you doing here?'

'I've been doing some research. After what you told me I couldn't stop thinking about it, I spoke to the Archbishop and an old friend who has some knowledge on these matters.'

'What did he say?'

'Well, I'm not sure you would want me to repeat such bad language.'

'He thinks I'm a crazy old fool?'

'Yes.'

'What about you? What do you think?'

He looked over at the house and crossed himself without even realizing, which confirmed what Missy suspected.

'This is not something we can go into lightly, you understand that don't you? I fear that if you go in there, alone and call it out, you won't necessarily remove it.'

'And?'

'And, you will die.'

Missy laughed, not just a small laugh. It was a real, come from the heart, belly laugh.

'What's so funny?'

She shook her head. 'Nothing, I'm just nervous.'

He folded his arms across his chest and arched an eyebrow.

'Bless you, thank you for coming to see me. I guess I've already resigned myself that death is inevitable, I'm just hoping that the big guy in the sky takes pity on me and lets me in. I don't want to spend all of eternity with a beast that smells like a gone off side of beef.'

It was his turn to smile. 'I admire your bravery, but really what we need to do is get your friend out of that building. I want you both somewhere safe, where you can both be blessed and out of harm's way until I'm fully prepared to go in. Just a few hours will do. It's not much to ask is it?'

Missy decided not to argue with him, for what difference would another few hours make? It had been here a long time. She pulled out her cell and rang Emilia.

'Grab a few things, I want you to come outside and meet me. We kind of have a backup plan.'

Emilia didn't answer and for one dreadful moment she wondered if her friend would do as she'd asked, she was probably more exhausted and tired of this than she was. Then the front door opened and she saw Emilia. Missy waved to her. There was a loud crack as though a bolt of lightning had struck the chimney of the house. Missy looked up to see chunks of masonry begin to cascade and that one of the large chimney pots was balancing on the edge of the roof. In a matter of seconds it was going to collapse directly onto Emilia. Father Anthony began to run across the road, but it was too far. The heavy, stone chimney came crashing down. Missy screamed. Unable to look she turned her head. Not seeing the pair of strong arms that wrapped themselves around her friend's frail shoulders, dragging her back inside the entrance of the house. The chimney pot whistled past her head, hitting the concrete steps with such force it shattered into a million pieces, taking a huge chunk out of them. She heard Anthony's voice as he shouted.

'She's okay, she's not hurt. You stay there.'

Not about to argue with him, she watched as he clambered over the shattered chimney pot to help Emilia over it. Behind her was Mikey, he waved at her and she mouthed *thank you* to him. The two men towered over Emilia as they half led, half carried her across the street to where Missy was standing.

Mikey spoke. 'It's scared, so it's trying to fight back the only way it can. We need to send that mother-fucker back to where it belongs once and for all. So what's the plan?'

Siren's blared in the distance, there was quite a crowd gathering to look at the mess across the road. Anthony hailed a passing cab and bundled them all into it.

'Saint Patrick's Old Cathedral, please.'

They sat in silence until the taxi stopped outside the church. If the taxi driver thought they were an odd bunch he never said anything. Two old women, a black man and a priest. Missy smiled. There was a joke in there somewhere. As it was they were an unlikely bunch, united through fate to do God's work and she found a small measure of comfort in that thought. Anthony paid the cab driver and ushered them out, instead of walking to the huge front doors he led them to a red door further along. Opening it with a key he held it open, waving them through before closing it behind them. Missy looked around at the beautiful, leafy garden. It was like they'd stepped through a doorway in time, back to when there were no cars polluting the city streets. There was a narrow, twisty path and Anthony led them along it until it opened up to an imposing, rough, cut stone building that mirrored the cathedral. It too had a blood-red door steeped with shiny, green Boston Ivy growing around it. Anthony opened the door with another key.

Stepping inside he shouted, 'Father, I have some visitors. Is it okay to come in?' They were greeted by a gruff voice and Missy wasn't sure if it had sworn at them. Anthony smiled. 'He sounds like an ogre, but he's not. He hates being disturbed, but I think he will want to hear what we have to tell him.' Missy wasn't so sure, but right now they needed all the help they could get and if she had to talk to a miserable son of a bitch priest then she would. Anthony led them into the most beautiful, oak panelled library that Missy had ever seen. She'd thought the library at Emilia's house had been wonderful, the hours she'd spent in there choosing which books to read were too many to count. This had floor to ceiling shelves and glass display cabinets full to the brim with books. Sitting at the desk near to the window was a grey-haired man wearing a roll neck jumper despite the warmth of the day outside. On his gnarled, liver-stained hands was a pair of fingerless gloves. He peered over the top of his wire rimmed oval glasses and Missy wondered where she'd seen him before. He looked so familiar or was it because it was the middle of summer and he was dressed like Ebenezer Scrooge? He looked at them in turn, spending the longest moment staring back at her.

'What are you doing bringing this band of trouble to my door, Anthony?'

He was blunt and Emilia looked at Missy, her face a picture which in turn made Missy laugh. Mikey who hadn't spoken a word since he'd dragged Emilia out of harm's way looked at Missy as if to ask 'What the hell?' She shrugged, they couldn't argue with the man. They were trouble and he didn't look the least bit interested in them.

'I think you're going to want to hear this lady's story. This is Emilia Carter. She lives in the house on West 10th Street.'

Missy wondered how on earth that was supposed to explain anything, but for the first time Father Morgan's eyes opened wide as he sat up straighter.

'The house?'

Anthony nodded. Father Morgan stared at Emilia as if she'd suddenly grown another head or a pair of wings.

'You're Emilia Carter? Well, I never, you still live there. How long has it been?'

'All my life. Why, what do you care?'

He laughed and his face broke into a smile, he didn't look quite so terrifying.

'I care more than you would ever know. You don't remember do you? I completely understand why. I've been keeping a watch on that house since 1952. I didn't know if it was a rumour or if that meddling Mrs Smith had only made things worse.'

Suddenly Missy remembered where she knew him from, he was the priest who had paid them a fleeting visit. He looked a lot different now, and then she caught sight of her reflection in the large mirror on the wall above his desk and had to do a double take. For a split second she was looking at her much younger, prettier self. She blinked and that woman was replaced with the grey-haired, wrinkled woman she was today. That was what life was like, it went in the blink of an eye. A wave of sadness engulfed her; she'd wasted so much of her life being afraid. She turned to Emilia and wondered if she felt the same. It was a testament to God and their stubbornness that they were both still alive.

Emilia was staring at the man, who pointed to the couch. 'Please, sit down. Forgive my grouchiness, I'm no longer a morning or a people person come to think of it. I spent a good many years of my life doing God's work until it got too much. Now I take care of the library, it's my pride and joy. There are books in here the Vatican have been trying to get hold of. They're not getting them, I can tell you that. Well, not at least until I die then I can't do much about it. I also have some books in here the big guys don't know about and wouldn't be too happy with.'

Missy wondered if the grumpy guy was senile as well, it was Mikey who finally spoke.

'What has this got to do with the situation we're in now and why would you be watching that damn house. Who are you?'

Anthony stood up, his face burning. 'Sorry, how rude of me.' Missy shook her head, they were all a little bit highly strung today. She crossed the room to where Father Morgan was sitting and held out her hand.

'Missy Green, former housekeeper for Miss Emilia and the gentleman is Mikey who is a current tenant in the house. What's your name because I refuse to spend the next hour calling you Father?'

'Missy, Mikey, Emilia.' He nodded at the three of them. 'You can call me Charlie. If you aren't an unlikely bunch of heroes I don't know who is. You don't look anything like Venkman, Stantz and Spengler.' He began to laugh so hard at his joke it made him start coughing. Emilia and Missy stared at the man as if he was speaking a different language. Mikey started laughing.

‘We aint afraid of no ghost. Man, we definitely don’t look like Ghostbusters and that’s because we aint.’

‘You might not think so, but I have bad news for you. I guess you’ve heard the saying God works in mysterious ways. Well it’s true, sometimes he has a sense of humour. This is probably why he’s chosen you three to take a stand. I take it the entity your brother summoned, Emilia, on that fateful night never actually went away. That you couldn’t see it, but you knew that it was there. Lingering in the background, biding its time. You’ve been living under its shadow for a long time, but that’s what they do. They’re like a cancerous tumour sucking all the goodness out of your body, your mind, it’s probably been oppressing you all your life.’

Mikey who had never spoken more than a few words to Emilia until the other day looked at her, she began to blink manically as a tear fell from the corner of her eye. Missy reached out her hand, clasping hold of Emilia’s.

‘I should have known, I should have investigated it myself. I trusted that Mrs Smith had done the job for the church, she prided herself on helping the people the church wouldn’t. I was too young and inexperienced.’

‘Why wouldn’t the church want to help anyone living with such a horrible thing?’

Father Anthony spoke. ‘It would open up the floodgates for every crackpot in the entire world. Of course, the church is well aware these demons exist. But to publicly announce it would cause panic and every mentally ill person who needs a psych evaluation would be dropped at our door. We don’t have the capacity to fulfil that role. What we do is take each case on its own merit, we have to investigate, send out a psychologist to assess if the person is off their meds or not. When we have proof the

Archbishop then gives his blessing for an exorcist to step in.'

Emilia's body shook and her voice trembled. 'If I'd have asked the church to help would they?'

Charlie nodded. 'In this case, at the beginning probably not. I'm sorry, I should have been honest with you, but I was young and very inexperienced back then.'

'Why?'

'Your brother displayed all the signs of a classic psychosis, the police reports said as much. That he was having a psychotic episode on the night he killed Mae Evans. They didn't believe it had anything to do with devil worship or summoning a demon despite the pentagram drawn in blood and the presence of the Ouija board. The cops prefer things to be cut and dried, they would have been torn to shreds by the papers if they hadn't sent your brother to Greystone's.'

Emilia sat down, she was wringing her hands and Missy felt bad.

'Why didn't you speak to us or the police if you thought there was something going on?'

'I did, I spoke at great length to your father. It was him who gave me permission to see copies of the psychiatrist's reports. On paper it seemed as if the police were right.'

'But...?'

He let out a loud sigh. 'I didn't think they were telling the whole truth, something about it wasn't right. I went back into your house with your father, I couldn't get any further than the first floor. I felt as if I was going to have a heart attack and die. I got clammy, I felt sick, I was dizzy and the smell of rotting flesh and sulphur was too much for me. I'm ashamed to say that I ran out of your house and never went back. I was young, scared and fascinated so I began to research it as much as I could. Mrs Smith told me that I should stop being a dress-wearing bible basher and face the truth. That there were things in this world beyond the church's control.'

Missy looked at him. 'She was right, she had to battle to close the portal that James opened up. She told me afterwards that she'd had to call on all of her spirit guides to help her fight it. If you'd helped her would it have made a difference?'

He shrugged. 'Mrs Smith did a very good job, better than I would have done. I wasn't a trained exorcist back then.'

'But you are now?'

He nodded. 'Yes, although I've stepped back from that line of work. I'm too old to be fighting with anyone, let alone a demon.'

'Are you going to help us?' Missy needed to know. For the love of God he didn't look any younger than she was.

He paused, looked at Anthony and nodded. 'I'm going to advise you.'

Mikey began to laugh. 'And what the fuck good is that going to do? Pardon my language, Father.'

'I have been teaching Anthony everything he needs to know.'

Missy stood up. 'Forget it, the church didn't help last time. We don't need your help this time. You're telling me you've had a vested interest in that house for sixty five years. Yet you're going to hide away in the comfort of this house and let us do the rest. For Christ's sake what's the worst that can happen? In case you haven't noticed between the three of us we're ancient, we all got to die some time and I'm afraid it could be anytime. Why the hell would you want to send Anthony in to do a job you could do with your eyes shut. You're putting him and us at risk. Have you done this before, Anthony?'

She turned to stare at him, her arms folded across her chest. He shook his head. 'No, but I can. Charlie has taught me well.'

She shook her head. 'Jeez, what a pair of assholes. No offence guys, but I think we'll manage. Emilia, Mikey, let's go.'

She turned to walk out of the door when a voice bellowed at her.

'Stop.'

She turned around and felt her heart sink. Charlie wasn't sitting in a conventional chair. He wheeled himself around from behind the desk and she stared at the missing gap where his right leg should have been. Now she felt like an asshole. She hadn't noticed. How would he even get up to the attic?

'I have an unfortunate disadvantage due to the diabetes I developed in my seventies and yes, you're right, I'm pretty sure that at some point in the near future one or all of us are going to die, but not at the doing of a demon. I would like nothing more than to go in there and do battle, it would be fun to have one last showdown with one of Satan's creatures. I'm also no fool. I'm a weak link in the chain and it would seize the moment the minute it sensed I had entered the house. This is between Emilia and you. The pair of you fought it the first time and did a pretty good job of sealing it inside the portal. Whoever decided to reopen it knew exactly what they were doing. '

He waved an old, cracked, black leather book at her. 'The ritual requires three sacrifices, now I don't know why a third wasn't done after the last one. Maybe it's because they got cold feet or got locked up for something else.

What I do know is that it's getting stronger, which means something is happening. I wouldn't be surprised if another sacrifice was imminent.'

Mikey looked at the priest and shook his head. 'I can't believe I'm hearing this. Sacrifices, demons, Ouija boards, that's some bad shit going on there. How do I live in a house of evil and not know any of this?'

Charlie shrugged. 'Some people are oblivious to it all and some people are very sensitive. It's life. Some people like mustard on their hot dogs others don't.'

The room fell silent as they all contemplated the fact that this was all very real. It was Emilia who broke it.

'I've had enough of this. So, Charlie, what the fuck do I have to do to claim my house back?'

Chapter Forty-Three

Maria could feel the soft, sagging mattress under her. How had she got into bed? Had she passed out and Frankie had found her? She tried to open her eyes, but one of them was sealed shut. Blinking the other she tried to focus on the darkness that surrounded her. The air in the room was heavy with the stench of decomposition and she felt her stomach clench, her gag reflex kicked in. As the back of her throat filled with bile, her tongue moved forward and stopped. She couldn't move her mouth or her tongue to be sick. She lay still, trying not to breathe too deeply because then the smell would penetrate her nostrils again and make her sick. The gag choking her to death on her own vomit. Her chest began to fill with the fluttering, wings of panic. There were only two times in her life she'd ever felt like this, both in her childhood. She didn't panic. As an adult it was one of her rules, but the alarm bells were ringing in her head. She knew that she was in a dire situation that was going to end badly if she didn't stay calm. She closed her other eye, she would pretend she was still unconscious. She needed to think, she wasn't in her bed because that was much firmer, so she was in an unknown place that smelt strongly of death with a gag in her mouth. She knew it was futile, but still tried to move her arms and legs as slowly as she could without alerting her captor to the fact that she was awake. The rope bit into the soft, flesh of her wrists. Fear rushed through her veins, she was not only tied and gagged, but spread-eagled on the bed. She was cold, but not shivering so at least she was still fully dressed. She still had some dignity which was good. If her asshole colleagues were going to find her body she'd still have some pride. Bad enough to die this way, never mind be gawped at and photographed a thousand times by the jerks she worked with. This thought alone was enough to focus her mind – it wasn't going to happen, not like this. She hadn't really got a good look at the guy who had been in her apartment. She tried not to shudder at the thought of Anya's decomposing head in her cooler. Anya. Jesus, she knew exactly where she was, and she had to stifle a cry. She was in the attic apartment of the house on West 10th.

There was movement in the corner of the room, she didn't dare to open her eye. She waited for him to come closer and wondered if he had an axe and how much it was going to hurt. A loud, long scratching noise filled the air and a vision of Freddy Krueger who'd scared her shitless as a teenager filled her mind. The sleepless nights she'd had because of those films were too many to count and now some maniac was going to kill her. She was too scared to move. The only thing she could do was headbutt him if he got near to her and hope she could untie herself in record time. She waited, not daring to breathe out. The scratching didn't happen again, but the smell seemed stronger, more potent and it made her eyes water. After a few minutes she gently tugged her arms against the rope, there was a little movement. If she could work up a sweat, she might be able to make her skin slippery enough to pull her wrist free. She was glad of the gag in her mouth because it stopped her crying out in pain at the friction burn the rope was causing. She paused when she heard a low growl that sent a shiver down her spine, it sounded much bigger than a dog. She carried on, writhing both wrists against the rope, the soft, tanned skin of her wrists was now a burning, red mess. Any minute now she would break the skin and the blood would begin to seep through. She didn't care, if it gave her enough moisture to pull her wrists free she would deal with the mess later. Friction burns were the least of her worries; a homicidal maniac was her main priority. She tried to remember the layout of the apartment. There was a kitchen, living area not too dissimilar to hers. The bedroom was off the kitchen. This was a top floor apartment, it would have to have a fire escape. If she could make it to the window and climb through, it would be okay. She had no weapon on her, but if she had to she would fight with her bare hands until she found something suitable to kill him with because he wasn't getting away a second time. This time she would finish it for good. No more women were going to be killed in this apartment. A door closed from elsewhere in the apartment and she felt her heart skip a beat. If he was outside the bedroom who the fuck was inside?

Chapter Forty-Four

October 1952

They watched from the window, their hands clasped in each other's, as the police entered the house opposite, guns drawn. In turn every single light was flicked on as they searched each room. Emilia knew it was pointless, the cops would never find the thing that was hiding in there. It didn't care about their guns or harsh language, they would come out of there scratching their heads and rolling their eyes at the two crazy broads who'd over-reacted to a noise. The house was lit up like a beacon, every window glowed brightly, casting out the shadows. Mr Smith was watching in fascination from the front step. Mrs Smith whispered, 'As soon as the cops leave, I'll take you both back over.'

Emilia released a small cry and she felt the warmth of Mrs Smith's arm as it wrapped itself around her.

'I know you're scared, but I can deal with this. I can send it back to the dark, depths of hell, but I need your help. So I need you to be brave, the cops will never find it in a million years. They won't be looking for it, they're looking for a man made of flesh and blood. Not a monster made of smoke and shadows.'

Missy looked at the woman to see if she was teasing them and felt relieved to see her face was as serious as hers.

'You can't tell Mr Smith what is going on though. He will be mad and I don't want to upset him. Father Morgan might help us, but don't rely on it.'

Emilia asked. 'Who's Father Morgan?'

'The priest who came to visit you, they're very good friends and normally I wouldn't ask because the church is a pain in the ass when you need instant action. They have more pull than the Whitehouse, yet need everything in writing, so I'm not holding much hope. It might just be us girls.'

The officers spewed out of the front door, faster than they went in. Their faces confused, they shut the door behind them and scrambled to get onto the sidewalk. As far away from the house as they could. Mrs Smith watched them and nodded. 'Uhuh, something went down in that house, but I bet your bottom dollar they won't spill.' She left the two women and they watched as she marched down her steps to where the cops were standing. Emilia turned to look at Missy.

'I'm scared.'

'Me too, but we have to do what she tells us otherwise we won't be able to live in the house and we can't let it scare us away. That's what it wants. Didn't she say they live off fear? Well maybe it's time we took a stand.'

'You think so? You think that we can fight a monster made of smoke and shadows, Missy?'

'Yes, I do. We have to.'

They waited for Mrs Smith who was pointing her fingers at the chest of the cop in charge. It was Mr Smith who ran over and grabbed his wife's arm, gently pulling her away. Missy watched them for a little while and then turned her full attention back to the house, all the while they had been arguing the lights had been turning off, one by one and the top two floors were all in blackness even though the house was empty. They went back inside to the safety of Mrs Smith's house and waited for her to call the priest.

When Mrs Smith entered the room, she had Father Morgan behind her, but there was no sign of Mr Smith.

'Father tell these poor, terrified ladies what you told me?'

He looked as if he wanted to be anywhere other than standing right here, he glared at Mrs Smith.

'Well, I, um, I'm not sure that I can do anything to help tonight. I need to speak to the Archbishop, this isn't something I can just go in and flush away.'

'Basically, he's saying he's a coward and won't do anything unless he's been given permission.'

'No, not at all. It's just… you know Amanda that it isn't that straightforward, there are certain protocols that have to be followed.'

'For Christ's sake Charlie, grow a set of balls and help these girls out will you? Look at their faces, how can you turn your back on them?'

He shook his head. 'I can't help, you know that and neither should you.'

'Right, well the least you can do is to keep Mr Smith entertained whilst I go and do it.'

'Amanda, you promised no more.'

'I did, until it happened on my own doorstep. Charlie, you might be afraid to break the rules, but sometimes they must be broken. I can't ignore it and besides, I kind of feel as if it's taunting us, taking up residence in the house across the street.'

He shook his head and left them to it, Missy expected to see him leaving and walking down the street as fast as he could. He didn't, instead she heard the muffled voices of him speaking to Mr Smith.

Amanda turned to them. 'I was wrong, we can't wait until the morning. We must fight it now. Give me a few minutes, I need to call on all of my spirit guides to help me with this and it might take a little while for them to get here.'

She sat down on a chair and closed her eyes, Emilia wondered if they were in a strange dream. She didn't have a clue what a spirit guide was, but it sounded very important.

✪

When Amanda opened her eyes she nodded. 'They're here, all of them which is a relief and they agree with me. We can't wait any longer, it needs to be brought over here, out of it's hiding place to be sent back to hell. Once that's done we will go to the house and seal the portal.'

Missy looked at her. 'What do you mean it needs to be brought here, how do you do that and isn't it dangerous for you? What's a portal?'

'Well, I'm not going to lie. This is very dangerous, but I'm afraid it's our only option. If Mr Smith knew what I was about to do he would probably divorce me, he would be that angry. I'm going to draw it in. It won't be expecting a house full of guides and angels. That's good though, we'll have the element of surprise. A portal is a doorway between our world and another, in this case between our world and hell.'

Emilia shook her head. 'You can't do that. What about you and Mr Smith? You'll be putting yourselves at risk.'

'Honey, it won't be the first time and it won't be the last. Besides Mr Smith is oblivious to any of this, he'll be watching that television set we paid an arm and a leg for. He plays along with me, but he thinks I'm a little bit crazy.'

Missy wondered if the woman was nuts, but what choice did they have?

She stood up, clasping hold of their hands. 'Whatever you do, don't break the circle, keep tight hold of each other's hands.' She began to pray. When she'd finished she went to the dresser and pulled open a drawer. She returned with two sets of rosary beads and placed a set over each of their heads.

'Do you believe in God and all things good?'

They both nodded.

'Then we're ready. Now this might be easy and it might go without a fight because sometimes they do. When they realize there is someone who isn't going to let them through they cower and back down. Others, who are stubborn, will hang on for dear life. Are you both ready?'

The horror which filled Emilia's veins turning her body into a quivering wreck was too much to comprehend. What choice did they have? It was unlikely they would ever find another person so kind and brave to help them. She nodded. 'Yes, I'm ready.'

Mrs Smith smiled at her. 'Demon, I command you to come to me. I know you can hear me, I'm sending a beacon of light for you to follow. I have the girls, they are waiting for you.'

Panic filled Emilia as she tried to pull away from Amanda, she was offering them up to that monster.

Amanda had such a tight grasp on her arm she couldn't move. Looking at her, shaking her head she hissed. 'Don't break the circle.'

Missy who had never been so scared closed her eyes, she didn't know if Amanda was a crackpot. What if she really was offering them up? Her fingers, which had gone numb they were so cold, began to tingle as a warm feeling began to spread up them. It felt nice and as the heat spread up her arms and began to envelop her entire body she felt calmer than she had done in months. She opened one eye to peek at Emilia who had the same blissful expression on her face that she was sure if she looked in a mirror she would see reflected back at her. Amanda smiled and called out again.

'Demon, you have been called. It is your duty to come out of the shadows. I command you to show yourself.'

The light in the room began to dim, getting darker by the second and Missy's heart began to beat faster. The air in the room was getting heavy, oppressive. A huge thump on the floor in front of Amanda made the floor shake. Missy looked around. She couldn't see anything, but she could feel, hot, fetid breath on the back of her neck. The smell of rotting flesh was over-powering and her knees began to buckle.

'Tell me your name, demon? I've invited you into my house so you have to tell me your name.'

It growled, a sound so low and guttural that it made Emilia squeeze Missy's hand so tight she thought it was going to fall off.

'Are you shy, demon? You are not welcome into this house or the house you've just come from.' Amanda paused. 'Ah, I know you. I don't need your name, I already know it.'

The room was so dark that Missy could no longer see Emilia or Amanda even though they were standing inches from each other. There was a roar so loud that Missy's instinct was to cover her ears, but Amanda wouldn't let go of her hand and then a blinding, golden light filled the room. Clearing the darkness, it was so bright and warm it felt as if the sun had just risen inside the parlour. The feeling of love and warmth that enveloped them was enough to make Missy's eyes fill with tears, it was so pure and beautiful. Amanda whispered.

'Thank you all so much.'

She let go of Missy's hand and turned to Emilia. 'You can open your eyes now. It's gone. Back to hell. You're safe.'

Emilia stared at her. 'How?'

'I had a lot of help from some special friends. Now you have to go and seal the portal before it comes back.'

'But, how do we seal the portal? I don't understand.'

Amanda gasped. 'Oh my.' As her hand reached for her chest, Missy managed to catch her as she collapsed into her arms. The weight of her was too heavy to bear and she began to fall towards the floor, doing her best to keep hold of Amanda who was dead before they hit the floor.

This time Emilia began to scream so loud that it brought Mr Smith running from his room to see what had happened.

Chapter Forty-Five

Frankie was pacing up and down the hallway. While the CSIs were working Maria's flat, the elevator doors opened, and he saw the huge bunch of white roses before he saw who was holding them and knew it was Harrison Williams. He ran towards him, barrelling into his chest and crushing the roses. Harrison yelled as he was pushed back into the elevator. Frankie had his elbow pushed tight against his neck, choking him.

'I swear to God if you've hurt her I'll kill you with my bare hands. Where is she asshole? I'm giving you thirty seconds before I haul your ass in for kidnap.'

Harrison's face paled visibly as he tried to shake his head. Frankie moved his elbow so he could speak.

'What are you talking about? Where is she? I haven't seen her since this morning. My driver brought her here, I've been in meetings all day. Jesus Christ, I wouldn't hurt her.'

Frankie stepped back, the roses which were now a squashed mess of petals and leaves were all over the floor. He ran his hand through his hair.

'I don't know, she's gone. There's broken glass and blood in her apartment.'

Harrison pushed Frankie out of the way and ran towards Maria's apartment where he was greeted by an angry looking CSI.

'Buddy, you can't come in here it's a crime scene.'

'I need to see.'

'No, you don't. If you trample over my scene I'll shoot you. If you care about Maria you'll let us do our job. If you compromise any forensic evidence then you're going to slow down any chance of us figuring out what happened.'

Harrison's shoulders sagged, he turned to Frankie. 'What can I do? I have people I can contact. What do you need?'

Frankie grabbed his arm. 'How fast can you get a cell site analysis?'

'I need to go to my office, I have a tech guy there. He knows how to do all sorts of stuff.'

Frankie ran towards the elevator. 'Come on then.'

As Harrison ran towards the limousine Frankie shook his head. 'No way, we'll go in my car. That thing is way too slow.'

Frankie ran towards his car, pressing the fob to unlock the doors. He threw himself in, Harrison followed suit.

'Buckle up, this won't be no fancy, slow ride.'

Harrison tugged the belt across his shoulders and pushed it into the clasp. Frankie did a U-turn and sped off down the street to a symphony of blaring horns. Harrison pulled out his cell and began talking to his guy on the other end. When Frankie screeched to a halt outside the Manhattan Media Corporation he heard Harrison mutter 'Thank Christ we're here in one piece.' They ran into the building and past security, but Harrison didn't stop at the bank of public elevators, instead he ran towards a smaller set of doors at the end of the corridor and pressed his thumb against the keypad. Frankie watched in awe as the doors slid open to a much smaller, more intimate elevator. Harrison shrugged.

'Private elevator, perks of the job. I haven't got time to make small talk with everyone who works for me. Don't get me wrong I do talk to them, just not first thing in the morning. I hate small talk at the best of times.'

Frankie looked at the highly polished cherry wood and brass fittings and felt a grudging respect for the guy standing in front of him. Frankie didn't do small talk either, except with Maria – he would talk about anything with her. A sharp pain tugged at his heart at the thought of her name. For a moment he'd forgotten about her. Now it was back, the churning stomach was on double time and he felt queasy. The ride up was smooth and fast, Frankie felt his ears pop and knew they were high. The doors opened into a large room filled with people, computers and television screens. Nobody looked up from what they were doing, they knew better than to speak to their boss unless he spoke to them. It was how he liked it; this was where the behind-the-scenes magic happened. Frankie looked around then, realising Harrison was moving again, he followed him. Through a set of double doors to a smaller metal one, he pressed his thumb against another scanner which opened the door, it was a small office with almost as many computer screens as the huge one. This room had a kid who didn't look any older than twenty typing away on a keyboard. His fingers were flying across the keys so fast Frankie got dizzy just watching him. He looked up at Harrison, his shaved head and *Breaking Bad* t-shirt made him look like an extra off *Prison Break.*

'I need a number.'

Harrison pulled out his cell and rhymed off Maria's number. Frankie had to ask, he was a geek when it came to anything technical.

'How can you track it?'

Joe, who had a British accent, rolled his eyes at him.

'Mate, anyone can track a phone. It's not rocket science, there are all sorts of apps out there. Is it an iPhone?'

Frankie shook his head. ‘Nope, it’s a cheap cell. Maria is too tight to pay contract fees for one of those.’

‘Ah, that might make it a bit trickier. Still I can do it, I’ll use CCSS7. It might take a little longer if it’s not an up to date mobile.’

‘What’s CCSS7, I’ve never heard of it?’

‘Well, basically it’s a network interchange service that acts as a broker between mobile phone networks. By hacking into the system I can track the location based on the mobile phone mast triangulation. It will even let me read their text messages, I can log and listen to phone calls by using the number as an identifier.’

Harrison nodded at Joe. ‘Let’s just hope she has her phone with her, it definitely wasn’t in the apartment, Frankie?’

Frankie wasn’t sure, he hadn’t seen it. ‘I don’t think so, she never goes anywhere without it.’

‘Well, let’s hope this works then. All we need is a location.’

Harrison stood watching Joe over his shoulder until the kid turned to look at him.

‘Boss, you might pay the wages, but back up. I can’t work with you breathing down my neck, you’re putting me off.’

Harrison stepped back, he looked at Frankie who was surprised to see Harrison do as he was told. He wondered how often that happened. Probably not a lot. Maria must mean something to him if he was willing to be so compliant. He didn’t strike Frankie as the sort of guy who did what someone else told him very often.

Joe let out a whoop. ‘I’m in and this mobile is somewhere in a one mile radius of West 10th Street. I can get you her last messages up if you want.’

Frankie felt the contents of his stomach threaten to spew out of his mouth all over the fancy computer system that Joe was sitting behind. The blood drained from his face, Harrison watched him, horrified.

'What, what the fuck does that mean? It's bad isn't it, what's on West 10th Street?'

'A murdering son of a bitch, that's what. I have to go, wait here. I'll contact you when I have her.'

'No, I'm not waiting here. You can't get out on your own, you have no security pass or access to the elevator. You need me to get you out of this building.'

Frankie knew he was telling the truth. 'Move your ass then.'

Harrison ran towards the elevator, the door opened and he ushered Frankie in. Joe shouted. 'You're welcome, of course I don't mind.'

Harrison yelled back. 'Thanks Joe.' Just as the doors shut.

Frankie arched an eyebrow at him. Harrison shrugged. 'He's British, they're very odd about good manners. He's also the best computer guy I've ever had, so he kind of has free reign and he's only a kid.'

'I never said a word, it's your circus. Your monkeys'

'You didn't have to, I saw your expression.'

They reached the ground floor and ran to the staff exit, Frankie let out a huge sigh to see his car was still there and hadn't been towed by his over keen co-workers in traffic. He looked at Harrison and realized that maybe he wasn't just a rich asshole. He'd just saved them valuable hours that could mean the difference between life and death for Maria.

Chapter Forty-six

Charlie wheeled himself as close to Emilia as he could.

'I think you know what you need to do, whether you know how to do it is an entirely different matter.'

She shook her head, as it all came rushing back – that last evening when she'd been chased from her own home to Mrs Smith's house across the street. A glorious, technicolor, slideshow of complete and utter fear filled her heart as the images flashed across her mind. She gasped.

'We need to seal the portal, we never did. After that night when poor Mrs Smith died in Missy's arms we didn't do it. We were supposed to, but it all went horribly wrong. Mr Smith was so angry with us for coming to them for help. By the time the EMS and cops had been we forgot all about going back to do the ritual.'

Missy nodded. 'When we finally went home we were exhausted, the house felt different. Lighter, happier, it didn't have that goddamn, awful rotting corpse smell. Whatever Mrs Smith had done before she died, it worked. For a while, at least, I didn't notice it creeping back in. When Clarke died I left you and I'm sorry, I left you to deal with the consequences and you've spent all those years locked inside the house which has now become your prison.'

Emilia sobbed so loudly it made them jump.

'What do we need to do? I don't care if I die trying, I've had enough. I've lived under the shadow of that beast for far too long. I'm ready to fight it single handed.'

Charlie nodded his head, smiling at the same time. 'Now that's what I like to hear, fighting talk. I believe you're ready to do this, I truly do.'

He turned, wheeling himself towards a glass bookcase stuffed with cracked, antique, leather books. He opened the door and pulled one out, handing it to Emilia. You need this, holy water and salt. You go to the portal and make the sign of the cross with the holy water, then you seal the area with salt and repeat the prayers. First of all Anthony must go through the entire house, blessing each room with holy water. It will help to remove all the negative energy, it will stop it from leaving the attic whilst you go up and seal the portal. The page in the book I've marked are the prayers you need to say.'

She looked at Anthony. 'Will you even need to be there?'

He smiled at her. 'I'll be there to bring in the light and watch your back. I'll be your support.'

Missy shook her head. 'Shouldn't it be the other way around, shouldn't we be watching your back?'

It was Charlie who answered. 'In some cases, yes, the church leads the way. In this case I believe that Emilia's strength of character and the fact that she knows it so well will be to the advantage.'

'So, the church is copping out and letting a couple of seniors do its job?'

'To the contrary Missy, for once the church is being devious and playing evil at its own game. You must trust me on this one. Anthony will go in and do the prayers to cleanse the house. You will go to the attic and deal with the portal.'

Emilia nodded. 'Let's go now, I want it finished.'

Mikey looked at them both. 'What am I to do?'

Charlie spoke. 'You're the hired muscle, you make sure Emilia can get to the attic at all costs. Now gather round, I need to bless you all. Come, come, join hands and close your eyes. I want you to believe in the power of good and God more than you've ever believed in anything else.'

Chapter Forty-Seven

Maria's wrists were on fire, she could feel the wetness of the blood as it seeped down her arms from the rope burns. Gritting her teeth, she managed to tug one arm free. It was better than nothing. At least she could punch or poke his eyeballs out with one hand. Silent tears were running down her cheeks, she'd never felt such intense heat and pain as she writhed the other wrist against the rope. There was something in the room with her, but it wasn't anything she could see, it was something she could sense. She didn't even know where to begin explaining it when she got out of here to the guys, to Frankie. The pain in her heart at the thought of never seeing him again was like someone had taken a knife and physically plunged it into her heart. She loved him and had never told him, despite the fact that most of the time he drove her nuts. On a deeper level they were connected, they'd been through a lot. How ironic that after all the attempted drunken fumbles now he was finally a free man, she'd met Harrison. Not to mention it was quite likely she was going to die before she got the chance to make a life with either of them. Maria stifled the sob which wanted to explode from her chest. This was so fucking wrong, she'd spent the last ten years of her life hunting down homicidal maniacs to get them off the streets of New York to make it a safer place. Yet here she was in the world's smelliest apartment, waiting for an absolute psycho to come and chop her head off. *Well, not today Satan. This is not going down on my watch.* Her wrist slid free from the rope and she smiled to herself, she didn't touch her wrists as tempting as it was to rub them because she knew they were a bloodied mess. She wiped them across the bedcover to remove some of the blood, she needed her fingers to be dry. Sitting up she began to unfasten the ropes around her ankles, praying he wouldn't come back before she'd set herself free and found a weapon. Her eyes had adjusted to the darkness inside the room, she could make out a chest of drawers and a wardrobe on one side. The other wall had nothing against it, it was a huge expanse of white with a freshly, painted pentagram filling the middle. Her heart which was already racing began to hammer against her rib cage. She didn't want to believe in this crap. It was far easier to accept it had nothing to do with angels and demons, it was good old fashioned psychotic behavior. Humans were more than capable of committing acts of heinous behavior of their own free will. They sure as hell didn't need the excuse of being possessed by demons to do so. A scraping, creaking noise began to fill the room, Maria looked around, but couldn't see anything. Her fingers began working even faster to loosen the knots in the rope as she tugged one foot free. She looked up towards the pentagram and felt her entire body prickle with fear. There was a huge shape pressing against the inside of the plaster. She'd never seen anything like it, the plaster on the wall was bulging and she watched in fear as she waited for it to start cracking. For the first time in her life Maria felt the realization come crashing down on her that she was wrong, there were things in existence that couldn't be explained. The wall was bulging out so far that she didn't know how it was still standing. Free of the ropes she ran towards the door desperate to get away from whatever it was trying to break through the wall. She threw the door open and ran straight into the man that had brought her here. The surprise on his face was almost as wild as hers, suddenly he didn't look so mean and scary. Realising she had the advantage her arm shot out and she repaid the favour by punching him hard in the nose. She smiled at the satisfying crunch as her knuckles ground into face, the blood began to spurt from it and he stumbled backwards. Not waiting a second longer she ran at him and punched him again, this time her knuckles connected with his Adams apple and he fell to his knees, his eyes streaming with tears as he was gasping trying to catch his breath.

'How do you like that you asshole? That one was for Anya.'

There was a loud bang as the door to the apartment was hurled open, Maria had never been so happy to see Frankie. He rushed towards her, grabbing and hugging her close.

'I thought you were…'

'Yeah, well you thought wrong.'

He let go of her. 'Your wrists.'

'I'll live.'

She noticed a red-faced Harrison standing there taking in the scene before him.

'What are you doing here?'

Frankie – who now had the choking guy in an even tighter choke-hold shook his head.

'Well, it's a long story, but thanks to him we knew where you were.'

Maria smiled. 'With his stalking abilities that doesn't surprise me.'

He crossed the room and taking hold of her gently, he pulled her close.

'I don't know what to say, except I swear to God, I'm not a stalker.'

'It's okay, we're used to this kind of crap. Thank you.'

There was an almighty crash which vibrated the whole floor as the lights went black, and the temperature in the room dropped to sub zero. Maria, who had forgotten all about the thing in the bedroom, felt every nerve in her body begin to freeze.

'Run! We have to get out of here now. It's too big.'

The terror in her voice was enough to convince Frankie, who dragged the guy along with him towards the door. Maria grabbed Harrison's hand, tugging him after them. They reached the top of the stairs and she turned to slam the door shut behind them. Not knowing if it would make the slightest bit of difference or not, but if it stalled it for just a few moments it was better than nothing.

Chapter Forty-Eight

Frankie pushed through the front door, dragging his prisoner behind him. He was closely followed by Maria who was dragging Harrison behind her. Almost barrelling into them, standing on the top step was Miss Green, Ms Carter, the man who'd warned her to keep out, and a priest. Maria shook her head.

'Miss Green, what are you doing here?'

Missy stepped forward. 'Maria, what happened to you? You're bruised and bleeding.' The elderly woman reached out her hand, tenderly stroking Maria's cheek.

'I'm fine, I'll mend. What are you all doing here?'

Mikey stepped forward. 'Sorry to break up this reunion, but we have work to do. As much as I'd like to make small talk with the cops all day we have a pressing matter to deal with.'

Missy nodded. 'We're here to do something we should have done a long time ago.'

'You can't go in there, there's something inside.'

'I know, it's been there since 1952. Hiding, watching, waiting. Well, not any longer, we're here to send it back to hell.'

The priest walked towards the door and began to pray, while Missy and Emilia clasped hands and followed him in. Mikey crossed himself and turned to Maria. 'I have no idea how I got roped into this fucking mess. If I don't make it out you can put that on my gravestone.'

Then they were gone. Maria turned to Frankie who had the suspect in cuffs and was on the phone for back up.

'We can't leave them. What on earth is going on?'

Frankie shrugged. 'If I knew that I'd be living his lifestyle.' He jerked his head in Harrison's direction.

'But, they're old. Miss Green is a sweet, old lady. How can she fight that?'

She began to run in after them. Frankie yelled. 'Don't you dare! Get your ass out here now.'

She waved a hand towards him. Harrison shouted at him. 'What do I do? Should I go in after her?'

Frankie sighed. 'Knock yourself out, tell her I'm gonna kick her ass and get her put down in the basement with Layla.'

Harrison ran back towards the building. 'Who's Layla?'

'Pray you never have to meet her, that's who.'

And then he was at the front door, leaving Frankie waiting for a squad car to come and get the psycho he had cuffed to his right arm.

Emilia led the way, the house was dark. Much darker than she'd ever known it and the smell was back. It was so strong it made her eyes water. She turned to Anthony who nodded at her. He began to pray, at each apartment door he used the holy water to make the sign of the cross. Mikey who felt like a spare part stood watching. Anthony turned towards him. 'You keep watch. We'll keep on moving up until we come face to face with it or until it decides to come down to see what we're doing.'

Emilia gripped Missy's hand even tighter. She whispered, 'We'll take the staff stairs, maybe take it by surprise.'

Missy nodded, the fear in her eyes reflected back in those of her friends. This was it. There was no going back and she knew that. Emilia began to recite a prayer in her mind, it was one she'd made up, but it had served her well all these years. They broke away from Mikey and Anthony, hurrying towards the far end of the building and the hidden staircase. Maria came flying through the front door, pushing it shut behind her, she turned the lock. Harrison pressed his face against the glass, slamming the palms of his hands against it. He shouted.

'Open the door, Maria.'

She shook her head. He hammered harder on the glass, 'Let me in, I can help.'

'No. You can't. Stay with Frankie.' She ran towards the first floor where she could hear male voices. Mikey was standing behind the priest. Maria felt her heart skip a beat.

'Where are the others?'

The priest ignored her, his brow furrowed. There were beads of perspiration on his forehead. Mikey lifted a finger to his lips, he had no idea if the demon could hear them or not. He didn't want to blatantly let it know their plans. The air was heavy with anticipation, the smell was much worse. She whispered to the priest.

'What are you doing?'

He whispered back. 'Blessing this part of the house so it can't come down, we need to keep it trapped upstairs.'

She cupped her hand to his ear. 'Is it working?'

All the bulbs exploded at the same time sending glass flying, Maria and Mikey both ducked. Anthony wasn't so lucky and a shard of glass embedded itself in his cheek. He winced at the sharp pain, but he didn't stop what he was doing.

'You can try your worst, you won't stop me, demon. By the power invested in me by the Almighty you will leave this house.'

The roar that filled the hallway was so loud that the floorboards reverberated under their feet. Maria felt coldness begin to seep into her veins. For a second she was frozen to the floor. Then she heard an almighty smash from above and her instincts kicked in. Miss Green and Emilia were up there, alone with a mean son of a bitch, monster thing. She wasn't going to stand for it. She ran towards the stairs. Making it halfway up them before an invisible force slammed two huge hands into her chest, sending her flying backwards through the air. Her arms and legs began to windmill as she tried to slow herself down. She felt herself falling towards the floor and landed with a loud crash at the priest's feet. Stunned she lay there for a moment trying to catch her breath. Anthony bent down to her, he made the sign of the cross on her forehead with the holy water and blessed her. Mikey who was shaking his head held his hand out towards her. She took it and he pulled her up. Bruised and winded she didn't let it stop her, she was about to try again when Mikey whispered in her ear.

'There's a servants' staircase at the far end of this hall. I'll distract it.'

She nodded and watched as he climbed onto the first step. 'Come on, you bastard, you're big and tough when it comes to hurting women. What about men?'

Maria wondered if the man had a death wish, but she didn't stop to find out. She began to limp towards the second staircase. She heard a loud shout of, 'Holy Christ.' This was followed by an even louder thump. Putting her head down, she carried on despite the fact that her heart was racing faster than ever. She reached the end of the corridor and the false wall with the staircase behind it. Wondering if she'd make it to the top she began to run up them; these were bare, wooden, steps that would hurt like hell if she got thrown down them. She could hear the priest shouting and Mikey let out a yell, then the sound of pounding footsteps filled the house. She reached the next level and ran towards the attic staircase. There was no light up here, she couldn't see her hand in front of her face. Gagging, she tried not to breathe. Running up the narrow steps she pushed her way back into the room she hadn't long tried to break free from. *You must be crazy girl, you've escaped a killer to run back and fight a demon.* It didn't matter… she knew it was the right thing to do and she breathed out a sigh of relief to see Missy and Emilia standing in the room staring at her their eyes wide open in fear.

'Sorry, sorry, it's me. I have no idea where it is or what it's doing, but it's pissed off. Whatever you need to do, please do it.'

Missy spoke. 'We can't until the house has been blessed and it has nowhere to run. We need it to come back to the safety of this room and then we can seal it in the pentagram and send it back.'

A low, growl came from behind Maria and she turned to face the huge, black shadow that had come in behind her. The two horns on its head so large they seemed to be alive. It was then that she realized they were moving of their own accord. Every single belief Maria had her entire life was wiped clean from her mind. She heard a small gasp come from behind her and turned to see Missy clutching her heart. Her eyes wide, she was trying to suck in huge gulps of air but couldn't. Maria knew what was happening, it had happened to her at the library. That thing was squeezing the life out of her and she was going to die because she was too old and frail to fight it. Maria screamed in anger at the top of her voice and all hell broke loose. She heard the thundering of footsteps coming up towards them, and Mikey ran into the room followed by

Anthony. Both men stared at the black figure in the corner, then at Missy who was struggling to breathe. Anthony threw holy water over Missy and made the sign of the cross on her forehead. Then he did the same at the door, sealing them into the room with it. Maria nodded at Mikey and they both ran towards it. She had no idea how to fight something made from smoke and shadows, but she sure as hell was going to try. She ran towards it, grabbing at it. The smell of rotting flesh filled her nostrils; repulsed she wanted to run the opposite way, but her stubborn heart wouldn't let her. Mikey hit it from the other side and they both began to push it towards the bedroom and the pentagram on the wall, with Emilia and Anthony walking behind them, blocking its exit. Whatever they were doing was enough for it to release its grip on Missy and she fell to the ground with a thud. They kept on pushing. She could hardly hear the priest's voice as he shouted above the howling wind and roaring noise the monster in front of them was making. With one final roar they pushed as hard as they could, forcing it back into the wall. It paused. Its black body becoming one with the bricks and plaster. Emilia threw the rest of the holy water at it.

'Get out of my house. I forbid you from ever coming back. You are not welcome here. Take your twisted values and go back to where you came from. In the name of God get out of here now.'

She ran at the wall and made the sign of the cross, the pentagram on the wall burst into orange flames. The heat was so powerful Maria dragged Emilia away from it before she got burned, Anthony ran to the sink, filling up a jug he said a prayer over the water then launched it at the wall. Extinguishing the flames, smoke and steam began to rise from the bricks making all of them cough and splutter.

Maria ran to Missy, whose face was pale, her eyes were closed. She pressed two fingers against her friend's pulse which was faint, but at least it was there.

'You did it, you all did it. You sent it back. Missy, hang on – EMS will be here soon.' No sooner had she said that than a flux of footsteps began to hammer up the steps towards them. Maria yelled. 'Get me a medic now.'

Frankie ran into the room followed by several armed police. He looked at the smouldering wall then looked at Maria. She shrugged. 'I'll tell you about it after.' The cops looked around, confused by the unlikely trio of suspects who were standing with their hands raised above their heads. Maria shouted. 'They're good, they're witnesses, not suspects.' Two medics ran in and she stood up, leaving Missy in their capable hands.

'Take care of her, she's very special.'

A loud bellow filled the air and both Frankie and Maria grimaced.

'What in the name of holy fuck has happened here?'

Addison stepped into the now cramped apartment and his eyes fell onto Anthony.

'Jeez, I'm sorry, Father. I didn't know you were here.'

Anthony smiled. 'I think your initial observation was right, Lieutenant. What in the name of holy fuck has happened here.'

Maria giggled, it sounded so wrong coming from a priest, yet it also sounded very right.

'Sir, it's a long story.'

'What happened to you Miller? You look like shit.'

'I'd rather speak to you back at the station.'

Frankie nodded. 'Yep, you don't want her to talk about this in the public domain.'

Addison looked at her wrists. 'ER now, you can tell me after you've been checked over.'

Maria remembered her bloodied, burnt wrists and immediately the pain hit her. She nodded, she'd go and let them clean her up. She didn't want them getting infected, Frankie gently took hold of Emilia's arm to lead her out. The older lady looked shocked. Mikey followed, and he didn't look much better. Anthony whispered in Maria's ear. 'The attic still needs cleansing.'

She looked at him. 'Will it wait until investigators have finished?'

He turned and looked at the burnt shape of the pentagram on the wall. 'At least let me cleanse this room.'

The medics had a line in Missy's arm, an oxygen mask on her face, and were just transferring her into a chair to get her downstairs. She waved Addison over.

'Father Anthony needs to cleanse this room, it's vital that he does.'

'Are you shitting me, Miller?'

'No, sir. I'm not. If we don't then we'll be back at square one before we know it.'

He looked at her serious face and then the priests. Waiting for the medics to leave, he turned to the officers still lingering.

'Right, you lot downstairs. This is a crime scene, I need CSI here now and I need to speak to detective Miller and the good Father here.'

The cops did as they were told, they followed the medics down the stairs leaving the three of them there.

Anthony smiled. 'Thank you, Sergeant. If we don't cleanse the room it might be able to come back through the portal.'

Addison stared at Maria who nodded. 'You don't want that big-ass demon coming back through that wall, sir. It's mean as hell and it's really pissed.'

She passed the bottle of holy water and bag of salt to Anthony who then sprinkled it around the floor in front of the pentagram. He began to pray, making the sign of the cross with the water inside the pentagram. All the time Maria held her breath wondering if that thing was going to break out of the wall again and grab him, dragging him inside. When he finished praying and stepped away she exhaled. He turned towards her.

'It's done.'

'Are you sure?' Even as she asked the question she knew that it was because the atmosphere in the room was no longer heavy. It felt much lighter and the terrible smell had gone. Addison shook his head.

'Right, now you've messed up my crime scene get out. Father, thank you. I'm not sure what it is that you've done, but I'm sure it was very important. Miller get down to the medics now.'

He ushered them both out of the room, but she couldn't help turn her head for one last look. The pentagram had faded significantly to what it was. She knew that she was going to have nightmares for the rest of her life about this house. As she stepped out into the beautiful, bright sunshine Harrison ran towards her. He pulled her close, not normally one for public shows of affection for once she let him because she needed to be held. She looked over his shoulder at Frankie who smiled at her and she felt her whole body relax. Anthony, Mikey and Emilia were all standing next to each other like the three, wise monkeys. She pulled away from Harrison to go and talk to them.

'Now what?'

It was Anthony who spoke. 'Now Emilia can live her life, Mikey can live there without fear and hopefully Missy will make a full recovery. We'll all live to tell the tale.'

'What about you?'

'I can go back and tell Father Morgan that his theory worked. That with a bit of team work we did an excellent job.'

Maria laughed. 'You can say that again, thank you.'

Frankie caught her arm. 'I hate to break up this party, but Addison said we have to get you to the emergency room and get you checked out.'

'I'm coming.'

Harrison waved them over, he was standing in front of a stretch limousine.

Maria shook her head. 'I'm not going to the ER in that, but you can be a hero and take my friends home please. I'll catch a lift with Frankie, I'll call you when I'm done.'

He bent and kissed her cheek. 'Whatever you say, Maria.'

She laughed and walked towards a squad car where Frankie was leaning on the hood. He stood up and opened the door for her. She gave him the finger.

'What, what's that for? You don't mind Mr Look-at-me-I'm-a-millionaire opening a car door for you. Did you give him the finger?'

'That's different.'

'How is it different? Your loyalty should be to me, I'm your partner. If anyone gets to open a car door for you it should be me.'

Her heart sank. Frankie did give a shit about her and Harrison's relationship. She turned to speak to him and he began to laugh.

'I'm kidding, open your own door. What are you an invalid? You get a couple of friction burns and think you deserve to be treated like royalty. Not on my shift, Miller.'

She started to laugh.

'Frankie, you're an asshole.'

'I know, but you love me despite my failings?'

'I do, I love you very much.'

One Week Later

Maria took one last look around Miss Green's apartment, it would have to do. The air felt much lighter in here than the last time she'd been in. The light from the lamps lit every corner banishing the shadows which made her much happier. She hadn't been inside her own apartment either, Frankie had insisted she either stayed with him or Harrison whilst it was redecorated. For once she hadn't felt guilty choosing The Plaza over Frankie's, she didn't want Christy thinking her and Frankie had been carrying on behind her back. Frankie had filed for divorce and it could mean the difference between him getting his fair share or losing everything. She picked up the envelope addressed to her and let herself out. Walking across the hall and standing outside her own front door she took a deep breath. Frankie had wanted to accompany her, so had Harrison. She'd declined both of their invitations, she needed to do this on her own. Opening the door, the smell of fresh paint filled her nostrils, she'd take that any day over the smell that had filled the house, that was what her and Frankie now referred to it as; the house. Expecting to feel a rush of emotions as she stepped inside she didn't, it was her apartment which had been scrubbed free of all the blood, the glass was long gone. She stared at the hall closet, her palms a little sticky. Her childhood fear of monsters in the closet had turned into a reality for her, who knew that stuff was real. She'd faced the monster head on and lived to tell the tale. Grabbing the handle, she twisted it and tugged open the door, pulling the string to bring the light to life. It was empty and the crawl space she hadn't even known existed until Frankie told her about it was now filled with bricks and mortar. Nothing could hide in there, ever.

Satisfied she turned off the light and shut the door. Walking through the rest of her apartment she felt better, it wasn't much but it was hers. She liked living here and despite Harrison's best offers of penthouses in apartment buildings she could only dream about, she'd declined. She couldn't even detect the motion sensor cameras they were so discreet, or the intruder alarms. Tight security was the only compromise she'd agreed to, she'd lived here ten years and never had a bit of trouble. She expected to carry on living here with no more, she didn't know Harrison well enough to accept his offer of a luxury upgrade. Maybe if they stayed together and they had more than a no strings attached relationship she would. Who knows, but for now she was happy. She could come home and that was what she wanted most.

Opening Miss Green's letter, she read it through eyes which were so blurred it was hard to read the delicate, handwriting. She'd informed Maria that upon her death which attorney handled all her affairs and that she was to help herself to the entire contents of her wardrobe of designer clothes, bags and jewellery. This made her cry even more. After a few minutes she dried her eyes, tucked the letter in her kitchen drawer and went back down to where Frankie was waiting outside in his car for her. She nodded at him and he grinned.

He parked at the back of the station and looked at Maria. 'I'll carry the boxes, but you can deal with her. I can't face that this early in the day.'

'You're such a girl at times Frankie.'

He shrugged. 'Call me what you want, I'm still not doing it.'

She ran down the steps and hammered on the basement door, Frankie cringed behind her. The door flew open and

Layla stood there glaring at the pair of them for three seconds before leaning forward and grabbing Maria in a bear hug. 'Girl am I glad to see you, how are you doing?'

Maria hugged her back. 'I'm good thanks.'

Frankie coughed behind them and Layla gave him the death stare. 'You Conroy I'm not so glad to see, get those boxes signed in. I thought you were keeping them.'

Maria whispered. 'He was too scared to come on his own.'

Layla nodded. 'Good, that's how I like it.' She released her hold on Maria and followed Frankie to make sure he did as he was told. They left the basement and went up to the department, everyone stopped what they were doing to look at them both and then they began to clap. Maria grinned, her cheeks burning. She'd never been so glad to get the clap, it was reserved for near misses and heroes. Even Frankie began to clap, and she burst out laughing. 'Enough, thank you. It's great to be back.'

Addison's voice boomed across the department.

'Miller, Conroy, my office now.' Just like every other time Frankie let her go first. They went into his office and he pointed to the chairs.

'Now what are we going to do about this sorry mess, how do I file a report on it?'

They both shrugged.

'Jeez, you two are most helpful. What would I do without you both?' He walked to his door which he shut, not slammed. Maria took this to be a good thing. Then he sat down opposite her.

'I'm glad to have you back Miller, this department would go to shit without you solving most of the homicides.'

Frankie coughed. 'What about me?'

'Conroy, you know she does most of the work, but I'll admit it. You two make a great team. That's why I have something for you.'

'Sir, what have you got for us?'

'Well this is top secret, there's only a handful of people know about it.

'Know about what?'

'The strange case review team.'

Frankie looked at him. 'What the hell is the strange case review team? I've never heard of it, have you just made it up?'

'Keep your voice down Conroy, it's strictly a need to know thing. It's been decided by the Commander that you two need to know. He wants you two to run it, you'll get your own office. You can come and go as you please, no one breathing down your neck. What do you say?'

Maria shook her head. 'I don't know if I want to, what sort of cases?'

Addison squirmed. 'Well, it's stuff that we don't know how to deal with.'

'Like the thing at the house?'

He nodded.

'There are more cases linked to it?'

'No, not to that at least I don't think they are. I think those two old broads and the priest managed to get rid of that one and did a pretty good job as well. But yes, there are other cases not of dissimilar nature. They're out there, a bit on the woo, woo side. It's not something the NYPD likes to talk about or admit. Apparently, your handling of the case and the fact that you managed to not die has made them want you to take over and review them.'

Frankie stared at Addison as if he'd gone mad, then he turned to Maria. 'A bit woo, woo. What the fuck, did he just say that for real?'

Maria turned to look over her shoulder, no more working in this shit hole, their own office, their own hours. She looked at Addison.

'We're are own bosses, keep our own hours, keep our pay rate?'

'Maria, come on. You're not seriously considering it? That house scared us both shitless, I'm not too much of a big man to admit it.'

She smiled at him. 'Yes, it did. I never knew anything like that existed. I'd rather fight it head on than bury my head in the sand and pretend it never happened. Think about it Frankie, our own office.'

Addison nodded. 'Yep, oh and a yearly bonus for having to keep it all quiet. You know it won't be something you can talk about down The Cat.'

Frankie leant forward. 'How much of a bonus?'

'An extra ten thousand a year.'

'I'm in, what about you Maria?'

'If you're in, I'm in.'

Addison stood up and passed them a file each. 'Good, this is your next case. I'll show you where your new office is. I'll still be in charge, anything you need you come to me about.'

They both nodded, Addison began to walk towards the door and Frankie whispered. 'Ten K.'

Maria hoped the money was worth it as she stood up and followed Addison could you put a price on their sanity? She wasn't too sure if they could.

Harrison smiled at Maria, she didn't berate him for picking her up in a limousine. She wanted this to be special, it parked outside the entrance to the hospital and she got out. 'I won't be long.' She went inside, her mind a whir. Today had been both surreal and amazing, this was going to be by far the best part. She walked along the corridor until she reached the private room, knocking gently she pushed open the door and smiled.

'Maria, I've never been so happy to see you.'

Maria walked over and kissed Miss Green on the cheek. 'I'm even happier to see you.' She turned to look at the woman sitting on the chair. 'How are you Emilia?'

Emilia laughed. 'Much better now I don't have to come to this damn hospital every day.'

Maria took hold of the wheelchair Miss Green was sitting in. 'Come on then, your carriage awaits. I can't believe you two are going to be sharing Miss Green's apartment. It's amazing.'

Emilia grinned. 'Well someone has to look after her, it might as well be me.'

Miss Green nodded. 'Uhuh, that's true. It will be nice to have some company. And Maria, you really have to start calling me Missy. Miss Green makes me sound far too old'

Emilia shook her head. 'I hate to upset you Missy, but we are old.'

Maria laughed. 'You two better not argue all the time.'

Emilia grabbed hold of Missy's hand. 'Oh, we won't, at least not all the time.'

The End

A LETTER FROM HELEN

First of all, I'd like to thank you, my fabulous readers from the bottom of my heart for buying this book and I hope you enjoyed it. If you did enjoy it I would really appreciate it if you could leave a review. They make such a difference and are a wonderful way to let other readers know about my books.

If you want to know more about my other books you can find them all on my website at www.helenphifer.com You can also sign up for my newsletter there to keep up with my bookish news.

Since I was a little girl I've dreamt about visiting New York City. In 2015 I was lucky enough to be invited to a Black & White Ball at the Waldorf Astoria by my first publishers Harlequin. I like to think it was fate that it came at a time when I could make this dream come true. What can I say, three weeks later I was in New York and speechless. I've never felt more at home anywhere in the world than I did there, and I fell completely head over heels in love with it.

I knew I wanted to set a book on the streets of New York and as we toured the city and all its attractions the idea for tough, homicide detective, Maria Miller began to take shape. I was lucky enough to visit again July 2017, this time it was a research trip for the story that I knew I had to write. I dragged my poor husband Steve along on a two-hour walking ghost tour of Greenwich Village which I loved, he wasn't so enthusiastic, bless him.

The walk started in Washington Square Park, where I stood and listened to the most amazing pianist who did indeed push his piano home when he finished. I know this because I passed him an hour later, with his piano. He was so good I could have stayed there and listened to him all night. From there we toured the haunted locations of the village. The Fat Black Pussycat is a real bar, so are all the streets and most of the locations used in this book. There is a haunted house on West 10th Street which I'd read about and this became the inspiration for my story. The house and the haunting are a lot different to how I've portrayed it, but I'm a writer and making stuff up is what I do best.

helen phifer

Acknowledgments

I'd like to thank my fabulous beta readers and very good friends Jo Bartlett, Sharon Booth and Julie Heslington who are all brilliant authors. They have a whole array of best selling, fabulous books on Amazon so go check them out. They have held my hand through this process and made me believe that I could do it.

I'd like to thank my good friend Deirdre Palmer for helping me to format this book. I didn't have a clue what I was doing. Deirdre is another bestselling writer whose books are available to buy on Amazon.

I'd also like to say a huge thank you to the rest of the Write Romantics for their unwavering support. Jackie Ladbury, Lynne Davidson, Helen Rolfe, Alex Weston and Rachael Thomas. All of them successful authors, we got together five years ago, and it's been one hell of a rollercoaster ride. The pride I have at seeing all my super talented friends filling the Amazon charts is mind blowing.

A huge thank you to the amazing Gina Dickerson @Rosewolf Design for my amazing cover artwork. I've never had so much fun choosing a cover for a book, if you ever need one then Gina is your girl.

Thank you to the fabulous Jeff Gardiner for his editing of this book, it really made a difference.

A very special heartfelt thank you goes to Paul O'Neill for his amazing surveyors report and proofreading at such a difficult time. Also, to his gorgeous wife and a very special friend Gail. You have been my biggest cheerleader from day one and I can't express how much you both mean to me.

I'd also like to thank Trisha Sherwood for her excellent proofreading.

Thank you to Joanne Grainger, Donna Trinder, Nikkie Capstick and Kirsty Ann Dawson. You have no idea how much I appreciate all your support.

A special thank you goes to the fabulous Cara Alwill Leyba who motivates and inspires me every single day to be the best that I can be. Cara, reading your books changed my life and I can't thank you enough. You need to check out Cara's amazing podcasts and books, they really will motivate you to change your life.

As always, I'd like to thank Sam Thomas and Tina Sykes for being my go to coffee girls. Good friends are hard to come by and I'm very lucky to have you both.

As always, a very special thank you goes to my gorgeous family, who both drive me mad and fill me with more love than I know what to do with. I'm a truly lucky woman to have such an amazing, supportive tribe around me. One day we'll have a table big enough to sit around for Christmas dinner without having to bring out the emergency chairs.

Printed in Great Britain
by Amazon

41881440R00161